I0618561

DESTINED TO BE

By

W Parks Brigham

I would like to dedicate this book to my family and friends for their love support and constant encouragement. Thanks guys!

DESTINED TO BE

By W Parks Brigham

This is a work of fiction. Names, characters, places, and incidents are either the product of the author's imagination or being used fictitiously.

All rights are reserved. No part of this book may be reproduced, stored in a retrieval system, or transmitted in any form or by any means, electronic, mechanical, photocopying, recording, or otherwise, without prior written permission from the author and publisher.

Copyright © 2011 W Parks Brigham

All rights reserved.

ISBN: 0984806814
ISBN-13: 9780984806812

ACKNOWLEDGMENTS

First of all I want to publicly thank God for blessing me to still have the ability to write. Next, I would like to express my deepest thanks and appreciation for the love, support, and encouragement I've received from family, friends, and ex-co-workers.

Special thanks and recognition to:

My sisters Barbara and Dellanise and cousin_____ (too many to name) who told everybody and anybody who would listen, my sister /my cousin wrote a book. I know they got on your nerves, but thanks sisters and cousins. I like to thank Jeanne who introduced me to the Editor-In-Chief of Belle Magazine, in Chicago during a BBW Beauty Pageant. Right then and there she told me "We're going to support you my sister!" The rest is history. Many thanks to you Sonia Alleyne. Of course I was given celebrity status and became a who's who (still grinning) I sure miss Belle and I'm sure all of my sisters of substance do too.

The many book clubs who invited me out and made me feel like a noted author...celebrity status for sure. Thanks ya'll.

The many readers who supported me in purchasing my first book. I also want to thank those who took time to write letters to let me know how much they loved and enjoyed reading my first story. Those readers who were speechless when I answered my own phone or returned their calls. You were absolutely priceless. Thanks a bunch. All the new friends I met during the course of promoting *Senseless Misconceptions*. I dare not call names, because I would hate to leave anyone out. I met some wonderful people who made it possible to put my book out there, have a local television interview, and my magazine debut. Thank you all fro the bottom of my heart.

Linda Anderson who traveled with me and promoted *Senseless Misconception* better than I did. She would have the people pumped before I even made it inside the book store. Thanks Linda.

Special thanks to those wonderful people who took time out of their busy schedule to edit my second book. Special thanks to my telephone group who allowed me to bend their ears and listen to Kellie and Gregory's story unfold.

Special thanks to J&E and Neblett Enterprise for providing information on operating a business.

Last but not least I want to thank the many family and friends who stayed after me time after time to start back writing. I know I tried your patience. Thanks for not giving up on me. I pray *Destined to Be* was well worth the wait.

.

CHAPTER 1

"Baby girl, it seems like I've waited for you all my life," he whispered as he held her tight. He couldn't resist nibbling her ear while caressing her bare shoulder. Lord, this man feels so good, she thought as she leaned against his muscular body. Ring!

Not again whined Kellie Kincaid as she turned over to pick up the receiver, nothing but a dial tone. One thing that could make her blood boil was for someone to call her at the crack of dawn...on a Saturday....with the caller ID saying unknown, and then have a dial tone when she picks up. Especially when they're interrupting her.... She couldn't even finish that thought. But it was true! She never gets to finish her dream. Someone or something always interrupts her. Kellie shook her head in disgust. Lusting after someone who's probably never given her another thought since that day is sick. If she didn't stop this madness she was going to check her own self into the nearest hospital. She desperately needed some mental evaluation for her behavior which was that of a blatant hussy. Now she really was losing it. Kellie chuckled to herself because she knew she sounded just like her Auntie E. Maybe Kat and Gracie were right. These dreams never occur until after she's read one of those romance novels and she had just finished a real spicy one. Instead of having a healthy relationship, Kellie preferred reading about someone else's. That was safe and smart as far as she was concerned. She had witnessed her fill of romance that would last her for a good long time and she didn't care what her buddies thought. Kellie had seen enough friends go through changes, trials and tribulations behind men. She did not have to experience that first hand again and she was leaving the past behind. After all she was young at heart at the time. What did she truly know about real love? Lord, she just wished she could let go of her dream. Kellie Kincaid couldn't stop the smile that was now spreading across her face as she thought about her hot steamy fantasy. She did enjoy...Okay, so her friends were right fluffing her pillow, she was just not playing with a full deck.

That's all to it!

***

Her flawless ice tea complexioned body that was silky smooth to the touch awakened and electrified every nerve in his rock hard body. She held onto his powerful chocolate cream frame for dear life ... afraid that this too was nothing but a dream. As his dark piercing eyes gazed into her dreamy brown amber eyes, the blood in their bodies were ignited into a passionate blazing fire that could only be put out with the union of their inflamed bodies and souls. Joy and pure happiness was disclosed as they savored in each other's ecstasy as they began their journey that would take them to....Ring!

Kellie moaned as she turned over to lie on her back. She glanced at her clock on the wall, she couldn't believe the time. It couldn't be eight already she thought, closing her eyes tight as if to shut out the beginning of a another day. It seems like she had just laid her head down and now it was time to get up.

"No," sung Kellie as she stretched and fluffed her pillow. She wanted to snuggle under her worn out designer covers and try to recapture her dream that she's had for the last few months. She couldn't get up now, she was right in the middle of the good part. This time it was so real. She could actually feel him on top caressing and kissing her feverously. At that very moment her body was in such a bothered steamy state that she felt embarrassed. Kellie rose up and looked around as if someone could actually hear her thoughts. Yep, her buddies were right she needed to get a life besides Kincaid Transportation Services. But if it wasn't for the business she never would have met him. Laying back down, she smiled recalling the incident at the airport five months ago. As usual she was rushing to catch her flight back to Houston. She had attended a four-day conference for one of the professional organizations she belongs to in Dallas. Making it to the airport just in the nick of time, she was the last one to board the plane. That's how close she came to missing it. There was no time to check her garment bag with all the security check going on. Although she had the smaller pieces to her set she still didn't like carrying any kind of luggage on the plane. It was enough just trying to maneuver herself down the small aisles without knocking someone's head off. To carry luggage plus a purse was just a bit much. Especially if you're the last one to get on the plane! As if that wasn't enough, she had to ride coach! Thanks to her buddy Gracie, she missed her first class flight and had to settle for the next best thing…fly coach.

Kellie cringed as she remembered how she almost snatched this brother's arm off when her hanger on the clothes bag caught a hold of his bracelet. She could have died! And he was just that, someone to die for braids and all. She never thought much about brothers in braids and earrings unless of course you were *Eric Benet*. And he's even given himself a new look. For all she knew he might have been one of those "wanna" be rappers. But the brother did look good. Humph, he was simply gorgeous with short braids sprawled over his head and small gold hoops in his ears. Everything about him with his smooth chocolate cream complexion expelled personality, success, sophistication, charm and lots of sex appeal. Her lips turned into a sheepish grin at her present thoughts. It was a sin the way she still carried on about that incident, but she had to admit she couldn't shake it. She could still hear the soft rasping whisper he used to ask for his arm back. It was like he was trying to save her from being humiliated in front of the passengers. But it was too late, she was embarrassed, but because he was such a gentleman about the situation she managed to save face. He released his bracelet, and assured her there was no damage and not to worry. While making her apology she found herself gazing into piercing dreamy dark eyes that held her for eternity. Okay, a few seconds, but it felt like eternity. She couldn't help but notice his sexy eyebrows that had just the right amount of thickness that formed a perfect V right in the middle of his forehead. *She had only seen eyebrows like that…* Her eyes shifted down to the direction of the husky sensuous baritone voice that lulled and soothed her racing heartbeat. She envisioned a beautiful enticing smile that was perched upon two luscious lips that were made for kissing instead of talking. What was it about a black man with a light shadow on his face that says I'm sexy instead of I need a shave. Everybody can't wear that look, but this brother was doing a good job.

Kellie shook her head as if she could actually erase her thoughts. She might as well, because one thing for sure, she knew that brother has never given her a second thought. But she was still having steamy hot fantasies about him. If the truth be told, she had secretly asked God to let their paths cross once again. She knew that was really asking for the impossible, but if anybody could she knew God was the one. And deep down inside she wanted him to make it possible. For once she needed to admit her true feelings and be honest with herself. She longed for a love of her own and since their run-in she's wanted HIM! Boy would that give her some serious business! Kellie smiled to herself as she thought about how everyone would react, especially her dear cousin.

Humph, since she completed high school her life has been work and very little play. On the completion graduate school Kincaid Transportation Service has monopolized a great deal of her life. She had little time for herself or anyone else for that matter, unless it was church oriented or family. The saying was, "Call Kellie, she'll do it." So her life pretty much consisted of church, work, and any and everything for others. It's not that she didn't mind doing for others. But between her aunt and sister, her life had been dominated by them thinking she needed them to dictate what her life should be. The bottom line, she's happy with her life and wished they would accept that and leave her alone. Auntie E was always after her about dating and having a social life. Kellie tried to convince her she did have a social life; it just wasn't what she considered to be such. She knew her aunt only had her best interest at heart, she just wished she had someone else to look after besides her. It wasn't like she doesn't do anything. She tries hard to attend all of the church functions, and she even joined the church singles' group. Whenever her schedule permits, she attends their activities as well. She also hangs out with her sisters and their Sorors at times. It's just that serious dating is not on her mind right now! She's experienced that dating drama a few times it just didn't work out. Too much fuss that she could do without for a while! Humph... forever! She just couldn't make Auntie E understand she had no time for all of that foolishness. It's not like she's over the hill. She still had a whole year before she turned thirty. Kellie knew a lot of her friends were married and had families, but that didn't mean she had to travel down that avenue. She had other important things to do with her life, than becoming a wife and mother... like a successful businesswoman. Besides, she was not domestic at all and didn't cook nor like cleaning house. She has a housekeeper that comes twice a month to keep her place up. What would

8

she do with a husband and children? She didn't see marriage and children as a priority right now. It's not on her to do list at the present, maybe later in the future. Much…Much later! A wicked thought crossed her mind. *Unless she runs into him again!*

Kincaid Transportation Service was a major priority for her at the moment. She had just talked Uncle Kel into spending a small fortune in leasing new vehicles to expand their services and venture out into other transportation areas. She couldn't afford to get laxed with KTS now. They were getting ready to have one of the busiest seasons ever with graduations, weddings, and church conventions. Although the holidays were further down the road, their limousine and bus services have been booked until the following year. Even though the economy was suffering, KTS was holding its own. She had to give Uncle Kel credit, he was a shrewd businessman. He has kept them on top for a long time. They have provided services for the Houston area for many years. Thanks to her, their latest contract with The Grandeur Inn Project was a major financial win for their transportation business. When the Inns in the Hobby area heard about their services, additional contracts were developed.

Kellie was proud of her accomplishments. Uncle Kel said she was truly an asset to the company. She had worked hard to improve and put Kincaid Transportation Services on the map.   Since the radio contracts, their limousine service was a household word. They were receiving advertisement at a discount for their service for two of the largest radio stations in the Houston area. .

***

Might as well get up she thought, as her phone started ringing. Kellie knew if it wasn't Auntie E now, she would be calling in a few minutes. She had promised her aunt she would give her two hours at the Saturday tutorial they held every week at the church. What's so amazing, she didn't know how she managed to get drafted for so many projects. She made a special point not to plan anything this weekend, but somehow she let her aunt volunteer her to tutor math. "*It's not like you have something to do,*" sang Auntie E. Kellie made a face as she thought about their conversation earlier in the week. Just what did she mean by her not having anything to do? Like she goes around telling her everything she does or what she has to do. Her business is just that her business! But her dear aunt knew just how to get her, start her whining song that truly got on her nerves. The continuous ringing of the phone caused Kellie to give up on trying to ignore it and answer it. Besides, everyone knew she was at home trying to sleep as late as she could. Humph, Auntie E no doubt!

"Hey sister, what cha doing?"

"Oh noooo," thought Kellie out loud after she removed the receiver from her mouth. She walked over to her chair and flopped down as if Nisey herself was sitting there. It never fails. Nisey Kincaid Hamilton can always sniff out when she's taken a day off for herself. At least try anyway. See Auntie E doesn't know what she's talking about. No social life. How can she, when she has to baby-sit doing her free time. Knowing Nisey she was probably calling her in route to her house at this very moment.

"Too late, I heard that," said Kellie's older sister on the other end. This was a blessing in disguise. Boy was she lucky to catch Kellie home like she didn't know she would be there. Where else would she be? She eats and breathes KTS, even on Saturdays. Nisey Kincaid Hamilton you know you're not right! She didn't fault her for wanting to be a successful businesswoman and wanted her to be the best in whatever, but that's all she does is work. Kellie Kincaid thinks just because she gets to rub noses with celebrities at different concerts and parties she's having a social life. But as their chauffeur! Pleassse… Sometimes Nisey hated the day she promised her parents she would look after her little sister when they moved back to Edna Texas to take over their grandparent's family business. She tried so hard to get them to stay, but their argument was the city was too much for them and they were way over due to go home. Besides, they were tired of the headaches and the hustle and bustle of this metropolis city. What headaches? What hustle and bustle? Nisey Kincaid Hamilton couldn't live anywhere else. When she left little bitty Edna after finishing high school, she never looked back. She loved Houston Texas to death. She had a wonderful husband, three beautiful children and a lovely home. Who could ask for more? She better ask for more and get a baby-sitter before her husband Robert gets back.

10

"Kellie, little sister, I need a huge favor."

Here it comes. Boy did mom and dad make life difficult for me when they moved back to Edna, she thought. "What do you need this time sister?" Kellie and her two sisters use to refer to themselves as big sis... little sis... and baby sis... that is   until their eldest sister went off to college .Lynette immediately put a stop to that country nonsense and sister it has been. Kellie was glad because she was tired of being referred to as baby sis!

Nisey began her begging song, "Well sister, I need a baby-sitter for the weekend. Robert bought tickets for the Lover's Only Concert and Auntie E is busy this weekend and would not be available. Please...say you'll do it?" She said that in one breath. Nisey knew she needed to get everything out in the open quick and in a hurry. She was desperate and almost to her exit. Something must be wrong, thought Nisey. Kellie usually stops her after she hears the *pl* in please, this time she got out the entire word and still no response. Nisey held the phone, which seemed like forever. There was still silence. She couldn't stand it! "Kellie, are you still there?"

Got cha worried huh, thought Kellie to herself. She loved her nieces and nephew, but the whole weekend. Kellie squirmed in her seat, "Nisey not the whole weekend. Can't you pick them up after the concert?" She crossed her fingers but knew it was in vain. No, it wasn't anyone's birthday and their anniversary was last month. What could possibly be the occasion?

"Sister, you know the concert will be over after ten. They should be in bed by that time. Robert also made reservations at The Grandeur Inn for a late dinner."   Nisey paused for a second, she knew Kellie was thinking...What? Before Kellie could ask, Nisey decided to put her mind to ease and said, "My husband is taking me on a date! You know that's what two people of the opposite sex do for companionship, enjoyment, entertainment, pleasure, fun! Get my drift?"

She thinks she's so smart, sajd Kellie to herself. "What time are you dropping them off?"

"Thank you sister, I knew I could count on you. We're right outside."

Ugh... one of these days you won't be able to, vowed Kellie under her breath as she got up to greet the little people. Right then and there she made a promise to get some business and she didn't mean Kincaid Transportation Services!

***

Once again Kellie was alone, and had her place back to herself. Her nieces and nephew were home with their parents regardless of their whining. Kellie loved her brother-in-law. If it had been left up to Nisey she would have had to bring the kids home after church. She didn't have the heart to tell them no, after all she was their favorite aunt. Thank God Robert insisted they go home so they could get ready for school tomorrow. The twins had asked for spaghetti today and she certainly didn't feel up to cooking. Her kitchen was only a show place, as a matter of fact her whole townhouse was nothing but a showplace, inspired by the Home and Gardens channel. Everything was always in place thanks to the cleaning service provided by the building complex, worth every penny. That was one of the reasons she wanted to buy in the Rancho Bee District. The amenities and security along with the location was great. She was five minutes from her job and had access to the expressways. It's generally peaceful with everyone respecting each other's privacy.

Kellie grabbed a couple of slices of the left over pizza, cheesy bread, and punch to take to her favorite corner where she takes most of her evening meals. The cozy and modest L-shaped spot was located near the stairs and downstairs powder room. She used it as an all-purpose area with her computer and office equipment set up on a short wall unit alongside a slender bookshelf for her books. In the corner was a compact media center that held her flat screen, DVR, CD's, and stereo system. On the longer wall was a combination sofa and chaise with accent pillows in soft shades of blue, pink, and yellow with an abstract throw that pulled her the colors together. It was just the spot to relax and unwind with a good book or watch a little TV.

***

Kellie was ready to call it a day. She wasn't able to do exactly what she had planned for the whole weekend, but she did have time to pamper herself with a soothing and relaxing bath. She soaked in one of her favorite bath foams of a sweet mixture of jasmine, water lily, and exotic fruit. Then she used the refreshing luxurious body crème and mist of the same essence and moisturized and perfumed her body. With her favorite PJ's on she pulled the covers back to climb in her bed. Before she could get one foot off the floor, the telephone rang. Looking at the caller ID she started her *now what* dance. It was Auntie E!

"Hello Auntie E."

"Don't you Auntie E me. I thought I told you I needed to talk to you after church and you left anyway. Are you trying to avoid me?" Kellie made a face at her telephone. What in the world did she want this time? She did the tutoring Saturday just like she promised even though she had the little people with her.

"Auntie E, I'm sorry, I'm not trying to avoid you. I had to get home quick so I could get Nisey's children's things together. You know they spent Saturday night with me." Kellie silently prayed that her aunt would not ask her to do something she didn't want to. She had a hard time telling her no. Auntie E had her and everyone else wrapped around her finger, well just about everyone.

"Okay, Kellie I understand. Now, Auntie wanted to ask you about the townhouse next door to you. Is the side gate still open leading into your yard and patio?"

Now she was really puzzled, why in the world did she need to know that? "Yes, Auntie E the side gate is still open. Why?"

"Well favorite niece, if you must know, I've been recommended by my dear sister-in-law to the new owner to organize and decorate the place. I want to take a peek so I can start the wheels rolling with a few ideas. And Kellie sweetheart, I could use your help."

Kellie knew the minute "favorite niece" slipped past her lips something was up. Her aunt thought she was THE interior decorator with the help of The Home and Garden's channel. Together they did a beautiful job and turned on her townhouse into a showplace. Her large open space was transformed into a living and dining area with a movable wall that hid her office and entertainment area. She has also helped with several other projects. They did work well together, but that was Auntie E's thing not hers.

Auntie E continued, "Delores said he was black, single, quite handsome, educated, and a legitimate businessman. He sounds like husband material to me. He has all the fine qualities a woman could ask for in a man. Did I also tell you that he and Delores go to the same church? That makes him a God fearing Christian man!"

Well, thought Kellie, she did say the three magic words Christian, single, and working. That was certainly husband material to her aunt. But first she had to make sure he wasn't hung up on the size of a woman. She was not about to waste one minute on anyone that narrow minded. Lord, how many times did her aunt and sister try to fix her up with eligible single man at church that they approved of? After a few dates, Kellie insisted that they let her handle her love life and back off. She was not desperate and didn't need their help. But her new neighbor did sound interesting. If he was buying the place next door, he had to have *bank*.

The townhouses located in the cul da sac were larger and pricey than the ones on its opposite sides with at least five to eight hundred square feet more.

Big spacious rooms, jack and jill bath, and a large complete master suite with a luxurious master bath, were major attractions for that particular floor plan. Those townhouses were sold before the ground had been broken. Kellie did have a decent size master suite, a small guest room, and a half bath upstairs. She remembers Uncle Kel saying the developers wanted to provide homes that would appeal to all ages with features that they could truly enjoy. Rancho B was a wonderful place to live with its resort atmosphere.

"Auntie E, how soon do you want to start? You know I'll be starting my vacation soon and I don't see how I can work it in my schedule right now with us closing out our busy season at the office." Kellie held the phone, which seemed like forever before she heard her aunt clear her throat. She knew

14

this was not a good sign of okay I'll find someone else, like Nisey for instance.

"Well Kellie, if you don't think you'll be available, I could ask Nisey. She's just not as creative as you and me. We think more alike and have pretty much the same taste. Nisey tends to be a little flashy. The job will not start until the end of the summer."

"That's right Auntie E," interrupted Kellie, "when it's time for my vacation." She hated to disappoint her even if she did impose at times. And she was right about Nisey, she did go overboard with her flash. "I tell you what, you check the place out and then you and I can brainstorm with some ideas before I go on vacation. How about that?"

"Kellie that will be just perfect, I knew you wouldn't let me down. I'll be fun and we'll get to spend some quality time together and have girl talk. Oh Sweetie, I think I hear your uncle calling, we'll talk more later."

Kellie disconnected her phone. She couldn't help but smile because her aunt was a mess and knew the wheels were already in motion for one of her love connections. This time she may just cooperate.

CHAPTER 2

Kellie had nothing but busy days for the last few weeks. Although their service with The Grandeur Inn Project was not to start until next month, their calendar was full with other new contracts. One thing for sure, she kept her promise about getting her some business and was starting today! Everything was ready, her aunt was going to babysit her plants and aquarium until she returned, since she was going to be next door. That worked out great and her aunt would not have time to change her furnishings around this time, since she'll be busy next door. Kellie almost hated she wouldn't be around to help out. The new neighbor's townhouse was beautiful. The furnishings that had arrived spoke of nothing but class. She couldn't help but think that maybe her aunt was right this time and might have to give Mr. New Neighbor some serious thought after all. It was somewhat strange though her aunt didn't know this man's name yet. She was too nosey not to have that kind of information. It's like it was a secret, but she would have to deal with that later. Whoever he was it was a fact he had good taste and was financially secured.

Kellie took one more look around and pushed her luggage out the door. She was taking it to work because her evening flight to Atlanta was at six. Her friend Gracie called last night to see if she was still coming. Kellie smiled to herself as she remembered her buddy's remark. *She'll believe it when she sees her.* Well Ms Gracie you'll get to do just that and I'll get to see what's really up with you.

Just last week Kat spilled her guts and revealed some shocking news. *Gregory Larson was relocating back to Texas! And to Houston Texas at that!* She was still having a hard time digesting that news, but it didn't concern her and she could care less where he goes. She was not that timid young girl

16

anymore. She was a woman bursting at the seams with much attitude and it was best he just stay out of her way. Kellie put on her designer shades and walked out to her silver BMW X5. She was going to leave silver girl at the bus barn and Clyde, their maintenance operator would keep a watchful eye on it. She had also requested one of the drivers to take her to the airport after work. That was the advantage of managing a limousine service. You could go to the airport in style.

***

Kellie Kincaid stole a quick glance at the clock on the wall. All the reports had been given and the managers were ready for the weekend including Kellie. She could hardly contain herself. She had planned a real vacation and it was starting right after the meeting, TODAY! That is if her favorite uncle close out and call it a day. Kelley Kincaid, who was her name sake and great uncle; was still going on about their new business ventures. He was proud and had a right to be. In the midst of Sunnyside Texas, he started and managed a profitable transportation service by carrying children back and forth to school for over fifty years. Uncle Kel often bragged about him being one of the first black men to own a bus service during the fifties. If he told the story once he's told it a million times. He loves to remind young people that he started out with a one bus and driver team that has now become a competitive transportation business. Now Kincaid Transportation Service has steadily moved forward and expanded into a prosperous operation providing services for adults and numerous businesses as well.

"Okay Uncle," whispered Kellie under her breath sighing to herself. "You're losing your audience." She noticed the puzzled looks the staff was showing on their faces. *It's time to go!* Uncle Kel had been going on for the last thirty minutes really about nothing. She couldn't remember the last time he carried on so, it's so unlike him...like he was giving his last staff meeting. Bless his heart, she thought. What can you expect from a seventy-five year old man who still had his office in the same little area where he started fifty years ago? Even with the construction for expansion and the new offices, he refused to move. The contractors had to build around him.

Those had been some trying days, and she'll never forget the day they did a complete makeover in his office with new furniture and office supplies.

Smiling to herself, she also recalls how he put up a big fuss about not needing a new computer or fax. The devil with the new millennium was his constant remark. Kellie can't count the times she's caught him playing spider solitaire. You had to give him credit though, he still has what it takes to manage a successful business. Besides, she knew Kincaid Transportation Service was his baby. All he had was Aunt Juanita and KTS. Although he has given her authorization to modernize their operation with the latest technology, he was still a part of every decision. Regardless of the many changes they have undergone, they have always kept his motto: To provide excellent service for every man's dollar. And that's exactly what Uncle Kel has done since day one.

"As I conclude ladies and gentlemen," he said finally, "with summer almost behind us and winter around the corner, we are looking forward to a busy and prosperous time. Now, I know I've kept you long enough, if there are no questions or concerns this meeting is adjourned. Everyone please have a good evening, Kellie, I'd like to see you before you leave."

There go my plans for the weekend, thought Kellie. Right at this very moment her vacation was supposed to start. She had three glorious weeks visiting old friends and her parents, doing whatever she pleased. And that's absolutely nothing during the last week. Kellie had been looking forward to her time away from everything. She knew that was about to change. Whenever he requests her presence he has an errand or problem that only she can take care of. Kellie went back to her office to get her luggage. Maybe if he sees that he won't hold her too long. Fat chance of that she sighed and shrugged her shoulders. She closed and locked her door and started down to her uncle's office. Whatever it is she'll have to take care of it when she returns from her trip.

Kellie took the short walk down the hall. She couldn't help but have that same satisfied feeling that he walks around with, glancing out the windows at the fabulous views thanks to her vision. Knocking softly on the door to announce her presence and walked in his office. There he was playing his favorite game that one of their clerks had taught him. That was how he became familiar with his computer. According to Cherri if he played solitaire for a while he would get the hang of it. Needless to say it worked. One thing

18

for sure she could count on him playing his game or looking at their web site. Well at least everything seems normal thought Kellie, as she addressed her uncle. "What's up Uncle Kel? I'm here as you requested."

"Kellie, glad you stopped by. I know you're in a hurry. I understand you're taking a little vacation for a few days."

Glad I stopped by… understand you're taking a vacation for a few days, what does he mean by that she thought. She had informed him she was going to take three weeks while business was a little slow. September to mid-October was always considered their cooling down period after the summer months. She wanted to get away before homecoming activities started. That was the beginning of their next busy season until after February. She hadn't had a real vacation in ages. And when she plans something big, she rounds up postponing or putting it off for KTS or family. But this time she was taking twenty-one whole well deserved days just for herself. Talking about getting a groove back…Humph, she didn't have a groove to get back, her plans were to get one.

"Uncle Kel…"

"Don't get your dandruff up, I remembered!" He interrupted her before she could say another word. Because of the closeness between them they were pretty much in tune to each other's thoughts and feelings. "What I did forget was where all did you say you were going? So it's no need to start that whining," he said. "I just wanted to be sure you were still going to New York, because I need a favor."

Kellie took a deep breath. So he did remember she was scheduled for a vacation. She told him yes, she was going to Atlanta and then New York. She and Gracie were meeting their friend Sandy Waters for a few days in New York and then they were going to her family's cottage in Martha's Vineyard. She was truly looking forward to their little holiday as Sandy likes to call them.

"Yes, anything Uncle Kel, just don't ask me to cancel my trip."

He broke into a hearty laugh and expressed he would never do a thing like that. He knew she had every reason to be a little uneasy with his request. So many times she's set aside her own needs and desires for the company and family. What he needed her to do was simple, check on a little something he ordered. He asked his old army buddy and wife who owns a jewelry store in Harlem to design a special ring and bracelet for Juanita as a 50th anniversary gift. Uncle Kel went on to explain that he wanted to give it to her next month when they celebrate their anniversary on a Caribbean Cruise. He knew Harold and Veverly Houston were excellent at their craft and could send a picture, but that wasn't good enough for him. He wanted Kellie to see the pieces and give her opinion.

Her uncle continued on with his next news; he was planning on going into semi-retirement as soon as she returned from her vacation. She would be gone just long enough for him to get his business in order. Kelley Kincaid had thought long and hard about retiring. His plans were to make a smooth transition for his replacement to take up where he left off. He was very confident that everything would be just fine. It was time for him to enjoy his last few years with his beautiful and devoted wife, Juanita. The cruise was the beginning!

"Uncle Kel," whispered Kellie. She couldn't believe what she was hearing. Of course she would do whatever he needed her to do, but Kellie couldn't get past his news. Taking a cruise was one thing but going into retirement. Where did all of that come from? Kellie gently sat down in the aged wing back chair in front of her uncle's desk with her mouth wide open.

"We don't have time to sit. What time is your flight?" Without giving her a chance to respond he continued. "We can finish this conversation on the way. Let me call the driver. And Niece there's more!"

CHAPTER 3

Gregory Larson gazed out of the picturesque glass window of the view that he had enjoyed for the last six years. The yellow glow of the sun was slowly slipping away as the day came to a close. Dusk was boldly settling over the architectural designed buildings and busy streets of Atlanta. He was going to miss this spectacular view. So many times he had watched this great city come to life and gradually become idle. Atlanta had been good to him. She welcomed him with open arms and unlimited opportunities, never questioning his past. Not that he had anything to hide. Who was he fooling? He had a questionable past but was given a second chance at making everything right. It's not every day a man his age was given such a great opportunity. Of course one had to take into consideration his hard work and sacrifices he's made over the years. After all it was just him. He had no one else to consider. He was flying solo. Gregory also had a vast knowledge in security operations and he was good at it. Due to all of his previous work experience and financial gain, Gregory Larson was moving on to higher plains to speak. He was about to fulfill one of his greatest dreams, return home as a successful businessman. Finally after twelve years, this time he was going home to stay. He had just purchased fifty-five percent of a profitable transportation service in Houston, Texas, which earned him the title of CEO. Because it was a family operated business, the owner did not want to put any kin out on the streets so there were some provisional conditions he agreed to. That was fine with him, that way he could still freelance in the security business contracting out for special jobs.

A self-satisfied smiled surfaced as Gregory recalled the meeting he had with the owner. He couldn't believe it when he learned this was the same Kincaid family he had a run in twelve years ago. Getting down to the real issue, he had bought into Kellie Kincaid's uncle's business and she herself was his right hand. Talking about a coincidence! He and Kellie Kincaid would be working together. *Ain't that a trip!*

It was true Gregory Larson was moving on to better things. But before he became completely on his own, he had to finish one more job for Harold Grimes. He wanted him to organize and set up the security team for two of the largest conventions he's ever contracted out that's scheduled next month. It was even agreed for him to come back and personally supervise the operation, which would also give his replacement, additional on the job training. Providing security services for conventions and conferences had been an asset to Harold's company. He had the utmost respect for Harold Grimes and he was going to make sure he didn't disappoint him in anyway. Not only had Harold given him a job, but he also allowed him to venture out into other avenues in the security business. He was one of the top instructors at the Grimes Security Academy. He specialized in rendering services for a variety of events and affairs regardless of the magnitude of the occasion. What he really loved about his job, was the fact he had been able to contract himself out frequently as a bodyguard. Now, that was truly tight as far as he was concerned, and profitable. Doing so enabled him to meet people from an array of economic status. He loved being security for people of different professions from the political arena to celebrities. This also made it possible for him to earn some serious cash which he was able to invest wisely. Kincaid Transportation Service was his biggest investment yet.

***

Gregory had been in the fast line for a while and was ready to slow it down. He was very much aware that this was a going to be a new change, but he was a team player and had a great game strategy. Besides he was getting the opportunity of a lifetime, to be able to move back to Texas in grand style. Under no circumstances would he be considered a dead beat or loser now. He was a respectable brother in the security business arena in Atlanta and up and down the east and west coast. One thing for sure he had to admit regardless of his many accomplishments and financial gain sometimes he felt a dim shadow lurking around causing feelings of emptiness. He couldn't help but think about the family he had been alienated from for the last twelve years…The family that never really wanted him around even for a little while…The family that turned their backs on him after he lost the only person that ever showed him true love and kindness.

Gregory Larson couldn't wait to see their snug faces once they realized the mistakes they made judging him because of what his parents were. It was due to their memory and his great aunt's that he's driven himself to be nothing but the best. His past was the driving force that has kept him motivated and strong. Although the scars were still there, he knew he had to let it rest if he wanted to continue to stay focused and be on top of his game.

Gregory knew it had been a challenge to forget the way he had been treated. He closed his eyes as those old memories surfaced. His great aunt had done her best giving him the love and support a child of six should have. Although everyone said she was too old to raise a child, she spent her remaining years trying to do just that. She did everything humanly possible to make up for all the unhappiness he had experienced. She had given him a good life and thought it was a sin and shame the way their kin had acted toward him. No young child should have endured that kind of pain and hurt, especially after being without both parents. After the death of his mother he was practically thrown away. Neither side wanted him around. The irony of the whole situation was he had been blamed for everything. If his mother hadn't met his daddy....If his daddy had left his mother where he found her. How in the world could he be held responsible for that? What had he done? He was just another innocent child and knew it wasn't his fault, but somehow his extended family had managed to put all the blame on him.

He had been labeled a bad seed at birth. Although he was not his father, he was still his son. It was a known fact that his father was the force that pushed his mother over the edge which caused her to become unstable most of her adult life. She couldn't live with or without him and his death caused an unbearable amount of pain which proved to be too much for her. That's when she turned to drugs to survive and the rest is history. She never got over losing his father.

Even with all his great aunt's efforts, he still had constant battles trying to keep his heart and soul from being in a dark place, while growing up. He was drenched with hostility and bitterness towards his family on both sides, especially after her death. That's when he was forced to really be alone. Gregory could actually see the angry faces of his kin as they stood at the door with the local sheriff. All he needed was a place to stay after his great aunt died so he could finish high school. They had forced him off the property before she was cold in the ground. If it had not been for Ms. Lois Bell he didn't know what he would have done except to become homeless. Now smiling to himself, he recalled how she told his Aunt Cheryl off after they found out his aunt had a will and left him everything. Some of the family members had gotten together to remove her furniture so they could put the property up for sell. That's when they came across an envelope with the necessary papers awarding him all of her life possessions. She even had a modest insurance policy that named him the sole beneficiary. Because she had never married and had no children everything belonged to him. After he turned eighteen, to everyone's surprise a sizable fortune was awarded to him. What a wonderful graduation present which was a major factor in turning his life around! He knew it was expected of him to waste every dime, but he didn't.

At eighteen years old he did the right thing by securing his money and moving on with his life. When the right time came, he invested which has placed him in a comfortable position to become a successful business man with substantial income. The investments he made in Edna have truly paid off. Although he was the one that was responsible for rebuilding Edna's black community, it was done confidentially. The bed and breakfast establishment and his shares in the savings and loan were his largest investments until the Kincaid business, and he's doing relatively well as far as profits are concerned. But the most important fact is that he was able to do something for the little town his great aunt dearly loved and make Ms. Lois Bell happy and useful in her golden years. She's the only one who is aware of his business ventures and has been sworn to secrecy.

Revisiting his past often brought back to mind that very day when vicious lies were spread all over town about him. He had been humiliated and his character was destroyed. Even his boys looked at him in a different way. Gregory never understood Kellie Kincaid's behavior that dreadful day and why she accused him of something so terrible. During the years growing up they had remained cordial friends so to say. She had no idea how special she was to him, and the fact that he had always looked out for her. That's why he offered her a ride to the gas station that evening when he spotted her walking

24

alone with a gas can. Man that was the biggest mistake of his life. When he got out of that mess he knew then he had to make a decision about his life and what he really wanted to do. One thing for sure he did not want to end up like his parents. That very day he decided to make some major changes and leave his so call hometown right after graduation and he never looked back. From then on Gregory Larson became somewhat of a loner and stayed to his self never letting anyone get close to him, that is until he met Sarge and Harold Grimes. He had to admit he did not know how he really felt about Kellie Kincaid after all these years…Whether or not he was still carrying that boy hood crush or resent her for the accusations she made. One thing for sure he was about to find out since he bought into her uncle's business. He couldn't wait to see the look on her face when he takes over. That's also why it's important that he put yesterday behind him for good.

It had not been easy letting go of the lies and forgetting about the family he did have. He was like everybody else he needed to belong. He wanted acceptance. But most of all, he needed to put the past behind him and was ready to start over with his family. Gregory knew this was the right thing to do. Forgiveness! He had to find in his heart to forgive and put the pain to rest. Thank God for his great aunt and Dr. Nell Armstrong. They both were able to help him survive and get past his demons. He never would have made it without them. It's because of his great aunt's unconditional love and support he's the man he is today. He must accept the fact that it's a new day and a new beginning!

***

Gregory looked around his office and knew he had done well regardless of his past. He had taken advantage of the second chance that was given to him. He has proven what kind of person he really is. His character and morals are unquestionable and he was proud of the fact that he beat the odds. He was now an independent black man with dignity and self-respect. He was confident that he could do anything and succeed if it was his desire. His accomplishments so far were outstanding for a small town wanna be hood. His financial portfolio was impressive with a variety of business ventures he's connected with. Vain was he? Naw, just sure of himself…and he had every right to be! Rubbing and massaging his scalp trying to loosen his short braids, Gregory thought about the six years he had spent in Uncle

Sam's Army and the education he received from Georgia's fine schools of higher learning. They had been the right combination for his success along with an abundance of blessings from above! He also had to give a lot of credit to Sgt. Charles Johnson. If it had not been for him he probably would have been locked up or dead. He took over Ms. Lois Bell's job so to speak.

Yep, he had every right to be proud and yes, maybe his ego was inflated. Naw, just a little bit…He laughed quietly to himself and cleared his mind. He turned around in his chair and viewed his last files on his laptop. Today was going to be his last day at the Atlanta's office. He had prepared all the necessary information for his replacement. It was time to give another young brother an opportunity. Patrick, his replacement would do just fine. He had a great team to work with and after all he had been trained by the best!

All things considered he was going to miss Atlanta. He loved this city. This was definitely the place for any black man to get his head on straight and fulfill his dreams of prosperity. You just had to work hard at it! It was true Gregory had mixed emotions and was undecided about his true feelings about relocating to H-town. But it was settled, he had signed the contract weeks ago. Everything was in motion.

Glancing at his watch, he knew it was time to go home even if it was empty and lonely. Lonely! Where did that come from? Gregory Larson was alone, but not lonely. It was true he had no real family. Family did not apply to him. No one was looking for him to come home tonight or any night. No one was keeping his dinner warm. There was no one waiting to see how his day had gone. It was a given fact there was no one making a happy home for him. *What are you saying Gregory man? Are you ready to take the plunge? Make a commitment? Marriage? Has it come to this? What happen to your motto? Remember, you stand alone. Alone you stand! Besides, did you forget the past and who your parents were? Enough thought Gregory. He knew his life was meant to be alone!*

Yep, he was all alone in this fast pace complex world. He wasn't complaining, nor was he whining about his situation. He was alone by choice and that was a fact. Yes, he had a few meaningless relationships that he knew would never amount to anything serious. He knew that under no circumstances could he allow himself to get seriously involved with anyone with all his baggage. At least that's what he's always thought, but since that day…there was no need going there. His chances of meeting her again was the same odds as him winning the lottery which he's had yet to even purchase his first ticket to play.

***

Gregory Larson's life was still great considering. He had good friends that he was going to miss. His main man Harold who gave him his big break and the best secretary in the world was on the top of his list. They both had treated him like the son they never had and always wanted. Thank God their daughters were married with families of their own.

"Mr. Larson, are you all right?" Ask Delores as she peeped into his office. Delores Anderson had been his secretary for the last six years. They made a great team. They were so in tune with each other, they actually knew what the other was thinking or had a good idea what was on their mind. She walked over to his desk and set her bag down on the floor. "Thinking about your move?"

"How did you know?" ask Gregory as he flashed his million dollar smile. He stood up to take his last look for the day of the magnificent view that he's enjoyed for the last six years. He knew Houston wouldn't have anything close to the fantastic view he had grown to love. But that wasn't his problem. He had to admit he was a little afraid of his past hitting him in the face the minute he pulls up in the parking lot at Kincaid Business Park. But he knew it was too late for that kind of thinking, after all what was done was done and he should have thought of that before now.

Gregory knew he had been lucky making little overnight trips to Edna on small business ventures. He always made his appointments at night when most people where at home and settled for the evening. No one suspected that he was the one that had given the old neighborhood a new face lift. He had also made it possible for a few people to fulfill their dreams with their own businesses including his uncle and aunt. They were able to expand their little Laundromat and cleaners with new and better equipment which turned it into a real nice modern operation. He had done good things for the people in his hometown and one day they would all know. No more sneaking in and out of Houston or Edna. He was going to be there for good whether they liked it or not. As a matter of fact the second thing on his agenda was to pay the country people there a visit.

Gregory recalled the last time he sneaked into Edna. He had been right in Aunt Marie's face and she never recognized him. Of course he knew she wouldn't after all he had changed considerably. He had pulled up to the truck stop to make a pit stop before heading over to Ms. Lois Bell's place when she bumped right into him as he was leaving and she coming in. Gregory noticed she still had that honey drippy drawl that she used many times on Uncle Jay whenever she wanted her way, when she apologized for nearly running over him. He knew of all people she wouldn't have known him anyway, she would have been looking for a thug as she often called him to his face. Gregory shook his head, there was no need in rehashing that foolishness. He was putting all of those feelings behind him. The point was he had actually slipped in and out of Edna and Ganado Texas more times than he cared to remember. He had secretly attended both sets of great-grandparents' funerals, and not one time was he ever recognized. Jeremy and Ms. Lois Bell always kept him abreast of his family happenings.

The fact still remains he has had constant battles inside that was forcing him to come to some kind of decision about letting his past stay behind or face up to it. Gregory had to admit deep down inside he couldn't wait to see the people that had predicted he wouldn't amount to anything. Man, were they going to get the surprise of their lives when they find out he was the one who bought and fixed up a lot of the old run down houses in the old neighborhood. Right now he has maintained all of his business ventures in secrecy. He had preferred his identity to remain anonymous for a while. Yes, G-man was doing alright. He knew his great aunt would be so proud of him. He had survived and was now living a good life, even if he was alone.

"Surely you're not questioning your decision now," replied Delores in her matter of fact tone. She knew he had drifted back to his past as she watched the expressions change on his handsome face. She was going to miss him dearly. He was such a wonderful young man. The sadness and loneliness

28

she saw in his eyes at times tore at her heart. He just needed someone special in his life. It's not like she and the other sisters at the church haven't tried matchmaking. She never understood why he always preferred being alone and knew it went very deep. If it wasn't for Mr. Grimes's family and the church he would have remained a reclusive anti- social lonely hermit. Delores remembers six years ago when she had invited him to the church she attended. Not only did he accept the invitation but after service he placed his membership with the Westend Church and has been a faithful member ever since. The church family will truly miss him.

She always felt there was something special about Gregory Larson, yet there was a certain sadness about him that was disturbing. The move to Houston was going to be good for him. He'll make new friends and face old ones. It's not necessary for him to know she had everything under control, might say her last secretary duties for him. For starters, she was sending him to the church that her brother attends. There were lots of Christian activities going on and plenty eligible Christian women for him to choose from. If anyone could hook him up as the young people say, her sister-in-law Eula Harris could. If her only daughter wasn't married she would have done everything in her power to make him her son-in-law. Next, she found the perfect home for him. He would be living in the same complex of a nice young woman that attends the same church. As a matter of fact it was Eula's niece that was still single as she puts it. Delores smiled as she recalled their conversation, that Eula was simply a mess.

Delores walked over to the window. "It's beautiful isn't it?" She stood beside his six-four frame that was well defined in every way. He made her look like a young girl with her petite short frame. If she was single and twenty five years younger she would show these young women how to catch a man! He was such a looker. Delores didn't remember young men looking like that during her day. The bodies these young men have now days… umph… umph. Gregory turned around to face her. Sadness… long faced… downhearted… He had the look of a small child that was being sent away for doing wrong. She reached up and stroked his check. He had such a strong handsome face. "Now you listen to me," she started. "This new move is going to be the best thing that's ever happened to you. You're going to do just fine. We're all wishing you the best and you'll always be in our prayers.

Houston is getting more than they deserve."

Gregory knew he was really going to miss Mrs. D. She was always in his corner. "I don't know what I'm going to do without you Mrs. D. Give me a big hug." Mrs. D did just that and then patted him on the cheek.

"You're going to do fine without me. Besides I have someone in Houston that will take good care of you. She's going to take up where I left off." With a raised eyebrow Gregory gave her a suspicious look. He was very much aware of her many talents. Besides, being a wonderful person and friend, an efficient secretary, and a marvelous cook... her number one skill was match making. He knew Mrs. D would not rest until she had him engaged and married before the year was out. She had no idea he was well aware of her plans and he was staying clear of Eula Harris. She was as bad as Mrs. D according to Harold...they were close friends and sisters-in-law!

"What?" She knew that forget it Mrs. D look. Because of past experiences he knew her all too well. Gregory couldn't help but laugh, he knew that sweet innocent look was deadly. They held each other for a few more minutes and then let go. Mrs. D cleared her throat, she promised herself she was not going to carry on like a mother fixing to lose her son. She often took trips to Houston to visit her family and Eula promised to keep an eye on him. "Come on, it's time we call it a day, don't you think?" Whenever he was in the office they usually left together on Wednesdays... *International Bible class night* they like to call it. She had a million things to do and some last minute shopping before Bible class. He might have gotten away with telling Mr. Grimes he didn't want any going away celebration, but at Westend they were having just that. A surprise going away party for him had been planned the minute they knew of his new job venture. Gregory Larson need not think for one minute that he was going to leave Atlanta as quietly as he came in. Not if she had anything to do with it and she did! They left the building together as usual, both saying their good evenings to the building security guard. Gregory walked Mrs. D to her car.

"See you tonight Son," said Mrs. D as she fastened her seat belt. She checked the time and knew she would be running late as usual unless she could avoid a long line at the grocery's. Sis Twyla needed her to pick up the paper goods she was supposed to bring tonight. She wasn't sure what time she would be able to leave her job and didn't know if she would get to Bible class on time or not. Mrs. D waved bye to him and drove out of the parking lot.

Gregory watched her drive off. He was somewhat surprised, this was the first time she didn't ask him over for dinner. Although he was an excellent cook he still enjoyed an evening with Bro. and Sis. Anderson since this was going to be his last Wednesday night here in Atlanta. She did seem a little preoccupied as they were leaving the building. Probably thinking of her next victim since he was leaving, he thought. She had to mother some woman's son. Whoever she chooses next would be one lucky person. Gregory could only hope and wish for someone to care half as much for him, fat chance of that. Shaking his head to clear the thoughts that were trying to cloud his mind he turned to face his vehicle. It was no use to even go there. He knew it was wishful thinking. Although his dream had been very vivid and real to him, the fact still remains the same…it was just a dream. He didn't know who she was or where she was. That was just one of those once in a life time happenings. Never in a million years would they ever cross paths. He couldn't help thinking how wonderful life could be if she was in his corner. It was something about her that gave him the feeling that she was the one. Let's face it thought Gregory silently to himself, the truth of the matter, she only exists in his dreams.

Gregory turned the alarm off to his Escalade truck and discarded his briefcase and sports jacket in the back seat. He put on his designer shades and walked around to the driver's side and got in. As he fastened his seat belt he opened the sun roof. Since he was in no hurry to go home he thought why not just ride and take the scenic route. There was no reason to rush to an empty house and he means empty. All of his furnishings had been sent ahead to his new townhouse in H-town thanks to Mrs. D. All he had left were the things he promised to a newlywed couple at the church and personal belongings that would travel with him. Thanks to her, everything had been taken care of. Cruising out of the parking lot he knew then it was not going to be easy starting over. He slipped his favorite CD, *The Best O Teddy Pendergrass*. Teddy crooned out one of his favorites…*Can't We Try*. Man, was that the truth!

CHAPTER 4

With a grave look of despair and hopelessness Kelley Kincaid sat at his desk with his back turned away from the view that he had grown accustom to for the last fifty years. He couldn't believe the mess he had gotten himself into. He couldn't bear watching his livelihood drive away. He never dreamed in a million years that he would have to sell out. Kincaid's bus service had been a pioneer in the Sunnyside Texas community. He had built his one-man one school bus operation into a prominent business that provides all kinds of transportation service in the Houston area. His bus barn now held a variety of vehicles. It was his Kellie that talked him into expanding from just transporting children to providing the same service for adults. Thank God for that, at least they would still be able to provide transportation services just on another level. He was pleased that he was able to hold on to the business park and the additional suites, another one of her visions. If it had not been for Gregory Larson he would have lost everything including his pride and self-respect. If it hadn't been for Kellie and her business sense he would not have had anything to negotiate except school buses.

He was glad his namesake had the foresight to see the big picture in transportation than he did. She was a brilliant business woman with a creative discernment in management. Her clear sightedness and keen business intellect had advanced KTS right into the new era. He remembers her argument very well. Uncle Kel you're going to have to move into the new millennium and be competitive, she said. He had been sick and tired of the hype concerning the new millennium and this Y2K nonsense. But she was right on the money and hadn't even started college yet. With the building of the new sports arenas and the renovating of old warehouses into business offices, townhouses, and condominiums; her envisions of traffic jams and unlimited parking spaces, they were sitting on a gold mine. He had to admit she had some valid issues and he was glad he listened. He often kidded her by saying she was an old soul in a young person's body.

Kelley Kincaid couldn't contain his smile as he leaned back in his chair. That niece of his has always been able to lift his spirits whether she was present or not, and had a way of brightening up his world. One thing he regretted in his life time was not having children. But he and his loving Juanita had each other and their share of nieces and nephews. And it was a known fact she was his favorite. Why not, she was named after him. He knew she was often put up to pleading cases or presenting ideas from their staff. No one wanted to deal with Boss Hog! *That was his nickname behind his back. Of course he was quite aware of what he was called when his staff didn't think he was listening. He wore the name proudly, because he was the BOSS!*

Kellie's insight in expanding their business and offering additional services was a great opportunity and the answer to his troubles. Well at least most of them. He still had to put his school buses up for sale, which had been the beginning and main source of income back in the day. His new business associate did not want to have big school buses and had given strict orders to sell them. As an alternative, they could replace them with mini vans which would be more effective, less expensive and easy to service. Although selling the buses had dampened his spirits and sadden his heart he had to agree it was good sound business sense. His army buddy was right about that young man. Gregory Larson had been a God sent. He helped him save face and kept him from mortgaging everything he owned. Most of all he didn't have to tell Juanita and Kellie how naive and stupid he had been…an old man like him should have known better… He couldn't have begun to tell them what he had done. It was no way he could have explained his position. Hell, except for him being a fool. He had led them to think everything was fine. Kelley Kincaid had to admit it had been hard keeping it from those two, but he would have done anything to keep from dragging them into the mess he had created… including selling fifty-five percent of his business. All his precious Nita knew was he had a silent partner that bought into the company. She was blind to the fact that Larson practically owned it.

That young man had given more than enough to keep him from being financially ruined and provided him with a modest retirement. He would be forever grateful to that young man. Kelley Kincaid had been backed up all the way in a corner and stood a chance of losing everything. He had to admit he was a bit leery at first when he met Larson face-to-face. He reminded him of one of those rappers he had seen on *BET* from time to time with braids and jewelry. Larson explained he had just gotten off of a job, something about him being a bodyguard for somebody performing in Houston. During the next meeting he had transformed into the businessman his friend had spoken highly of. He was shrewd and highly intelligent in the business sense along with a very impressive portfolio. His credentials were impeccable. He would make any father proud or father-in-law for that matter he thought with a broad smile on his face. He was not going to play matchmaker, but that Larson and Kellie would make an excellent team all around. The old man shook his head, he knew that was farfetched. She was livid when he informed her of bringing him on as his CEO and President. He thought after he had agreed to lease the new vehicles she wanted, that would have sweetened the news, of course he was wrong. Well, she was going to have to get use to it and deal. It was out of his hands. Although he was sworn to secrecy, it was Larson and his money that made it possible to spend that small fortune. Besides, Larson was the man in charge now!

***

Kellie Kincaid blew out a long sigh as she took her seat in the first class section. She was glad she made her reservations earlier. The plane was full to capacity. It's nothing she hated more than being jammed right smack between two other people. Coach seats are nothing but a joke, she thought checking her bag. She needed her daily planner and magazine that she had been trying to get to for weeks. Besides reading romance novels she looked forward to *Belle* every month. She had a self-satisfied smile on her face as she recalled the first time she set eyes on a *Belle* magazine. There was a plus size woman on the cover wearing a swimsuit. But that's not what caught her eye. The caption said *Love Story! This time we get the man.* Now that was something! She was about to put the book back on the shelf when an attractive sister who look to weigh every bit of three hundred pounds told her she was missing a treat not reading that magazine. Kellie felt she didn't need to read about being a plus size woman...she was living that life and as far as

34

getting a man...please. But the sister was right about the magazine. She looked forward to the fashions and tips they had to offer, plus she enjoyed reading all of the articles in each issue. Kellie had to secretly admit she read the ones about getting a man too. She also loved reading the letters from the readers. Of course her heart went out to the ones who had been heartbroken because they were rejected by some man because of their size. As far as she was concern most men were fickle when it came to a woman's size and career choice. They were narrow minded and full of drama. She's made it her business never to entertain such nonsense and was better off without the complications.

Kellie knew she was called names behind her back. Maybe she did have a tiny bit of an attitude when it came to men. Who was she fooling? She at least needed to be honest with herself, but the kind of business she was in she had to have attitude. She had to maintain respect and make it known she was not somebody that could be pushed around or walked on...being a helpless female was not going to get it. Kellie worked with men and cars and had to make it clear she could hold her own and then some. Oh yes ma'am, she did just that. She's seen firsthand how some men can manipulate and run right over a woman in her shoes. She just couldn't go out like that. Kellie Kincaid has worked too hard and deserved more. If she runs across the kind of man she thinks she could work a strong partnership deal with, then just maybe...Okay, she was like any other single black woman... humph, she wanted a black prince too. And when she finds him, she'll snap him up with the quickness!

She closed her magazine. This time not even *Belle* was holding her interest. Boy did she have a lot to tell Gracie. Of course Kat probably knows already since Gregory and Jeremy were family. But she knew Gracie was not going to believe a single word she had to say. Humph, she could hardly believe it herself. She closed her eyes and carefully went over the whole conversation mentally. The vacation cruise was one thing, but retirement from his baby, KTS was unbelievable. Kellie was totally overwhelmed. Not only was he retiring, but he was dispatching his school bus...at least that's what he was calling it. He was selling the main source of revenue that started his whole operation fifty years ago. Kellie knew he was sentimental when it came to his school buses. She had tried so many times to get him to reorganize that part of the. It was a known fact that he actually didn't need school buses, mini vans could do the same job. But up until now no one was able to make him see that. Kelley Kincaid had been determined to do it his way and only his way. Kellie guess she can thank uhn uhn... no way was she going there.

The next disturbing news was him executing his last will and testament when she returns. She couldn't believe he was taking it that far. After he assured her there was nothing physically wrong with him, he continued with the inevitable. He had hired Gregory Larson as his CEO. Now that's when her mouth flew open. She was speechless. Kellie knew she wasn't ready to take on that kind of responsibility, but she would have given it her best shot, anything to keep HIM out of their family business. What in the world was he thinking? What made him even think of HIM? Where did he come from? Wasn't he supposed to be in somebody's prison, not somewhere developing some impressive portfolio as Uncle Kel had put it. She could handle everything else, but Larson, as in Gregory Adams Larson.

Kellie hadn't heard that name in twelve years. Why now? The mere sound of his name caused her to be sick. What made her uncle think for one minute she could work with him. Did he remember the ordeal she went through? Okay so he was not trying to attack her. According to him he was only trying to offer her a ride to the gas station...humph... the ugly remarks he made that got back to her was a reflection of his cruelty and cockiness. Until that particular day she always thought they were cordial friends. They always spoke to each other in passing. She was even thinking of asking...No, she was now going there. Lord, Uncle Kel what have you done? Kellie sensed nothing but chaos, confusion, and trouble. Kellie truly needed a vacation more so after today. She could still see her Uncle's smirk grin as he assure her she could handle the new transition hands down.

One thing for sure it wasn't over with yet. She was not going to allow her hard work and energy to dribble down the drain. Gregory Larson needn't think for one minute that he was going to waltz in KTS without a serious fight. He was definitely going to feel every bit of her wrath vowed Kellie as she batted her eyelids to restrain the tears that were threatening to fall.

CHAPTER 5

The pilot's announcement caused her to jump. She looked around to see if anyone was looking. Kellie couldn't believe she actually fell asleep, even though it was understandable. She was exhausted and emotionally drained from the extra work she's done. Kellie had chauffeured two weekends in a row for two weddings and an anniversary and had to admit it really wasn't work and enjoyed every minute of it. She took great pleasure in being around people in love especially newlyweds. Kellie was truly a romanticist at heart. That's something they probably won't see Gregory Larson doing. *Girl give it a rest, you're on vacation, she scolded silently!*

She looked at her watch as she fastened her seat belt, and prayed Gracie was there waiting for her. Even though she had taken a nap on the plane, she was still tired and sleepy. She couldn't wait to lay her body down to just rest. But knowing her Gracie, she probably planned a whole evening of entertainment, starting with dinner and then drag her to some comedy club. She did mention one of her favorite comedians was appearing at the Comedy Club House. Whatever was planned for her, she couldn't wait to see her girl!

Kellie and Grace met during their sophomore year in college. Grace had just transferred from a junior college to Texas Southern University. They had become roommates and have remained the best of friends. Once she received her pharmacy and graduate degree, she moved back home to establish a pharmacy in her family's clinic. Regardless of the hundreds of miles that has separated them, they have sustained a very close relationship. Its true KTS has hampered her traveling some, but they still manage to meet for weekend trips for short holidays during off seasons. Gracie also makes it her business to come to Houston at least twice a year for TSU homecoming and friends and family day.

Kellie had a satisfied smile on her face as she remembered their conversation last night. Gracie kept going on and on about how she couldn't believe she was actually coming to Atlanta. It was true it had been awhile since her last visit. But Kellie got the impression that Gracie's excitement was a bit much just because she planned a vacation in Atlanta. Yes...something was up. She couldn't quite put her finger on it but she was positive there was something going on. When she asked her about it, Gracie pretended she didn't know what she was talking about. They had never kept any secrets between the two of them and certainly they were not going to start at this late date. One thing for sure once they get to New York with Sandy, Gracie won't have a chance keeping a secret from the both of them. If anyone could get it out of her it would be Sandy. She had a gift for getting people to tell all. They have always teased her about how she would be a good talk show host. Sandy definitely had skills in that department. You don't have a prayer Grace Taylor, with the both of us, we'll get it out of you and that's a promise, vowed Kellie.

***

"Where are you Gracie," asked Kellie as she paced up and down the sidewalk keeping a close eye on her luggage. It sure would be terrible to have her luggage stolen. Then too that wouldn't be such a bad idea, she would just have to go shopping. Next to KTS, shopping was her next passion. Her closets were stuffed with enough clothes for three people. All the Kincaid women had that sickness. It had been passed down through the genes.

Kellie took a quick look inside the terminal once again. Maybe she parked the car and was inside, but that couldn't be. She specifically remembers Gracie telling her she would be out front at the arriving flight entrance. She couldn't use her cell because it died during the flight. Just as Kellie was about to take another look she heard someone shouting her name in the mist of honking horns and airport announcements. She turned around to see who was calling her, it certainly wasn't a female's voice and whoever he was recognized her from the back. Had to be someone that knew her too well, after all she had her back turned and they hadn't seen her face yet. A smooth deep baritone voice sung her name again. Such richness thought

Kellie as she faced the owner.

***

Kellie heard the front door close. At last she and her best friend were finally alone. She had spent the whole evening with Gracie and her fiancé. And once again she received another shocker for the day. She didn't even know Grace was seeing anyone special, certainly didn't know she had gotten serious about one of her suitors she was dating. She never said a word nor dropped any hints. Kellie couldn't help but be a little hurt because Grace had kept Carl L. Henson a secret. Out of all the times they talked not one time did she mention him. They were buddies and best friends even though they were miles apart. They talked on the phone at least once a week and left each other emails daily. One thing for sure he had to be someone pretty fantastic to capture her buddy's heart. Why the big secret though? She hadn't had a chance to share her own news.

Kellie peeped into the front room to make sure the coast was clear, but no one was there. She couldn't believe Gracie left without saying a word to her, boy did she have it bad. She had all the signs of a woman that was utterly in love. Kellie never thought she would see the day her buddy actually cook a full course meal, with all the trimmings. Gracie hated cooking! Yes sireee… not only was she deep in love, but with a preacher!

The noise of the door opening startled Kellie. She went back to the front and stood in the foyer with her lips tightly closed and arms folded trying desperately to hold back her smile. Even though she wanted to pretend she was hurt, she couldn't hold back the excitement and happiness she was feeling for her best friend.

"Okay bud-dy, you've been holding out on me," sang Kellie. "And I want to know why?"

Gracie was wearing a girlish lighthearted expression which was totally out of character. She was exhibiting the behavior of a schoolgirl in love for the first time. Kellie knew this wasn't the first time a man had captured her heart. She had traveled down the road of love before. Regardless of her being a plus size woman men were always knocking on her door. She carried herself with a certain flair that attracted them like flies. Gracie could

39

put a small woman to shame when she steps in a room. She had it all...beauty, brains, prestige, and money. Any black man that was about something would be honored to have her in his life. But it was always her decision not to get seriously involved. At least that's the song she's been singing up until now. This Carl L. Henson must really be something.

Without a word spoken, Gracie was airborne and floated right past her to the patio. With her arms still folded Kellie shook her head in disbelief and followed her to their favorite spot. They both took their seats in silence waiting for the other to speak first.

"Kellie"...

"Gracie"... The two friends burst into teenage giggles as they shed tears of joy. "I can't believe my girl is fixing to jump the broom," sniffed Kellie as they held on to each other. "You pulled one on me this time buddy. I just don't understand why you didn't tell me."

Gracie wiped her eyes with the tail of her blue jean shirt before she spoke. "Kellie you just don't know. I wanted to tell you but I wasn't sure just where all of this was going. It happened so fast." She told her the whole story as to when and how everything came into play. Gracie explained in detail how they were two of the five people who working on the committee for establishing the new senior citizen daycare center at the church. She and Carl's job was to design a proposal for the healthcare services they wanted to offer along with locating resources that would assist them in providing the best care. One thing led to another with them working late hours, grabbing a quick bite in between to having lunch or dinners at some of Atlanta's finest restaurants. The next thing she knew they were having Sunday dinners, evening strolls, taking in movies, and attending plays and gospel concerts. Gracie blushed at she ended her story because she too couldn't believe how she was acting. She was so out of character, but she had to admit she was in love and knew that's what Kellie was waiting for her to say. She felt compelled to give her just what she wanted to hear. "I LOVE HIM!"

Kellie couldn't contain herself as she clapped her hands. "Okay buddy, now let's talk about the good part. When did he propose? When is the big day? Can he kiss? Do you really have that deep down inside to your bones kind, that says I can't live without him? Have ya'll done the...Naw you don't have to answer that one." Both ladies burst in laughter!

Gracie grabbed her friend for another buddy hug, as they like to call them and answered all the questions in one breath. "Last night, the date has not been set, and yes to your other questions."

Kellie told her again how happy she was that she found her Ebony Prince. Gracie knew just where the conversation was going. She knew Kellie was still having those silly dreams. She really wished her number one buddy could find true love too and not in some kind of dream. Kellie didn't know it, but her time was coming soon. She was having a hard time keeping another secret...Gracie was going to introduce her to one of Carl's friends who was an excellent catch. The brother had everything going for himself too. The best thing about the new prospect was he had accepted a job transfer to one of the major insurance companies in Houston. Talking about coincidences, this has to be the one. She couldn't have planned it any better herself. Everything was set, even Carl agreed the two of them should hit it off. Gracie couldn't wait to set her buddy up. She deserved a real man and not someone that existed only in her dreams.

CHAPTER 6

"Kellie, baby you don't know how many times I've dreamed of us being together like this. It seems I've waited for this moment forever." Dragging sweet intoxicating kisses between her full bosoms caused sensuous passionate moans to escape from her trembling lips. Kellie held him captive tightly between her heavy thighs and arms as he caused her body to go through a series of stages that she had never experienced before. "That's it baby hold me tight," he whispered as he caressed her fleshy middle right down to her navel with tantalizing moist kisses. Her entire body shuddered as every nerve incited its own awakening. Together they rocked to the seductive rhythm of their favorite song, sung by their favorite artist Teddy Pendergrass. As they both encounter simmering hot passionate furies while soaring to high plains, he knew it was time to claim what was his. He was going to make sure she would never yearn for another as he reached for protection. Kellie was anxious. This was so new to her. She had no idea it could be so mind blowing. Sure she had read in books about how it was supposed to be and heard many tales, but this was far more than what she had ever expected. Each caress and sensuous stroke caused a struggle within her to maintain consciousness. Slowly losing the battle, she held on to him as if her life depended on...

"Kellie! Kellie!" She jumped straight up at the sound of her name and looked around at her surroundings. Focusing in on her whereabouts she tried to calm her erratic heartbeat. She took deep breaths attempting to calm her heated body down. Needless to say it was hopeless and caused her to become embarrassed. It's just a dream Kellie Kincaid! It's just a dream. She would be grateful if her mind and body could understand just that.

"Kellie is everything alright?" she asked. She heard strange noises coming from her bedroom. Gracie called herself letting her sleep late, but it was almost ten and they needed to get a move on if they were going to make it to the basketball game before it was over. This was Brotherhood Saturday according to the sisters from neighboring congregations. It was Westend Church's time to host the brotherhood's monthly meeting. Following their meeting and brunch they usually wrapped the day up with a game of basketball among the younger brothers. Sisters of all ages gather together to cheer them on and of course they complete the day with a picnic spread of all kinds of delicious foods. This was a golden opportunity to meet eligible, single, Christian men. It was Gracie's plan to stop by so Kellie could meet Carl's friend that she had picked out for her. But if her sleepy head friend doesn't get up her plans will be ruined.

"Come in Gracie, I'm up." Now you are, she said to herself. Struggling to get her mind and body in check, Kellie knew Gracie was right. She did need a man, a real man and soon. Maybe it was time for her to think about taking that same road Gracie was getting ready to travel down. Just one problem, she didn't have any prospects.

"Buddy are you going to sleep the whole morning away. We have things to do...places to go...and people to see." Kellie didn't have to say a word, the evidence was there, and her facial expression screamed out. *I dreamt about him again!* Ohhhhh it's a good thing I've made plans thought Grace to herself.   Looking at her buddy closely the sign I'm in need was plastered all over her face.

"No buddy, I'm getting ready to get up now. I was having a terrible nightmare, I'm glad you woke me up," lied Kellie. She couldn't dare admit to Gracie she was still having that stupid dream and it was becoming more passionate each time.

"Well get in a hurry sistah girl so we can get in the streets. I have our day already planned and it's time we get started." Getting out of bed Kellie rushed right pass Gracie and headed straight to the bathroom while hollering back she'll be ready in a few minutes. Gracie shook her head as she turned to go back down stairs. She really needed to get her plans into motion. Her buddy was pitiful!

It was a beautiful day. The sun was shining brightly in an azure blue sky with dancing fluffy white clouds as playmates. Due to a light wind they were able to enjoy a pleasant breezy ride with the top down in Gracie's convertible BMW. The view was breathtaking. Although fall was around the corner, there were signs everywhere indicating it was closer. The trees and lawns were already transforming into bright fall colors that added to the rich color scheme of the blooming year round flowers. This was the time of the year Kellie enjoyed visiting Atlanta. She always loved seeing the spectacular colors of the foliage. Kellie had never seen purple or red leaves on tall trees until she visited this great city ten years ago. She couldn't understand why she didn't come often. But deep down she knew why, but it was too late now. At this point things were going to change. Her number one buddy was getting married. Just like Kat she was giving up her freedom to become a wife and later mother. By the time Kat was twenty-six she was the mother of three adorable children and loved every minute of it. Grace would be next. Boy was that hard to believe.

With one of *Gladys Knight's* CD's jamming in the CD player they continued their scenic route to the church. In between singing along with *Gladys*, Gracie told her the kind of wedding she wanted. That's something they had never discussed during their entire friendship. Although Kellie had planned her own, it was a secret. Gracie had never shown any interest in such matters. When she expressed she had always wanted a fall wedding and actually had it written down to every detail, Kellie was speechless. She had truly underestimated her girl.

The best friends were both moving their heads side to side while singing one of *Gladys's* classics *If I Were Your Woman*. This had to be one of the best songs *Gladys* ever made thought Kellie as she continued singing in her *Gladys Knight* voice. They burst into giggles when she took her cell and pretended it was a microphone.

"Go girl," shouted Gracie. And she did just that. Throwing her head back with her cell phone at her mouth she ended the popular tune just as soulful as *Gladys*. "Buddy you're still good with your *Gladys Knight* impression." They both knew what the other was thinking, their college days when they would all get together and entertain themselves with talent shows. She was just about to make a request when her buddy announced they had arrived at their destination.

Gracie pulled into the parking lot that faced the church's park facility. They had a crowd as usual with brothers of all ages everywhere. The basketball game was in progress as several other activities were going on. She drove around to find the closest parking spot, there was none. It seems everyone was out today. It had to be more than just brotherhood meeting today. Surely this is not what goes on at these meetings she thought pulling up in a space that was made just for her small sports BMW.

It was evident they were thinking the same thing, when Gracie asked Kellie if she thought they did the same thing in Houston. Neither knew the answer to the question, but it was definitely worth Kellie's time to find out as they got out of the car. If anybody knew Nisey would, and she was certainly going to ask about it the next time they talk. Walking over to the court they took in the scenery. Everything had been set up for a fabulous time. They passed two barbecue pits filled with sausages, wieners, and hamburger patties on wheels. Ice chests were set up at the end of each picnic table, which were covered and flourished with all the necessary trimmings for a fantastic picnic. Kellie couldn't wait until it was time to break bread, she was famished. She spent her morning sleeping… correction dreaming instead of having breakfast. Her stomach was making sure she knew she hadn't eaten since last night. Of course she could miss a couple of meals, humph that was not her intentions. That's one thing about Kellie Kincaid, she knew she was a big girl and had no problem with her size. As they approached the basketball court she noticed on the opposite end was the children's playground. There right in the midst was a snow cone machine surround by little people. Kellie shook her head, no way, she was on vacation.

"Here Kellie we can sit and see everything," said Gracie stopping at the section that had been set up for spectators. Sitting down Kellie gazed at the brothers that were on the court. Such bodies, she thought as she raised her shades up to get a better view. I wonder where is that handsome preacher with the smooth sexy voice, she said to herself. "Oh there's my Baby," shouted Gracie waving wildly like some adolescent. Kellie snapped her head in her direction to see if it was still her friend Grace Taylor, sitting next to her. She ignored her and waved at her man that was sitting on the end of the court. Humph, he's not even playing thought Kellie. All of a sudden the roaring of the crowd caused them both to stand up to see what was happening. The crowd was going wild as they chanted Westend! "What happened?" asked Gracie. Kellie looked at her as if she had lost what little mind she had left. She knew darn well she was not into basketball, football, or any kind of ball for that matter. Watching men running, sweating, and falling all over themselves was not her. She drugged her here not the other way around. Surely she wasn't expecting her to answer that question.

She didn't have to answer. The woman behind them proudly informed them her eighteen year old Baby just threw a three pointer.

"See that's him with the black sweatband." She must be kidding thought Kellie, most of the men out there had on black sweatbands. They were all dressed practically alike except for the muscle t-shirts that exposed biceps and triceps. One team had on black muscle t-shirts and black shorts and the other had on red muscle t-shirts and black shorts. "Strut your stuff Baby," yelled the woman.

"Oh Kellie look at Carl dribble that ball." Gracie was now standing up cheering her man on. "You know he went to college on an athletic scholarship," she said proudly. "Go Baby! Go Baby! He's so cute, huh Kellie?" Lord where is my buddy, because this woman sitting here grinning like an idiot can't be her. Really she was acting like all the other ladies whose men were on the court, smirked Kellie to herself. *I hear a little jealousy uttered her conscience.*

Carl was just about to make a shot when this ebony prince swooped out from nowhere like a Dennis Rodman and snatched the ball right out of his hand. Kellie stood with the other sisters. It can't be she thought. Stretching her neck to see around Grace, who was now standing in front of her to voice her disapproval, she couldn't believe what she was seeing. Moving Grace out of her way, she could see clearly as her mouth flew wide open, it was HIM, the man on the plane in Dallas. The same one she's been dreaming about for the last few months. The one she was dreaming about this morning.

"What is wrong with you? You act like you've seen a buggerbear or something," whispered Gracie as she took her seat, with her eyes still glued to her buddy. Kellie likewise took her seat too.

It was HIM! Lord, she was trying hard to maintain control and hold in her excitement. He looked even better than before. He was at least six-four and had to weigh every bit of two hundred and twenty-five pounds. Thick solid muscles, bulging everywhere were now visible because of his sport's attire. Short braids were pulled up with a black sweatband which sat right above his sexy eyebrows that met in the center of his forehead. He was quite handsome even with sweat dripping from his smooth chocolate cream frame. He had grown sideburns that blended right into a shadowy beard. His mustache that curved around his sexy lips had the same thickness as his sideburns. He had to work out to have a body like that. His broad chest and back along with his powerful arms and legs were living proof. He was nothing but pure bulk with smooth muscles and easy on his feet. Just gorgeous! Absolutely gorgeous! His strong powerful legs ran up and down the court as he snatched the ball once again with his long muscular arms to give his team a six point lead. He was treacherous on the court.

Kellie tried desperately to hold in her excitement as she continued her thorough assessment of the fine brother. It was impossible because her treasonous lips turned up into a silly smile. At least Gracie couldn't see her insides were now quivering which was shameful how her body was reacting. But that was her secret for now. If she didn't stop this perspiring though everyone will know something was wrong with her, and it was not medical. It was a pleasant brisk afternoon and she was not running up and down a court. Oh Kellie you must get a hold to yourself. This is a perfect stranger you're lusting after. Kellie still had not answered her buddy. At that moment she couldn't bring herself to say one word. Gracie looked in the direction which held her undivided attention. Kellie knew it was obvious to her buddy if no one else. They knew each other just that well, at least up until now.

"What? What?" Kellie sounded like a child caught with her hand in a cookie jar. She knew she sounded silly and that's just how she felt. But that was HIM! Before Gracie could respond to her buddy the horn went off announcing the game was over. Westend had beaten Decatur by six points and it was a first. Decatur has a pretty good team in the brotherhood and has been victorious, but not today.

The man of her dreams had given his team a victory with his last six points. Everybody crowded onto the court to congratulate the winning team. Kellie followed the crowd keeping a close eye on HIM. In a matter of seconds he was surrounded by women. He must be that kind she thought watching him hug each and every. She should have known. Kellie closed her eyes as if she could easily erase him totally from her mind.

"Oh Sweetie, I'm so sorry your team lost the game. You were so good." Kellie shook her head as she watched and listened to her friend, absolutely amazing. It was just too hard to believe that people in love actually acted this way. Carl and Grace embraced like true lovers. They made a striking couple. She turned and looked the other way hoping she might catch a last glimpse, but he was no longer in sight. Probably left…

"Hey man, sorry about making that fantastic play on you." Kellie had only heard that rasping smooth whisper once, but she could never forget it. She turned to face HIM. There he was with several of his teammates, the man of her dreams. Once again their paths had crossed. Kellie's heart seemed to stop when he looked her way. His designer shades hid his dark piercing eyes that she so much wanted to see. She watched his lips move as he spoke to Carl. Yes, the lips that were really made for kissing instead of talking. She remembered well. Kellie closed her shielded eyes as she unconsciously licked her lips. Realizing what she was doing, she primped them and turned around to get her composure. What was wrong with her? She's seen handsome men before. Why was she carrying on this way? This didn't make any sense whatsoever. Taking deep breaths she turned at an angle pretending she had to block the sun out of her face. Thank God no one was paying any attention to her. Carl and Gracie were all hugged up while the handsome stranger from her dreams continued teasing him. Carl apologized for his manners and introduced him to Grace.

Right in the middle of his introduction his cell rang. Kellie blew a sigh of relief. She had such a strange feeling to come over her just as they were about to be introduced. Talk about being saved by the bell, he politely excused himself and turned his back. Even though she wanted to know just who he was, something fierce was pulling at her and she couldn't explain what. Carl continued his introductions with the other members from both teams. He turned back around to face them waiting his turn when his cell phone rang again. What rotten luck he thought as he excused himself one more time.

He started walking off a bit as he talked to the party. It was evident the conversation was not going like he wanted. His body stiffened as he walked further away. Must be a jealous lover thought Kellie as she turned away to face one of Carl's friends who was asking her something. His name was Walter. Kellie's eyes were still glued to HIM. She was glad she had shades on so no one could see her actually watching HIM… including the man himself. She certainly didn't want him to think for one minute she was trying to hear the conversation. Being the friend she is Gracie could sense something was up and suggested they all go over to the picnic tables and eat.

Thank God for his dark shades that hid his wandering eyes, he thought turning back around so he could see HER. He could hardly finish his conversation as his eyes traveled down Her large frame, thick and luscious. That's how he remembered the lady with the ice tea complexion that almost snatched his bracelet off his arm. Man, could he use a cool sip of HER right about now. That's not what he meant shaking his head trying to clear his mind. Breaking out into a sweat, he really needed to cool off. But it was HER! What luck!

He could still feel her soft caressing touch that unsettles him every time he recalls that incident. Sparks that set him on fire for HER. Just like she did that day when she innocently held his wrist while trying to rescue his bracelet from her garment bag. She was so apologetic about the entire situation. He only wished it had taken longer. Never in his life time did he think he would set eyes on HER again. Lord the baby had back and looked good too! He couldn't keep his eyes to himself as she walked off with the rest of the group. He watched the sassy sway of HER hips as his heartbeat danced wildly to each sensuous movement. Walter can forget about being with HER. He was claiming this woman as his own before the day ends. As they got into the food line she turned around to block the sun out of her face once again. Thanks again for the sun!

He continued admiring HER. She was a vision of loveliness in her Capri jeans, turquoise paisley print blouse, denim sandals, and turquoise jewelry. A matching scarf was wrapped around her head with small curls peeping out. Wait a minute, that's not the way her hair was the last time he saw HER. With a puzzled expression on his face, it then registered... she had on a hat that day. Yep, grinning to his self as he remembered precisely her entire outfit. He was not one to pay that kind of attention to what a woman wears, just as long as she looks nice. But he remembers that day well. She had on a black velvet hat with a silver pin that was used to pin the rim up in the front and a stylish black pantsuit that she wore with grace.

She pulled at her ruffled V-neck top which exposed a little cleavage and stopped midway her hips showing off her God given blessings...ample hips and a luscious bottom. He never understood sisters that tried to hide their main assets. Of course he's met some that didn't have a problem and believed in flaunting it. Now those were some bold sisters he thought, and enjoyed watching them too, even if some of them didn't have it together. Although he's dated women of all sizes from small to large, he has always admired and appreciated plus size women. And he was truly taking great pleasure in viewing the scenery she was providing at the present time.

What he really wanted to see were those dreamy dark amber colored eyes that danced lively when she gets excited. Like the day she hooked his arm. That was just one of the many things he remembered. He smiled at that very thought as he continued enjoying her alluring beauty. Her full figure and cool ice tea complexion complimented her outfit in every way. The sister looked like a million bucks as his eyes traveled down her large voluptuous frame. He liked what he saw. Such nice long thick legs too. The better to hold you tight... Where did that come from? Okay my brother, pull yourself together and stop drooling. He was acting like a horny teenager. Willing his body and mind to behave, he took deep breaths to steady his erratic heartbeat and gain control. After all, this was the woman that has constantly plagued his mind since their meeting.

"G-Man, are you listening to me. I need you!" screamed the frantic

50

woman on the other end of the phone. He snapped, all he heard was she needed him. His mind was elsewhere.

"Jacquè, I hear you baby, what's up?" He knew it was too good to be true, leave Atlanta without doing one more show for Jacquè. At least it will be all over once he moves. He hoped she was not up to her old tricks trying to entice him into staying. He had enough of that kind of life. Yes the money was good, in fact he had benefit very much, but he was through with that line of work. It's not like she couldn't get someone else to do these little jobs. A number of brothers could use the extra income.

"One of my people had an emergency and I need you to fill in." Before he could say a word she continued, but this time she started in on him with her flattery request. "G-Man you know you always bring the house down and have the women going crazy. Please help me out this one time. You know the money is all-good. We can turn it into a going away party, your last time modeling in Atlanta. Please sweet thang, I'll be forever in your debt." She patiently waited for an answer.

"Okay Jacquè, you can stop with the song and dance act, where and what time?" She was right about one thing he would be leaving and all of this will be behind him.

"I wonder what's that all about," asked Gracie as they stood in line. "And I might add you've been acting mighty strange. Do you already know him? I could have sworn you were hawking him during the game." Gracie waited for a response. Kellie totally ignored her. Just as she was about to start on her again one of the servers asked her what would she like to have. After being served they found the perfect spot to eat their lunch and take in the view. Kellie looked around to see if he was still there. She spotted him over by the court talking to another one of the players, and then he turned and left practically running. Of course thought Kellie, not only was he a womanizer he was also rude.

CHAPTER 7

G-Man was steaming as he pulled out of the parking lot. This was the first time he decided to stay and play a little ball and socialize. As a matter of fact Harold was the one who invited him to play. Something about them needing a secret weapon so they could finally beat this team today. Harold was aware of his skills. He did play a little ball in college. He was certainly going to give his man a call and a big thank you. Today had been incredible until his old friend Jacquè called. Now he didn't have time for anything thanks to her whining as usually. He had to rush to take a quick shower and change clothes to make it to the hotel on time. G-Man smiled to himself as he thought about HER and how he would love for them to take a long hot bath. He visualized the two of them soaking and caressing each other in their favorite bath foam. Soft music playing in the background, scented candles for light, and chilled apple cider for sipping, and a tray of fresh fruit would provide the perfect ambiance. G-Man shook his head to stop his imagination from running away. Mrs. D was right, he did need someone special in his life and thank God he finally found her. Man did he regret not being able to have lunch with them and hope the tickets for the show will let them know how sorry he was for running off like he did before they could have a formal introduction. Before he hung up with Jacquè he insisted on having runway seats for some personal friends. They would be waiting for them at the door. G-Man was planning on showing them the time of their lives and couldn't wait to see HER. For once he was looking forward to the fashion show. This time his payment would be them exchanging more than just names for sure.

***

The phone was ringing off the hook as Kellie and Gracie walked in the house. Gracie couldn't imagine who it could be. She just left Sweetie and she had already talked to her parents and gave them the details about the wedding.

"Where in the world have you two been," shouted Sandy. "I've been calling you for the last four hours. Neither one of you even answered your cells. I was getting ready to put out a missing person bulletin on both of you." Sandra Waters was known for exaggerating. She was their drama queen!

"Hello to you too Sandy," said Gracie motioning for Kellie to pick up the other receiver. "Kellie and I are just getting back from the basketball game. You know, I told you about it yesterday."

"Did you tell her yet," asked Sandy cutting Gracie off.

"No, I did not. I was saving that for you to do."

"Tell me what! What are you two keeping from me?" Kellie knew it. Something was going on and once again she had been left in the dark.

***

Kellie couldn't believe it. Sandra Waters was married and moving to Europe. She and her husband were stopping in Atlanta so they could meet him and see her before she leaves the country. Now that was unbelievable! What was next? What other surprises were in store for her in the month of September. Kellie was excited and couldn't wait to see Sandy and her husband. She wondered what was he like, to have her friend all bubbly. All she could get out of her was that he was absolutely wonderful. The love bug had given her a serious infection that could be treated only by Dalton Ashton Jr.

***

Kellie was being summoned by Gracie. The guys would be there in a few minutes. She checked herself in the mirror as she ruffled her short natural curls. Before leaving for her vacation, she told her stylist to give her a new look. Bronwyn had out done herself this time. She loved her new haircut, just the right length where she could style it in many different ways. Natural short hair was much easier for her to manage than the long hair she had been wearing all of her adult life, especially since she's always on the go. She was very pleased. Kellie heard her name being called again. Let's face it she thought, Gracie was as bad as Sandy. They both had a bad case of *"I love you's."*

Walter had invited all of them to Georgia's Annual Greek Fashion Show Extravaganza that was being held in Atlanta this year. Kellie smiled to herself, at least she hadn't thought about HIM. Well not much! No telling what kind of business he was into hiding under the name Christian. She must do something about the mix emotions she was having. It was strange no one had mentioned his name or said anything about HIM. Maybe he was new to the church. Kellie had to admit she was curious, after all she had been having sizzling hot dreams for months. A knock on the front door interrupted her thoughts, signaling it was time. Taking one last quick look, she turned the lights out and hurried downstairs.

"Wow! Don't you look beautiful," exclaimed Walter. "Doesn't she guys?" As usual the betrothed couple was engaged in a little lip lock. Walter and Kellie chuckled. Gracie and Carl faced them with big wide smiles. Kellie came to the conclusion it was no way they were going to last until December. Not these two…The power of love!

Kellie turned to face her date and thanked him for his compliment. This was her first date in months and she wanted to look especially nice tonight and she did. It's amazing she had to come all the way to Atlanta to get a date. Anyway, she had on a new dress she had purchased last year and forgot it was in the closet. Kellie loves shopping and her closet was full, so it was easy for her to forget what was in there. Nisey and Lynette always teased her about being ready if she didn't get to go with all the clothes she had. Of course they couldn't talk, they were the ones who got her started.

When she packed for her trip she was a little bit concerned whether or not some of the pieces she selected would still fit. But she must admit she made some excellent choices in spite of her not trying everything on before she left. Kellie had not been counting her calories lately and may have put on a few pounds. Who was she trying to fool, she only counted calories when she was only around certain family members and sometimes she didn't do it then. She had accepted the fact that she was a big girl years ago and that was that. Once upon a time her wardrobe was drab and dark, but not anymore. Her closet was full of vibrant colors of the rainbow and any dark pieces she owns are sexy and eye catching like the one she was wearing tonight. She had been one of those big women that bought into the idea that dark colors were slenderizing. Needless to say she learned regardless to what you put on you cannot hide your size. *As Gracie always said people can see how big you are, so what are you hiding?* Therefore Kellie Kincaid adopted a whole new attitude about being overweight and made it her business to maintain good health by eating healthy and exercising periodically. Her flawless complexion allows her to wear pretty much any color she chooses. Yes, she was blessed with a large healthy body that was well proportioned from her head down to her feet. Nothing was small about her, and she's learned to love and accept herself for who she is.

"You look quite handsome too," complimented Kellie and he did.

Both men were striking in their black designer's suits with white collarless shirts and black shoes. The ladies looked at each other and agreed silently they had some handsome escorts. Of course Kellie and Grace were gorgeous in their knee length black strapless dresses, both exposing long beautiful legs, manicured feet in silver sandals with matching bags. Gracie's black satin dress had a sweetheart neckline and balloon skirt. She selected a shiny silvery chiffon shawl for a drape and matching silver jewelry which were perfect accessories. Kellie on the other hand chose a sheer metallic shawl in fading shades of platinum to add pizzazz to her soft satin midriff waist band dress with its flowing full skirt of layered chiffon. Her trillion cut silver jewelry set and bracelets dazzled her outfit.

"I hate to interrupt a good thing Bro. Henson, but it's time we get a move on. I would hate for someone to take our table." With that said Gracie grabbed her keys and they left, but not before she gave her buddy a smile of approval.

***

The hotel ballroom with its plush gold carpet was simply breathtaking. Beautiful green plants and exotic flowers with a sparkling waterfall right in the midst were placed in opposite corners to set a festive and romantic atmosphere. Crystal chandeliers hung from the ceiling reflecting vivid hues of multi-colors onto the tables accenting the décors and symbols which represented the Black Greek Sororities and Fraternities. A real stage and runway was set up with colorful illuminate lightening on opposite sides like the ones you see at the upscale fashion shows in New York. Huge baskets filled with roses of various colors were on each side of the stage. Waiters walked around with trays that had a variety of appetizers and drinks. This was truly going to be a gala affair, thought Kellie as she took in the total picture. Dollar signs flashed before her. Ways for KTS to make money was always on her mind and she could see them making a small fortune providing limousine services for such an occasion. She would have to check into this. Maybe the Greek organizations in Texas could do something of this magnitude with Houston being the first host. Kellie would have to mention this to her aunt and sisters who were Deltas. She never took the time to pledge during undergraduate and kept putting it off after graduate school.

They were escorted to seats right on the runway. Mmmm. Walter had some very influential friends for sure she thought taking a seat. He was being such a gentleman as he held her chair which was needed.

"Girl what do you think?" whispered Gracie. Kellie looked at her buddy and gave her a sweet smile of approval. Finally she found someone she could really be interested in.

The show was just about to start. The mistress of ceremonies made her way gracefully to the side of the stage where she would enlighten the audience with vivid details of the designs that were featured in the fashion exposé. The sound of light jazz in the background was the cue the extravaganza was beginning with a grand parade of the models wearing clothing that represented the designers that would be featured tonight. Cheers and applauds filled the room with excitement as they walked the runway. Just as everybody thought all the models were on stage, out strolled HIM. He was escorted by two beautiful women... one on each arm. Kellie's breath was caught in her throat. Breathe fool. He was more handsome than she could ever imagine. Ump... ump, she thought as she watched him take smooth confident strides. He was drop dead gorgeous. Lord Ha' Mercy...

The two escorts stopped midway the runway. Reaching for a long stem red rose he continued his cool confident stroll alone as the women in the audience went wild. Kellie was speechless. His four buttoned black designer's tux and white-collar band shirt looked like it had been made especially for HIM. It was a perfect fit. It had to be his personal suit. Broad shoulders swayed seductively to the music as he took lengthy leisure strides on powerful legs to where she was standing. Kellie didn't realize that she too was standing at the runway with the other women who were chanting something. Spellbound by his presence, she couldn't hear anything but the sound of her heart beating rapidly. It felt like it had traveled up to her throat. Her full bosom was keeping time to each note of her sporadic breathing. She was losing control of her body as their eyes locked. Close up she could see a small scar above his left eye. She never noticed that before as she yearned to plant tiny kisses on it. A broad smile spread across his handsome face as he stopped in front of her. The crowd became absolutely still as they waited and anticipated his next move. In a squatting position, he gave her the rose and tenderly kissed her trembling lips with such warmth. She couldn't believe her arms as they reached up to HIM. Then with a mind of their own, her fingers gently caressed the scar and his left cheek right to his sexy lips that were made for kissing. Lord, she had been hypnotized. He was fascinated as he took her hand and kissed each fingertip affectionately. Flying flickering sparks fused electric currents from him to her as he slowly returned her hand. It was no denying it, a room full of people witnessed the fire and chemistry that drew them to each other. He stood…smiled… and winked as he turned around to join his lady escorts. He knew at that very moment it was fate itself that brought them together. The crowd applauded wildly as he left the stage.

Kellie was still in awe as she returned to her seat. All the days of her life she's never made a spectacle of herself in public. Lord not like that. She needed a cold drink. She was here with one man and carrying on with a stranger. Kellie knew that wasn't true, he's invaded her thoughts and had been constantly in her dreams for months. It was the inevitable, and she had to find out his identity. Her secret thoughts caused her to smile inside. *He likes her! He actually likes her! He had made a point of seeking her out and…* Lord, what was she going to do?

"Buddy are you alright?" asked Gracie as she leaned over to look her in the face. Kellie still couldn't speak. She nodded her head like somebody's small child. For once she was speechless! "We must talk later. You've been acting pretty strange today. What is it about this man?" Kellie looked at her friend for understanding and sympathy. She couldn't explain her behavior right now. Not in the presence of their dates. Gracie gave her a comforting smile and patted her hand. She knew they would discuss in detail about tonight and she could wait. But she had to admit she had never in all the years they had been friends see her react in such a manner behind a man. Okay, he wasn't just any man. The brother was fine!

Kellie looked over at her date. Embarrassed was an understatement. Just as she found the words to apologize the models strolled out again in casual and sports attire. Her heart started pounding rapidly again as she anticipated seeing HIM. Relief, and thank God he was not in this group. She silently prayed a prayer of thanks because she needed to regain her sanity and pull herself together. She looked over at Walter…

"It's okay Kellie, he has that effect on all women." She still told him how sorry she was, and it was downright rude for her to behave in such a manner. She gave him a sweet peck on his cheek. After all he was a very nice person and was being a good sport about the whole situation.

"Do you know him?" asked Kellie as she took a sip of her tea. She was curious and wanted to get it out in the open. Maybe if she had a name to go with the face and body then perhaps she could. Perhaps nothing, she thought, a name was not going to help her in anyway. Walter leaned over to tell her his name, but the crowd started up again.

She didn't have to see HIM. She felt his presence as the crowd chanted. Every bone in her body said he was near. There he was this time alone! He strolled down the runway dressed in a designer's jogging suit. Black nylon pants and a matching jacket that was zipped covering his sexy body. Red and gold bands were down the leg of his pants and on the sleeve of the jacket. He wore black athletic tennis shoes that were also trimmed in red and gold. He was matching from head to toe. He continued his stroll with the audience watching his every step. Reaching into his pocket he pulled out a cell. The commentator announced he was making a date with some lucky lady in the audience. The women went wild when he pointed out into the crowd pretending to hold a conversation with someone. He continued his dignified stroll down to the end of the runway. On his way back he paused and honored Kellie once again with his sexy affectionate smile. It was a shame she never heard the commentator say his name nor describe his apparel. Well, this time she behaved sensibly. She looked at Walter again as she sipped more tea. She really needed nothing but the ice.

"They call him G-Man, but his name is Gregory Adams Larson. We all attend the Westend church." She went into a spasm of coughs. Her tea went down the wrong way. "Kellie are you alright?" Walter tapped her lightly on her back and Gracie handed her a napkin. Her eyes watered as she tried to catch her breath. She could barely be heard as she tried to speak. She needed to hear him repeat his name again. Truly he didn't say what she thought he said. Walter didn't have to oblige her, the commentator did that as she requested HIM to come back to the stage. The ladies wanted HIM to unzip his jacket. Kellie understood well this time as the women chanted G-Man... Honoring the ladies request he came back to the front of the runway. All the ladies were standing including Kellie as they were charmed by his every movement. Making eye contact with her he slowly unzipped his jacket exposing a solid sculptured six pack. No wonder the ladies made their request. She gasped... her eyes began to tear as he stood there tempting her with his flamboyant seductive smile. Who did he think he was?

Kellie grabbed her purse and quickly walked out fighting back tears. She had made a fool of herself once again with that Gregory Larson, this time in front of strangers. It was no way she could work with HIM now. She had to make Uncle Kel see that before it was too late. Something had to be done.

Gracie followed her with the men behind them. Kellie looked for the ladies' room. She didn't want to explain her action to anyone but her buddy. As a matter of fact at this very moment she didn't want to see another man! Kellie entered the ladies' room with Gracie on her heels. She was so caught up she didn't know she was being followed, but in all honesty she expected that kind of loyalty and support from her best friend. Gracie knew the story behind Gregory Larson and was aware of the ugly things he said about her. It was Gracie who was instrumental in helping her heal those old wounds and insecurities. Together they restored her confidence and rebuilt her self-esteem. Although Kellie was still a little apprehensive about dating, she still managed to date a little in college and occasionally now. There were never any serious relationships. It's not like she didn't want someone special in her life. She was like any other healthy woman. She wanted her chance at love and happiness too, but she was not willing to go through the drama and endure the heartaches all for the sake of love. Gracie tried so many times to make her see that anything worth having was worth a little pain and drama. Her philosophy was no drama…no pain. She didn't want to drag up the past. Besides, she wasn't sure if it was love she had for him or just a school girl crush.

Kellie closed her eyes tight trying to prevent the tears that were starting to surface. She hadn't cried over that whole mess in twelve years and she wasn't about to start now. *You suck it up Kellie Kincaid! Sh*e looked at her friend who had watched her emotional transformation and knew exactly what had transpired in her buddy's mind. She could tell her girl was battling with feelings and emotions that she's kept under lock and key. Gracie sat down beside her and turned her so they could have a buddy cuddle. She tried to speak but didn't for fear of becoming an emotional wreck. All she could do was shake her head in disbelief and allow her friend's closeness to ease some of the pain and hurt she was now feeling. At that very moment everything became crystal clear as Gracie held her tighter. She realized Gregory Larson was the man she had the little mishap on the plane. It was Gregory Larson…the man in her dreams. Kellie sensed that her friend now knew. What she hadn't been able to tell her was her Uncle had also hired him as his CEO and the two of them would be working in the same building.

G-Man exited the stage back door and went out into the lobby. He had to find HER. He couldn't let HER slip pass him this time. He kept wondering what could have possibly happen? Was it something he had done? He thought she had been receptive to him and was experiencing the same magnetic force. Although he had often dreamed of what it would be like to kiss HER, he never imagined a simple touch of the lips could be so… so… potent. And when she touched him it was pure heaven. It was all he could do to contain himself and not turn a sweet kiss into something disgraceful.

60

He would have embarrassed them both if the visions that flashed in his mind had been disclosed. He had kissed a many lips but none of them left him feeling so alive. He was lost for words and that's the way she left him lost and confused.

Walter and Carl were standing by the ladies room door. Both were puzzled as they stood waiting for them to come out. Neither understood nor had the slightest idea what was going on...what happened...or why Kellie became so upset. It was clear she was fascinated and taken with Gregory like so many women. The difference was this time he showed the same fascination with her. It was obvious he was attracted and drawn to her the way he publicly displayed his affection. Walter should have been upset, after all she was his date. But it was Gregory who gave them the tickets to invite them to the show. Their plans were to take them to the comedy club house for an evening of laughs and good food. What really surprised them was Gregory Larson's behavior. He was totally out of character. He was not the cool dude from Texas tonight.

"There you are," said Gregory as he approached his friends. "Is everything all right? What happened? Is she sick?" Walter and Carl shrugged their shoulders, they didn't have a clue. Gregory continued questioning the guys as he paced in front of the door. "How long have they been in there?"

Walter looked at his watch. "It seems like forever, but in reality it's only been a few minutes. I do wish we knew what's going on."

"Me too," added Carl as he looked at Gregory. "I guess you really shook her up with that little demonstration," he said smiling. They had become good friends over the short time span, and he's learned to love him like a brother. Although he had Walter in mind for Kellie, it looks like Gregory is the one she wants or at least interested in. And it's obvious the feeling was mutual. Carl just had to comment on his actions, because that was so unlike him. He did not have anything to say nor an explanation. It was too deep for him to put into words at the time. Besides, he was too worried and concerned about her. Gregory looked at both men who were still wearing the word confusion stamped across their foreheads. It was true in the short time they had been friends they had never seen him act in such a manner. And the nerve of him to tell Walter he had an interest and to bring HER to the show was presumptuous. He didn't mean any disrespect or harm, but he couldn't help himself. It was fate that caused their paths to cross and he was going to take full advantage of the situation.

"I'm going in watch the door," he ordered. Gregory Larson walked in and found both ladies. She was standing in the mirror gently patting her face with a paper towel. Her eyes were closed. He could see she was upset and was trying to pull herself together. But why? What had upset her so? He could sense she had genuine feelings for him. They were being drawn into a magnetic field that they could not deny. She had to have felt the strong powerful force that was pulling them together both body and soul during their kiss. She did feel compelled to respond by touching him in a tender loving way. He had been relieved that she didn't think he was being too forward. He didn't believe in putting on that kind of show, well not until now. He needed her to know she was special!

Kellie opened her eyes and blinked them several times. They had to be playing tricks on her. She couldn't believe it! Gregory Adams Larson was standing in the door of the ladies room. Kellie angrily turned to face him.

"I..." was all that passed his lips. Her hostile glare caused him to become uneasy and silent. She was ready to explode. The nerve of HIM, coming into the ladies room, she thought. He already caused her to make a fool of herself in front of a crowd of strangers. Now he was humiliating her more in front of new friends. No Sir! She didn't think so! Not in this life time and no other life thought Kellie as she marched right up to HIM. Gracie followed and stood beside her offering support like they had done so many times in the past.

Kellie didn't care how good he looked standing there exposing his muscular and fleshy chest that would cause any woman in her right mind to lust... imagine the sensations you would enjoy with each tantalizing caress. She didn't care how his strong powerful arms cried out to her for comfort...or how enticing and pleasant his male scent was...how sweet his kiss was...how the touch of his smooth silky chocolate cream skin caused every nerve in her body to tingle...and...Kellie was all worked up and on the verge of bursting apart. She was ready to lash out and finally give him a piece of her mind, but how could she. She gazed into his handsome face and gorgeous potent eyes that disclosed confusion but concern /uneasiness-but thoughtfulness / frustration but patience / aggravation but calmness and stamina.

"Whatever it is I'm sorry," he said before she could utter one word. His husky sensuous voice was cautious but caring. His demeanor was soothing and comforting as he sneakingly eased all the explosives from her enraged body. Kellie tried to keep up her disposition of annoyance, anger and resentment, but it was useless. How could she when she saw such warmth, understanding, tenderness, and concern for her well-being. Okay, so she couldn't give HIM a piece of her mind this time but she could do this... Kellie took a deep breath and sashayed right pass HIM without acknowledging his presence at all. Her girl Gracie was right behind her.

Walter and Carl were standing guard as they came out. "Kellie is everything alright?" asked Carl.

"We were worried," added Walter as he walked over to be by her side in case she needed him. One thing for sure it was Gregory who had upset her.

"I'm fine, I just want to go home." Kellie apologized for spoiling their evening, and asked Walter if they could have a rain check on their date. She expressed the desire to see him again for HIS benefit, since he was standing there with the same confused expression.

"G-Man, we've been looking all over for you. Jacquè is having a tantrum," shouted one of the models from the fashion show.

Gregory ignored him completely as he watched HER walk off with Walter. He faced Carl. He needed some answers and wanted them now. Before he could say anything, Gracie grabbed Carl by the arm to leave. "Carl, can you give me just a minute? That's all I need," he pleaded.

Carl didn't understand himself what was going on, but he felt they owed Gregory some kind of explanation. "Please baby," he said trying to appeal to Gracie's sensitive side. He knew Kellie was her girl and they had a strong bond, but he hated not to yield to the brother's plea and knew she was not leaving his side. She was protecting her girl to the end, but from whom? He felt it was only fair to let him know something, but what?

Gracie knew exactly what he needed to know and told him, "Kellie Renee Kincaid!" and walked off. Carl looked to him for a clue as to what the devil did that mean. There was a still silence between them. He sensed then there was some history there but he knew he would have to find out later. He shrugged his shoulders and caught up with the love of his life. He would have to get back with him later.

Gregory didn't know how long he stood there trying to register what just transpired. She did say Kellie as in Kellie Renee Kincaid. Well now, said Gregory to himself. Ms Kellie Renee Kincaid. He hadn't laid eyes on her since that day she blew up at him with accusations that he was in the dark about. Boy does she look different, he thought smiling to himself. The last time he saw her, she was plain chubby with no shape as far as you could tell. The baggy clothes she wore back then hid whatever figure she might have had. Man does she have some sexy curves now. Talk about pleasingly plump... and he meant very pleasing. He also loved the way she was wearing her hair. It was very becoming and gave her a natural exotic beauty that was unforgettable. Gregory had an appreciative grin on his face as he shook his head to clear his thoughts. He knew it wasn't any use in him going there, at least not right now. Besides he had tasted her wrath years ago and didn't plan on ruffling her feathers any more than he had to. According to his resources she was a shrewd businesswoman and responsible for turning KTS into what it is today. If Mr. Kincaid hadn't made that bad business deal he wouldn't have been able to buy in. Gregory couldn't help wondering how she took the news of him being the new CEO for the Kincaid Business. He had a thought, that's probably why she reacted when she learned who he was. That's why she was so angry and upset. Well Ms Kincaid you and I are going to get along just fine. We're going to become the best of friends. You'll see. Wishful thinking my man, he thought to himself. Out of all the women that have crossed his path she's the one that's set his heart and soul on fire. She's unnerved his very being. And it was not looking good at all.

CHAPTER 8

"Okay Aunt E I'll be right over to help you. Yes, Auntie E I promise, I'm getting up now, good bye." Kellie hung the phone up. She hadn't been home but two days before she was summoned. Her aunt expressed she was happy she came home early. Kellie was so sure her decorating job was just about completed. Humph, all she had done was arranged the furniture in the living and kitchen area and unpacked some of the boxes.

Of course she knew it wouldn't have been long before her aunt find out she was back. After all the drama she decided to cut her vacation short and return home. With the way things had gone down she needed to get out of Atlanta. Of course Gracie was upset about her leaving so early, but she would be back for the wedding that was now the last Saturday in September instead of the end of December. Even Sandy and her gorgeous new husband had postponed their leaving so they could be there. Kellie knew her girl was not going to hold out that long anyway. Together they were able to carry out her plans expediently. Everything was being held at the church where Carl is the assistant minister which couldn't have worked out any better. He had a member who was relatively new in the wedding consultant business and was eager to offer her services at a very good price. She was hired to take care of the remaining wedding preparations. Since the wedding was pushed up everything was going to be simple but beautiful and elegant in Gracie's colors cream and coral. They were fortunate to find their wedding apparel which included dresses, shoes, and accessories that accommodated their unique personalities and body types when they took their short visit to New York. Kellie was also able to purchase a couple of white dresses for different church functions and take care of Uncle Kel's anniversary gifts for Aunt Juanita.

All things considered Mrs. Taylor and Gracie were pleased which made it easier for her to leave. Besides, if she had heard one more word about Gregory Larson she was going to have a breakdown. She couldn't get over his boldness calling and sending her flowers as a peace offering, that's what the card said. Humph, she refused to read it, but that Gracie did. To make matters worse she and Sandy were actually harassing her to talk to him and listen to what he had to say. Love had definitely taken over their senses. Kellie could remember when they didn't believe in giving someone like HIM a second chance at nothing but getting out of their faces. Now they think she should allow him to show what kind of man he's become. They literally sung a song to the tune of how people can change, especially since they were practically adolescents at the time. Humph, adolescents nothing…he was a senior and she a sophomore.

According to Carl and Walter there was nothing but good things said about him throughout the brotherhood. He was very good with the youth and senior citizens at the church, and was a great friend always available when needed. Big deal she thought, if he was all that why don't he stay in Atlanta where everybody loves him. She was not interested in how much he's changed and how virtuous he was…most of all she didn't want him in her life!

Kellie knew she was not being truthful with herself nor her friends. She had to at least be honest and admit she was having mixed emotions where Gregory Larson was concerned. And Lord his kiss was to hard to forget. She was still having a difficult time shaking its affect. Kellie hated admitting he was nothing like the boy who was trying to impress his friends twelve years ago. Humph, it wasn't any use in treading those waters. That was behind her and she was going to have to deal with the situation she had been put in. After all he was only going to be in the same building. It wasn't like they would be working together.

***

"Auntie E can't we take a break," begged Kellie. They had been at the new neighbors for two days. Today made day three. All morning they unpacked bathroom accessories and kitchen utensils.

"Okay Kellie, but we need to complete the job, he's due here Saturday

66

sometime." She started toward the living room. "Where are you going?" asked her Aunt. They had been using the patio entrance from her place to his due to the adjoining gates from the previous owners. She suspected he would probably change that. Besides, she didn't see any sense in going all the way home just for a nap, they were practically through except for the master suite.

"Upstairs to take a little nap."

"Kellie are you crazy, you can't sleep in his bed!" shouted her aunt.

"Auntie E I can change the linen and wash the ones I sleep on. He'll never know the difference."

She knew her niece and it was useless taking it any further. "While you're taking a short nap I'll go check on James. I left him at home. He didn't feel like going into the office today." Kellie turned to face her. That was the first time she mentioned him being at home. "There's nothing wrong he said he felt like being lazy today. Besides Charlotte, Felicia, and Latonya can take care of any problems." She knew her cousins could do just that. They had good business sense and were raised to take over J & E Enterprises. They were practically running the family janitorial business anyway with the assistant of other family members. After Kellie was satisfied that he was okay she continued toward the front of the house. Before her aunt left she gave instructions to let the workers do the rest of the unpacking and cleaning while she napped.

Kellie shook her head in disbelief. It was still hard for her to comprehend she was actually spending the remaining of her vacation time decorating some bachelor's home. She moved into the living area that was cluttered with empty boxes that needed to be discarded. She turned her nose up as she mumbled to herself. Auntie E had made such a big fuss over this particular job. Humph, it wasn't like this was her first time being employed by someone with a little money, she was good at her craft.

Kellie had some preconceived ideas about the new neighbor already and felt they probably wouldn't hit it off anyway. She could already tell he was one of those stiff neck brothers with an attitude that was always looking straight ahead because he had money. He probably had that all eyes on me syndrome. He certainly wouldn't appreciate a sister like her that didn't need a man to support her financially. She had that under control. Perhaps that's the kind of man he is. Yep, thought Kellie. It's possible he thinks women are helpless creatures that must be told what to do, how to do it, and when to do it.

Who are you trying to fool? You know you're not being fair. Kellie was quite impressed with the new neighbor and knew the minute she stepped in his home it was much more than a bachelor's dwelling. After unpacking several boxes she knew he had class, but laid back. His CD collection alone that she arranged in alphabetical order said that much. He had become more interesting by the box, she chuckled. She knew the real reason for her sour grapes attitude was simple, Gregory Larson. Kellie just wanted to be angry with someone because of the way things were going down for her. Humph, his statues and paintings exhibited tranquility, compassion and humanity. Mr. Neighbor's home was absolutely beautiful. He had excellent taste and fine furnishings. The townhouse had been freshly painted a rich coat of vanilla cream which offset vivid hues of chocolate, blue, and green. The downstairs was completely furnished in contemporary pieces of dark to light woods that provided comfort elegance and style. There were three bedrooms, two baths, and a small open loft upstairs; every area in his townhouse was furnished except the two guest bedrooms.

Kellie had taken the last box that was left out to the trash bin. She looked around one more time before she called it a day. The task was finally completed with the help of J & E workers who had done an excellent job assisting them. Auntie E had called to see how things were going. Kellie knew she was checking up on her. Auntie E was surprised the job was complete and she was getting ready to go home and turn in early. The finishing touches for the downstairs and the master suite were done and ready for her inspection.

Kellie hadn't realized it had gotten so late. She had paid the workers and allowed them to leave hours ago. Before she knew it she was caught up in the last minute details. But Kellie had to admit she did have her reasons for staying later without the workers. She had gone through his boxes marked personal. Kellie couldn't help herself. The suspense of finding out anything about him had her curiosity at its highest peak. She just knew there had to be pictures of him and his family. One thing for sure Auntie E was right about being able to tell a lot about a person by his furnishings and personal property. Mr. Neighbor was also a private person. All that sneaking around, and all she did was draw up a blank. The boxes marked personal was just that…toiletries, colognes, etc. She was disappointed that she didn't find one picture or paperwork with any names. At least an idea or two about who he was and how he looked, not that it mattered to her. She was left with one assumption; all his business was on iPod and a Blackberry.

Kellie knew she had to be satisfied with what she did know and wait for his arrival. After all she did have his keys. He would have to come by her first. That was another great idea since Auntie E and the family would all be in Center for the weekend. Kellie assured her aunt she would be responsible for making sure he got his key. She would also give him the grand tour of his new home. She knew that wasn't really necessary but that would present a good impression. Mmmmmm… maybe she'll have a nice meal waiting for him. Okay, girl you're going too far, remember you don't like to cook. She ignored her conscience, because she had a feeling she was going to start liking to. Hummm…she might even invite herself to join him. With that in mind she came to the conclusion she was going to pursue Mr. Neighbor. Maybe this will help with getting her some real business. Grabbing her things she coded in the alarm and left through the patio door. She had to commend her Aunt on a job well done. Kellie wouldn't dare say this to her, but they really did make a great team. She knew she complained a lot but deep down inside she loved creating and designing fresh new ideas.

***

Gregory Larson was tired and very weary from his travels. Although he had enjoyed the scenic view of the southern states he was happy to finally hit the Texas highways and even happier when he reached the outskirts of Houston. He hadn't driven this far in years. But his Escalade truck had given him a smooth entertaining ride. He jammed all the way with some of his favorite artists. He had himself one *helleva* concert all the way home. Home, man did that sound good. It was true he loved Atlanta and the people there but he was glad to be back in H-town. Everything was going to be different this time. He was in a mellow mood even though he was tired. His girl *Phyllis*

Hymen had just finished singing one of his favorite. His mind wondered back to Chicago when he had the opportunity to visit the actual club she did her last performance. Her picture was a part of the many archives which hung on the wall. That was one of the fringe benefits in being a body guard for celebrities. You get a chance to hang out with certain cliques and work in some famous establishments. It was also easy money and had served its purpose well. He had had enough of living out of suitcases in hotels and eating their food unless he went to *Ma and Pa* diners or restaurants. Now he enjoyed eating out in upscale places about as much as the next person, but the fast pace he was living was getting to him. He knew if he didn't slow down trouble would be next. That's when he decided to take a job with GAL. That way he could still hire himself out, but with a selective group. It was time for him to draw the line and be more selective with his clientele.

Gregory was glad Mrs. D had hired a moving company and her sister-in-law to put his home in order. All he had to do was unpack the things he had with him and a couple of boxes with some special pieces he didn't want to trust with a moving company which would be shipped later. Mrs. D was taking care of that also. Even though he provided pictures for Mrs. Harris to give her some ideas as to how to arrange his home, at this point whatever she did would be fine with him. All he was interested in was taking a hot shower and lay his head down on his own pillow.

For the last few weeks he had lived in and out of hotels. After the fashion show he went to the west coast on two security jobs. As usual, according to Harold, *In the Basement Music Group* wanted him for the assignment. Their regular security person took sick and he was highly recommended for the position which was profitable but very stressful. Whenever he does security assignments for singers and models it's a twenty-four seven job. But he always survives and enjoys every minute of it. Once again he received a nice cash bonus and free tickets for the Houston concert that was coming up sometime in the spring. All of that was good, but once again he had put GAL's name out on the circuits for providing excellent service for any job. Harold was very pleased and hated to see him go, but he understood well about wanting to have your own business. Gregory did agree to do special assignments for GAL from time to time. He owed Harold

Grimes his life and would always be eternally grateful. Grimes had always been there for him when he thought it was just him against the whole world. He was responsible for keeping him on the right track.

***

Finally Kellie was able to relax. She had truly out done herself these last few days. Not only did she finish the new neighbor's place, but she had rearranged her own living room and changed her bedroom's décor. She had purchased new bedroom clothing with matching bathroom accessories when she and her aunt went shopping for their client. At first she was going to whine until they went into a little shop that had everything you thought you wanted for a dream bed and bath. She was past due for a new change and was glad they had gone into the specialty shop.

Kellie had decided to add more vibrant colors for a charming exciting atmosphere. As she looked around at her handy work, she still couldn't believe what she had done. Her chocolate chaise was given a new look with a throw of vivid shades of turquoise, orange and apple green and small accent pillows to match. She also accessorized her room with new candle holders, wall art and an area rug. Her smile of approval validated her new bold and bodacious style.

She was feeling pretty good right about now. She had accomplished more than she anticipated and was pleased with the ending results. Now it was time to pamper her tired body with a soothing relaxing hot bath in one of her favorite bath foams and then lotion herself in the body crème and mist of the same essence. This time she was using a fragrant scent of gardenia blossoms enveloped in peach tea leaves. Mmmm, it was just the right aromatic therapy to insure a peaceful sleep. She couldn't believe she was still dreaming about that man. You would think after she found out his true identity she would be over that. She was shame to say the dreams had escalated. The vision of his sexy hard body...his touch...the feel of his lips...and Lord his cologne of fiery spices and blended musk was embedded strongly in the core of her soul. One time she woke up calling his name. *Lord what was she going to do?* She knew what, she was going to be sociable with Mr. Neighbor since he was new in town. According to her aunt he didn't have family here. Kellie just hoped he was not one of those men

71

that valued the outside appearance instead of getting to know the person on the inside.

She put on her PJ's, pulled the covers back and crawled in bed. Kellie was ready to call it a night and sleep late in the morning. Her mission had been completed. Now she just wanted a good night's rest so she could be fresh and alert when she makes plans for Mr. Neighbor. She had already put in fresh flowers and an assortment of green potted plants in attractive pots. All that's left is to surprise him with a nice dinner welcoming him into the neighborhood. Mmmmmm...I wonder what does he like to eat she thought. Most men appreciated a home cooked meal period. It's true she didn't cook, but she was still good at it. Her mother made sure her girls were good in the kitchen, she just preferred not to be there. Her delicious meatloaf, au gratin potatoes with cheese sauce, fresh snap beans and cornbread should stimulate any man's taste buds. And for dessert she would honor him with her famous dump cake. *You go girl and work your show sang Kellie.* Batting her eyes as she succumbs to sleep, once again she was pleased with herself.

***

Gregory took the 288 exit from downtown and headed south. He would be home in twenty minutes at the most. He had called Mrs. Harris earlier about his key. She informed him that her niece that lived next door had his key and he could pick it up there. Of course he sensed matchmaking was in the air. To prove his suspicion Mrs. Harris disconnected before she informed him of her niece's name. But that was alright, he would call her back before he knocked on some stranger's door. He didn't care whose niece she was, it wasn't safe or a smart thing to do. His lips turned up in a smile as he thought of Mrs. D, she did say Mrs. Harris's niece was single. Well they both can put their matchmaking to rest. He was not falling prey to any of their schemes. Mrs. D was in Atlanta and he would certainly stay clear of Mrs. Harris. Besides he couldn't begin to think about getting involved with anyone at the moment. His hands were going to be full with his new business and Kellie Kincaid. It wouldn't be long before they faced each other. She was going to have to talk to him whether she wanted to or not. They would be working closely at Kincaid Transportation Services.

Gregory had a silly grin plastered over his face. Every time he thought about her and their kiss he found himself grinning like an idiot. Maybe they could have lunch or dinner together before she comes back to work, might as well get everything out in the open. He knew better than that, Kellie Kincaid didn't want anything to do with him. He tried talking to her and even sent flowers to apologize and hopefully soften her up before she left Atlanta, but she refused to acknowledge him in anyway. If anyone should still be angry it should be him. After all it was his name that had been dragged in the mud. Gregory knew his attitude and actions had a lot to do with the way he was treated. He had to admit he had been an angry and hostile teenager back then. He knew he had an evil side that was dead and buried, and that's the way he wanted it. Gregory Larson had worked hard to turn his life around. Nevertheless it was difficult keeping that side of him buried with his Aunt Marie and people like Kellie Kincaid reminding him. In spite of everything he had done well and couldn't wait to see his aunt and her reactions to the man. But first things first and that's Ms. Kincaid. More than likely she's been running down his name since she's been back from Atlanta and probably still at it this very minute. He had a pleasant thought, she couldn't say anything negative about him in Houston. It would be a reflection on the Kincaid's precious company. Yep, he had Kellie Kincaid right where he wanted her. Well almost where he wanted her.

The truth of the matter, despite the way she felt about him he wanted Kellie Kincaid all for himself. Gregory had to confess she has consumed his waking thoughts for months. He had actually prayed to God for their paths to cross and his prayers had been answered. The moment he laid eyes on her at the park, he knew everything would fall into place. Even with her refusing to talk to him that had not stopped his feelings from growing. In spite of their past history he had become more determined to win her respect first, then her love. *Gregory knew his work was cut out for him, but he knew they were destined to be together and fate was on his side.*

CHAPTER 9

Ring! Ring! Nooo...moaned Kellie. She couldn't believe the night she decides to turn in early the phone rings. Just her luck! Without looking at the caller ID, Kellie answered in a low whispering sleepy voice hoping whoever was calling would get the hint that she had turned in for the night.

"UH...uhn...my sister. Wake up! I have several bones to pick with you!" It was Kat and Kellie knew exactly what she was talking about. She had told her about her visit with Gracie, she just didn't mention anything about running into Gregory Larson. Needless to say not one time did she reveal the real scoop. He's the man that was on the plane and the same one that's in her dreams.

"Kat, I..."

"Don't you dare Kat me. I'm your cousin and I've been your best girl for how long now?" Kat didn't give her a chance to answer. "Since we were old enough to know what it means to be best friends."

"Kat..."

"Naw, I have to hear everything second hand. When were you going to tell me Kellie? When? If it hadn't been for Gracie and my aunt I would still be in the dark about what you've been going through. And Gracie said you made her promise not to mention somebody's name. Now what's that about?" Kat went on and on about what she heard. One thing for sure her source had been very resourceful and had it all down to the last detail. Kat's Aunt Lois Bell didn't hold back anything. And that big mouth Gracie! Kellie was sure Kat knew the whole story plus information that she wasn't even aware of...she just wanted to hear her version...well all except HIM.

According to her Gregory Larson was the one responsible for getting some prominent businessmen from Atlanta to finance major projects in their home town. Kellie did recall hearing something about VIPS from Atlanta had set up some kind of program with government assistance and Edna's Savings and Loan for minority. Kellie's family owned restaurant was also able to get on the band wagon. Their business which was located on the highway between Ganado and Wharton, was expanded and received a new face lift. They were also able to keep their Ma and Pa Café in Edna that was still pulling its weight in profits.

Kellie had to admit he's demonstrated skillful business strategies and was an unknown blessing to her family and their little hometown. Not only had Gregory Larson initiated the renovating and rebuilding of the black community in Edna, but he helped Ms. Lois Bell get a loan for her Bed and Breakfast business. Accommodations with a country flavor were provided for men and their families for weekend hunting trips on the Harris property. Beautiful landscaped parks encircled the property with picnic tables, adult swings and playgrounds for the children. A man made pond for fishing and water activities were positioned behind the facility. To offer an atmosphere with complete peace and relaxation, private areas were set up for those guests who wanted seclusion. It was an extraordinary place and business was fantastic! That was another brilliant plan which was an absolute winner, and responsible for putting Edna on the map as an ideal tourist town.

Kellie had always thought of Ms. Lois Bell's place as her own little private getaway. Just to be able to eat Ms. Lois Bell's cooking was reason enough to pay her establishment a visit every time she went to Edna.

"Kat, I was planning on coming down and spending the last week of my vacation there and tell you in person. But thanks to Auntie E we've been so busy working from morning till late evenings trying to get the new neighbor's place ready. So I had planned to come one day next week. It's been rough and very time consuming. I've been so tired all I can do was take a quick shower and get in the bed. Today we finally finished the job. I took a good soak and turned in early. I promise I had every intentions of calling you every night since I've been back, but I just didn't have the time."

"Okay, I believe you, now start from the beginning and don't leave out one itty bitty detail!"

"Kat it's just too much to get into this time of night." Kellie looked at the time on her radio.

"Well if you would stay in touch like you use to and keep me informed. What's going on with you anyway, Kellie. It seems like we're drifting apart. I know I stay busy with Jeremy and the kids and I know you have KTS, but we've always found time for each other and I miss that." She knew exactly where Kat was taking this conversation. After twelve years you would think she's put all what's happened behind her, but no, not Kat. She was such a martyr. That was such a long time ago. It's over and done nothing but puppy love anyway. Kellie has never revealed the real reason she became so upset that day. Poor Kat had no idea it was not behind her wanting him. She just allowed her to think so. It was safer to keep all that a secret. No real harm was done except her heart had been broken. In reality it only made her stronger, or as Gracie said hard. Besides it's in the past and that's where it will stay!

"Kat not tonight, I have so much to tell you and I need you to hear me."

Kat wiped her eyes and pulled herself together. "Okay Kellie, I'm ready," she said with a slight quiver in her voice. Jeremy and Kellie have both said she should let the past remain behind them. But because of her happiness and being blessed with a wonderful handsome husband and three beautiful children she couldn't help feeling guilty at times. She had everything and Kellie only had KTS. Kat knew her inside out and better than anyone. She was aware of her wants and desires. She was like any other healthy woman. She wanted her prince charming and babies. They both use to always say they wanted two children…one of each. Kat was fortunate to have two sons and a daughter. She loved being a wife and mother and knew her best friend has the same desires. At times she couldn't help feeling she had stolen Kellie's true happiness when she and Jeremy became more than friends.

It was Kat's idea to hook her and Gregory Larson up in the first place, because she wanted Jeremy for herself. If only she hadn't included that troublemaking two-faced Devin Bryson. He was the reason why her plan fell apart like it did. Thanks to Devin she had been double crossed, blackmailed, and nearly lost her best friend. And poor Gregory Larson was innocent and took all the blame. Probably to this very day he has no idea what all the commotion was about and how in the world he became involved. What's really pitiful...Kat has never had the heart or courage to admit her part in the whole mess. And thank God Devin Bryson has not shown his face in Edna since. Kat was glad when Gracie told her she had found someone she thought Kellie would really like. It was so good to hear that they had had several dates while she was in Atlanta, but something was going on. She could sense uneasiness and tried to get Gracie to tell all, but she insisted that Kellie would have to be the one to inform her about the rest of her visit.

Kellie started her story at the very beginning making certain not to leave out any details. She verified it was true about her uncle hiring Gregory Larson as his CEO and the two of them would be working in the same building.

"Kellie," interrupted Kat. "I know all about KTS. Tell me about the man you met. Gracie wouldn't give me any details about him. She said you would do that." Good old Gracie thought Kellie. She would leave the hard part for her even if she did make her promise not to say a word about HIM. Kellie dreaded telling Kat about meeting the man in her dreams. She was aware of how Kat felt about her dreams and knew she thought it wasn't healthy. Kellie now wished she had kept everything a secret. But with Gracie knowing her so well she couldn't have gotten away with keeping that hidden. Besides she knew the minute his name was announced that he was the one. "Well Kat, do you remember the man I met on the plane a few months ago?"

"You mean the one you've been dreaming about?" squealed Kat. She loved it as her anticipation and excitement soared.

"Well I met him again in Atlanta."

"Girl, get out of here! When...Where...How...Now girl don't you leave out anything. I'm warning you!" threatened Kat running her words together. Kat was as dramatic as Gracie. She continued with the when's, where's and how's, but not for long. Someone was trying to get her line. "Ignore it Kellie," demanded Kat. "This is too juicy and amazing. I can't believe you actually met him!" Like an obedient child she continued where she left off. Several minutes had gone by without Kat interrupting her, she was absolutely quiet. Then Kellie really got to the good part that is until she found out his true identity. "Oh Kellie I'm so happy for you. He singled you out among all the others. There must be some mutual chemistry there. How did you feel? Did you two exchange info? Have you heard from him since you've been back? Have you called him yet? You know women do that now. Knowing you…you probably gave him your don't you dare try to talk to me look." Finally Kat paused to give her a chance to comment. There was a dead silence. Kat waited nothing! "What's wrong Kellie?"

Kellie was lost for words…she was overwhelmed and her mind was crammed with all kinds of thoughts. How could she tell her the man was the one and only Gregory Larson? The only man whose kiss caused her to become breathless, her heart to flutter, her body to stir, and her skin to tingle; and it happens every time she recalls their physical contact. He's constantly in her thoughts and what's worst, she still moans his name in her sleep. The man that she's never wanted to have anything to do with. Lord what was she going to do, as she said his name silently in her mind? She's attracted to HIM. No that's an understatement, she wants HIM. Lord, how could that be?

"Kellie…Kellie what is it? What's wrong?"

"She finally spoke. "No we didn't exchange numbers." "Why   Kellie,   it sounds like there was a love connection there?"

"Because of who he is." She couldn't imagine what in the world that was supposed to mean. There was a stagnant silence then her cell rung. "Kat let me see who this is, hold on for a minute."

"Kellie Renee Kincaid, where have you been? I've been trying to reach you for the last twenty minutes. What good is having call waiting and caller ID if you're not going to use it?"

"I'm sorry Auntie E," was all she could say. She dare not tell her Kat was the reason why she didn't answer, for fear of hearing another lecture for sure.

"Never mind, the young man…" Before her aunt could get another word out the doorbell rang.

"Auntie E someone is at my door."

"That's probably him, the young man for his key. That's what I was calling you for." The doorbell rang again followed by a knock.

"I thought he was coming this weekend. Today is…"

"I know what day it is, niece."

"Okay Auntie E let me go." Kellie knew it wasn't any need in saying more. She seemed just as surprised as she was.   He wasn't due until the weekend. Today was just Tuesday. Kellie looked at the clock, okay it was almost the next day just minutes before midnight. She wouldn't be able to surprise him with that dinner after all. Oh yes I can, she thought. She could take it to him as an act of kindness and as a special welcome to the neighborhood gesture. "Just a minute," she said on the speaker. She had to get Kat off the phone. "Kat I got to go. The new neighbor is here to get his key." She made sure she turned the speaker off, there was no need for the new neighbor to hear their conversation.

"Not until you tell me who he is!" shouted Kat.

"He's Gregory Adams Larson, alias G-Man!"

"You said who?"

"Kat you heard me. Now I have to go. I'll call you back when he leaves." Thank God for the doorbell. Of course she left her speechless when she hung the phone up. That'll give her something to think about. Talking about bringing up the past…

Kellie put one of her caftans over her PJ's and rushed down stairs. She grabbed his keys off the table and looked in the mirror to ruffled her short hairdo, turned off the alarm, and unlocked the door. Opening it she began to apologized, "I'm sorry you had to wait." He had his back turned but that didn't matter to her, she would have recognized HIM anywhere including on her front porch.

"Hi neighbor," he said trying to restrain the excitement that was threatening to explode like an over inflated balloon. He crossed her threshold even though she had not extended the invitation. Man was he surprised when he called Mrs. Harris back and she informed him her niece Kellie Kincaid had his keys. No sir, saying he was surprised was a joke. He was pleasantly shocked no stunned! Regardless, talk about luck! Not only did he catch her off guard, but he was getting a chance to see her in her own comfort zone and natural self. Even though Gregory was like most men who appreciated a sister who enhanced her God given beauty with make-up, he takes great pleasure in seeing them in their natural state. And Kellie Kincaid was beautiful with or without all the extras.

He stood there invading her space sexy smile and all. She was spellbound and speechless with her mouth wide open. They were surrounded by a hush silence. Life itself was standing still. Kellie couldn't believe the trick her eyes were playing with her mind screaming Gregory Larson was her new neighbor. He continued standing there with a well satisfied look plastered over his handsome face. She silently scolded herself for even acknowledging that, but it was true. Gregory Larson was drop dead gorgeous! Kellie blinked her eyes several times to make sure they were not deceiving her as she struggled to hang on to what senses she had and stay calm. Lord, she gazed into a pair of piercing dreamy dark eyes which revealed exhaustion that pulled at her heart. Not once did he take his weary eyes off of her.

Although Gregory was enjoying every minute of watching her facial theatrics it was late and he was dog-tired. He had made a sixteen-hour drive only stopping when it was necessary. He knew he would see her later. And she definitely needed some "me time" to get over the initial shock, he was going to be her new neighbor as well. Man life was wonderful. While showing off his sexy smile and using his deep sensuous baritone voice he finally spoke, "I believe you have something that belongs to me."

Kellie just stood there like a zombie in a trance. Did her treacherous lips actual smile at HIM? The idea of her being betrayed caused her to practically throw his keys at him. His instincts signaled alert, he caught her hand and instead they fell to the floor as she snatched from his grasp. She felt stunned as his touch triggered sizzling sparks throughout her disloyal body. Her breathing was becoming uneasy and heavy. Lord if she needed this man out of her house. They both bent down to retrieve his keys and again touched. This time something caused her not to pull back. Their eyes locked. She kept saying over and over in her mind she didn't understand. Her puzzled and confused look gave her away or did she speak the words aloud and was not aware.

"What is it you don't understand Kellie?" he asked as they continued to hold hands. *"The inevitable...destined to be, or fate itself."* He pulled her closer to him but made sure their bodies didn't touch, she didn't resist. He's going to kiss me again she thought. She closed her eyes as if that would stop the inevitable. That was a joke as she felt his closeness. Once again he teased her with a gentle kiss on the lips. "Good night Kellie and sweet dreams." Leaving her standing in a daze and that much more confused, he turned and walked away.

CHAPTER 10

Kellie had just finished holding a telephone jam session with her two best buddies and was emotionally drained. She wanted to inform them together the identity of her new neighbor at one time. She did not have the energy to repeat what happened over again. It was bad enough she had to tell Nisey and Lynette at separate times who put her through the third degree. Gracie and Kat weren't any better. Before they hung up she was made to admit there was some forgiveness in her heart. She couldn't believe Kat's sudden attitude about him. She sounded like she actual wanted her to date that...*If he ask me!* Lord where in the world did that come from. Kellie shook her head, just like Gracie said; the main issue was he had invaded her world and he was someone that couldn't be taken likely.

***

It has been a whole week since Gregory Larson moved to Houston and next door to Kellie Kincaid. She had avoided him the entire time. With her vacation ending she would soon have to face him. Through inside sources she found out Mr. Larson had already started visiting the business park and the different offices thanks to her cousin Cynthia. Her sources also informed her a big meeting had been called for Monday morning to update the employees about the new changes that were going to take place immediately. Kellie still couldn't believe Uncle Kel would put her in this predicament and then call it quits. He could call it semi-retirement if he wanted to, but she called it plan old quitting. What were they going to do about their other business ventures that they were anticipating in the near future? She had some new ideas about providing transportation and carrier service in the downtown area and the outskirts of Houston. She knew the rail provided public transportation but it was not as convenient as it could be.

Houston's downtown was beginning to resemble New York and Chicago with congested traffic and limited parking even for connecting with the rail. They would need more compact vehicles and staff. Kellie guess now she would have to go through him. Well, at least she'll only have to deal with him at monthly board meetings since she would be operating the hotel transportation service. Kellie was glad she would not have to look him in the face every day. That was a blessing itself!

***

Gregory Larson leaned back in his chair with his arms resting behind his head and eyes closed. Instead of taking a much needed and well deserved rest, he started the groundwork for a smooth and friendly transitional takeover at KTS. At least that was his intentions. All morning he's been reviewing the financial reports and so far everything was in order. There were a few changes they would have to undergo, but nothing drastic. Although he owned fifty-five percent of the company he was going to let the Kincaid name remain visible. The name was respectable and well-known in the business arena even if it was threatening bankruptcy. As a matter of fact Gregory had insisted that Mr. Kincaid refer to him as his silent partner when they drew up the contract. It was written in the agreement to keep his identity a secret. He was not ready to go public as the owner. Besides several of his business ventures were done anonymously. Gregory empathized with Mr. Kincaid and the position he had been put in. Despite the fact that he was a victim, he still put his company in jeopardy. Thank God for some crafty business maneuvering, together they were able to reposition KTS's financial status and move forward with some new innovative goals and plans. Let go of the old and add on some new so to speak. Gregory was excited about his new business and was looking forward to working with the Kincaid family.

Gregory's eyes had only been closed for a few minutes before his mind wondered to what has become his favorite pastime...Kellie Kincaid. The mere thought of her brings smiles and heart-warming feelings that were slowly developing into something special. One thing for sure he had plans for her. He needed her by his side for many reasons than he cared to admit at the moment. Gregory knew he had a fight on his hands but it wouldn't be the first time. He had a lot at stake, the success of his business and his...A knock on the door interrupted his thoughts. It was his secretary who was highly skilled and proficient. He knew the minute they met they were going to get along just fine. He just hated that she was going to retire along with Mr. Kincaid, but she assured him she would get him a qualified replacement.

"Mr. Larson, a Mr. Grimes is on line one. I'm sorry but I knocked several times, I guess you didn't hear me."

She got that right he thought. Gregory had drifted off to *Kellie Land* and once again was thinking of another way he could get to her. He should have been shame of himself for the way he purposely put on a show while washing and waxing his truck the following morning after his arrival. He just wanted to get a glimpse of her.

She was babysitting a couple of little people and was letting them exert themselves riding their four wheelers up and down the driveway. Of course she pretended not to see him. But he knew better, the little people detoured to his drive several times and were very friendly. She tried ignoring him but that was impossible with her nieces and nephew extending the hand of friendship. Little Robert was like any other man child interested in cars and trucks. He was so sure when he put him in the back of his truck to help him she would have said something...anything. Instead, after a while she sent the girls after him. Gregory couldn't help but laugh when the girls tried repeating what their aunt said. He wished it was some way they could break the ice before she returned to work. He really would like to start where they left off in Atlanta before she discovered his identity. All he had were memories of their first meeting and that night. He wanted new memories and he knew it was going to be left up to him to make that possible. Its evident there's something between them whether she wanted to accept it or not and it's growing more every time he sets eyes on her. A big grin spread across his lips as he thanked Mrs. Williams and reached for the phone. It won't be long Kellie.

***

Gregory Larson could hardly open his eyes. It seems like he had just laid his tired body down. He looked at the clock by his bed. The time it showed couldn't be right. He had slept the whole morning away, but that was easy. His home atmosphere was very cozy and comfortable. Mrs. Harris and her niece were incredibly talented. Her niece...Kellie Kincaid, he wondered how she was doing this fine day as he punched his pillow and covered his head. Gregory still found it hard to believe he was not only going to work side by side with her, she was also his next door neighbor. That fact kept him grinning.

H-town was having some wonderful weather thought Gregory as he glanced out his bedroom window. He had decided he was not going into the office today. All this week he had kept late hours planning, setting up agendas, and schedules for the meetings that were to take place next week. A special meeting with the management staff was Monday morning. Everything was set along with a couple of new contracts, which should impress Ms Kincaid he thought. Gregory Larson has set into motion a plan that would insure them a prosperous business regardless of the economy. But he needed her to assist him in running KTS. She was an excellent businesswoman and would be an asset to him in more ways than one. He must have her by his side.

Gregory made his way down the stairs and put on his teapot. Looking out at a spectacular view from his bay window, he could see he had picked an excellent clear and sunny autumn day to stay home. The gentle swaying of the tree branches and small shrubberies were signs that it was a pleasant breeze out and a perfect day for lying around relaxing or taking a ride. As he looked over at his favorite spot, he smiled. Dang, that's all he's been doing lately. He couldn't help it.

Although Kellie was next door her presence was visible throughout his home. She was responsible for the area he favors the most along with the master suite according to her aunt. He loved the way she had the table set for two in front of the bay window, which was perfect for dining. He was thankful and wished he could find a way to show her how much he appreciated her hard work. He had a mind of just walking right up to her door and invite her over for tea. He could make up some kind of story about them going over the agendas for next week, which actually wouldn't be a lie. Yes, it would be a good idea, but business was not what he wanted to discuss. Plus, it was too nice of a day for that. What he really wanted was to have a day of leisure with just her, R & R day which would be a first for him. There had not been many days like that for Gregory Larson. His plate has always been full to the rim with this project or that assignment. But now he can focus on one mission, making sure KTS prosper and to continue to grow and win Kellie Kincaid's heart. Okay, in all honesty he knew that was two missions. Gregory wimped out on his idea of marching up to her door and decided to drink his tea and enjoy the view instead. Maybe he'll catch a glimpse of her, but he knew that was nothing but wishful thinking.

Gregory hummed the tune that was on the radio as he flipped the channels on his TV. Nothing was on as far as he was concerned, not even a good western he thought and stretched out on his sofa. He loved the old black and white cowboy movies except when the settlers and Indians were at war. He never cared for that kind even when he was a boy watching TV with his great aunt. They had some great Saturdays watching old westerns, eating popcorn, and drinking kool aid. He had some fond memories of the times they spent together and would always cherish them.

Startled by a strange noise Gregory jumped straight up. He wasn't supposed to have fallen asleep, but of course he dozed off anyway. He looked at his watch and realized he had been napping for nearly two hours or so. His plans had been to rest his eyes for a few minutes before he took to the highway. He had decided to go ahead and leave this evening and spend the weekend with Ms. Lois Bell. Gregory shook his head to make sure he was awake and alert. Although he had slept late this morning he must have been more tired than he realized. He heard that unfamiliar noise again. It wasn't a ring, and sounded more like chimes. Gregory smiled it was his doorbell and his first visitor.

***

"Nisey Kincaid Hamilton, you didn't! I've been avoiding that man ever since he moved in. It's enough he lives next door as it is and don't forget I'm going to have to work with him." Kellie couldn't believe her sister had actually gone over to that Gregory Larson's introduced herself, welcomed him to Houston, and invited him to the church they attend. Was she crazy? She had already had her full of HIM. She certainly didn't want to see him Sunday right before she returns to work.

86

"Relax Kellie, he's not coming this Sunday," exclaimed Nisey as she took a seat in the rocking lawn chair across from her. "He's going to run down to Edna and see Ms. Lois Bell. So you have a little more time to get it together. Sister, you need to get a hold of yourself, you're beginning to come unglued. I don't know why," she said as she observed her behavior. Kellie sipped her tea as, Nisey continued. "I understand he's quite a catch and Lord he's fine." She fanned herself as if she was having hot flashes and poured herself a cool drink.

"Remember sister, you're a married woman. And you already have a fine husband."

"Oh, so you do admit he's all that and then some." Nisey knew she was pressing her luck, but she couldn't help trying to get a feel of her sister's honest thoughts about Mr. Larson. Their Auntie E was dead set on making them a couple and solicited her help.

"Nisey please don't you start with me too."

"I don't know girl, he seems like an ideal prospect to me. I think he would make a wonderful husband. You two could be great together especially since you're both working for KTS. Besides, it time for you to settle down and have a family. And put those romance novels down and get a real man." Kellie couldn't believe what she was hearing. Did Nisey forget she reads them too? As a matter of fact they share books. The look on her face said it all. "I'm married, and there's a difference," she explained in defense.

"I'm not looking for a husband and if I was, I certainly don't want HIM. And furthermore, we're not going to entertain your last remark period." Kellie knew exactly where this conversation was heading. Nisey was being as bad as Auntie E with that matchmaking stuff. She thinks she has real skills since she's played cupid numerous time with a good standing record. All of her matches were still happily married. At least that's how they look to the public.

Kellie picked up a piece of fruit indicating she was done with this conversation and ready to move on to something else, like whether or not she had talked to their Uncle lately. "Nisey have you talked to Uncle Kel lately?" Nisey was chewing a piece of pineapple and couldn't answer so

Kellie continued with another question. "You know if I didn't know better I'd think he was avoiding me. I think something is definitely up."

"What do you mean?" asked Nisey between chews. "I haven't talked much to him except speaking to him at church. I did talk to Aunt Juanita a bit this morning. You know they're getting ready for their vacation and that's their whole conversation."

"I know," said Kellie, "but something is still going on with him. You know I'm supposed to handle the transportation for the hotels, at least that was my understanding before I went on vacation, but he won't discuss the position at all now. He actually told me I had to wait until the meeting that's being held Monday. Can you believe that? And I just know that Gregory Larson is behind the whole thing. Nisey I don't know what I'm going to do. I can't work with that man. He makes me sick."

"Really Kellie, I don't think you have anything to be concerned about, Uncle Kel knows how much KTS means to you. I wouldn't worry, besides it's nothing you can do. What you need to do is enjoy your last couple of days of vacation. You have anything planned for tonight," she asked while continuing helping herself to the refreshments. Kellie put her chicken salad sandwich down and gave one of her not tonight looks. "Relax sister I don't need a babysitter. I thought that maybe you and I could do something together. It's been a while since we've had a sister outing, how about we jump in the car and get busy?"

Kellie smiled at her sister, she was right. It had been some time since the two of them had done anything together. "That sounds like a winner let's clear the table and I'll get my purse."

Nisey walked out the front door with Kellie right behind her. Stopping abruptly she caused her to bump right into the door with a thump. Rubbing her head she turned around to see what caused her to stop. *Oh my goodness exclaimed Kellie silently to herself.* She covered her mouth to make sure her thoughts had not slipped passed her lips.

"You can say that again," agreed Nisey. She knew exactly where her sister was coming from even if she didn't say the words aloud. It was written

88

all over her face and her reaction was precisely the same. Husband or no husband Gregory Larson was one fine specimen made by the Creator.

"Nisey, I'm warning you. You better not make a scene. Ignore him and let's go."

"Girl I don't know about you, but any woman in her right mind couldn't ignore that man. You have to be inhuman to do such a thing. And it's no way in the world I can do that because I'm definitely human."

"Nisey, please don't," begged Kellie as she stepped in front of her sister attempting to get to the car first. "I'm the one who has to live here and he'll think I want him. He's that type and you know it."

"No, I don't know that and neither do you. You're just saying that. Besides he likes you sister. He had nothing but praise for you and your decorating talent. And you did something he's been wanting to do for a while and that's putting his extensive CD collection in alphabetical order. I can't believe you took that much time and alphabetized his collection. Sounds like you put in some serious attention on this job," she said with a smirk. Kellie knew it was nothing she could say that would not make her sound dumb, so she kept silent. Nisey continued, "And he also said he was looking forward to working with you at KTS. Sister look at him."

Gregory had just finished washing his truck before taking the highway to Edna. He had actually prayed that she would come out before he finished the job and thanks to the almighty his prayers had been answered. Of course he was looking his rugged handsome self in gray sweats that had seen their last days and were cut off at the arms and knees. Kellie shook her head to maintain clear thoughts. She knew Nisey was right. He was something to look at. But she still refused to acknowledge his presence as she continued walking to the car without Nisey.

"Hi Kellie, still enjoying your vacation?"

No he didn't she thought looking straight into his grinning face. He was on her side of the driveway, she mumbled to herself. He left her no choice but to speak or be rude. And if she were to be rude he'd think something of it. No way was she going to give him the satisfaction of knowing his mere presence sets her nerves on edge even if it was the truth.

"Hi Gregory, and yes I'm still enjoying the last bit of my vacation." No he's not, she thought as he walked right over to where she was standing. His steps were smooth but quick, he was upon her before she knew it. Lord all she could do was stand there wimping out once again with her mouth opened. What was wrong with her?

"Hi again Gregory", said Nisey with a big smile. She thought it was only right she stepped up and say something to get her sister off the hook because she was lost for words. She knew Kellie was overwhelmed and felt like she was backed up in a corner, but what Nisey didn't understand was why. She's been in tight spots before. Auntie E was always trying to match her up with somebody she thought was perfect for her, and she was also guilty. Kellie was a champ at brushing off a man in a nice way to keep from hurting his feelings when she was not interested. But this time she seems to be clueless as how to let this one know she's utterly unmoved by him in anyway. Unless there's an attraction, and she likes him whether she wants to admit it or not. Nisey continued her conversation alone, neither contributed. Instead, they both stood there looking goo-goo eyed at each other. Boy was her work cut out for her.

"Kellie and I are getting ready to hang out for a couple of hours. We would love to invite you but I know you're going to…Hey you two." She snapped her fingers and stomped her foot to get their attention and it worked. They turned to face her. If she had said something, they didn't know. Neither one heard a word she spoke.

"I'm sorry Nisey, you were saying," apologized Gregory. Kellie looked at her with that pitiful pleading look, like she use to when they were kids and she got caught doing something wrong. She knew Nisey Kincaid Hamilton was on top of it and was not going to let her get away with anything. Kellie had no explanation except there was an attraction.

Nisey repeated herself, "my sister and I are going to hang out for a couple of hours. We would love to invite you but I know you want to leave before it gets too late." Of course Nisey sang the words *we would love to invite you.* Kellie stood there looking foolish and vowed to fix Nisey. Humph, she'll need a babysitter.

"You're right, I just finished wiping my ride off." After I take a quick shower I'll be on my way," he said never taking his eyes off of her. She was a vision of loveliness. With the help of a gentle breeze he inhaled her sweet essence that was becoming to her personality. The sensual fragrance of mingling sweet fruits with fragrant flowers enticed his senses. Soft and sexy, that's how he saw her more so than ever now. Kellie was remained silent. Ooooh...but her mind was screaming all kinds of sensuous thoughts. She was so glad no one could hear them. Lord, how was she going to work with this man? "Maybe next time," he said interrupting her thoughts.

"We'll hold you to that." Nisey walked over to the driver's side and opened her door. Gregory immediately opened Kellie's door who was standing with that confused look that she's been wearing since he's come back into her life. Ooooh...but he was to close for comfort, him and his thick muscular bow legs and strong arms. Her nostrils were filled with his masculine aroma and sweat mixed with the scent of his body soap. Kellie had a dreadful thought, what if he tries to kiss her. It seems each time they've been in each other's presence he does just that. What could she do, he was the perfect gentleman. It was too late to stop him from closing her door and he also got an eyeful of her ample thighs due to her short dress. She held her breath in anticipation of his kiss. He closed the door with a smile, but not before he did what was expected of him and kissed her lightly on the lips and told them to have fun.

"Be sure to tell Ms. Lois Bell hello," said Nisey watching them. "Kellie, do you want to send Kat a message," she asked. Humph, he looked like she expected the kiss. Nisey vowed right then to forget about the matchmaking and not say another word. Why should she, it looks like nature was doing a good job on its own.

After her breathing returned to normal, Kellie told him to tell Kat and Jeremy hello and that she'll see them in a couple of weeks. Before she could catch herself she did what she always do when someone goes to Edna, and that's to tell Ms. Lois Bell to send her something sweet. But why did she say that to HIM! Gregory told them he would deliver their messages and the two sisters waved as Nisey backed out of the driveway. As they drove off Kellie was thankful for her sister this time. Her brain went numb and stopped working when their eyes locked. She promised herself to get it together and be the woman she's claimed to be and stop being a wimp! Kellie also did a silent prayer hoping Nisey would not bring up the kiss. And she needed to get him straight about taking liberty of kissing her whenever he pleases.

CHAPTER 11

Cruising home with *Maze* and the *Isley Brothers,* Gregory had decided to leave Edna right after morning service. Of course Ms. Lois Bell did not want him to leave so early. Needless to say she voiced her disapproval the entire time she fixed and labeled to go containers of his favorites. He assured her he would be making frequent trips from now on since he was back in Texas. The bed and breakfast was peaceful and his main get away spot for unwinding and relaxation. He thought it would be nice to have his own special retreat and decided to give his great aunt's old home complete renovations. During his previous trip he hired a contractor to add a complete master suite...build a new kitchen and bathroom... plus bring the home up to date with modernized conveniences without taking away its country charm. He was now actually looking forward to his own country home get-away. Although the trip was short it was very productive. The renovations were going according to schedule and the home would be ready in a couple of weeks, if the weather permits. Edna was just like Houston with the on and off again rain. He paid Louis the groundkeeper for the inn, to put the few antique pieces he had purchased in once the work was completed. On the whole he had a wonderful visit and spending time with Ms. Lois Bell was an added joy as always. As usual she helped him put things in perspective, especially after his visit with Kat and Jeremy.

Man, was his mind blown away after Kat took them back twelve years ago. She made him promise not to say one word to no one about what she revealed, especially not a word to Kellie. She felt it was her responsibility to tell her face to face, and she would real soon. But Gregory had an even better idea, neither one of them should bring up that situation ever again. As of that day it was buried and forgotten. Besides Sheriff Griffin had cleared him of all allegations and he left Edna Texas with a quickness. What's more he needed HER to accept him for who he is now regardless of the past.

Devin Bryson had set him up with vicious lies because he wanted Kellie Kincaid for himself. At least he now understands why she was so terrified of him that late evening. The nerve of Bryson, he had labeled him a rapist and had gone as far as to say he actually saw him attack a woman and force her in his car. That was a big joke, that's one thing Gregory Adams Larson has never had to do. It was the other way around, especially when his great aunt closed her eyes. Nevertheless, poor Kat has beaten herself up all these years behind this whole sordid mess when it was really Bryson's fault. And that's all it was! But it was Ms. Lois Bell that was responsible for pulling it altogether even though she was not aware of their conversation. His past had been instrumental in orchestrating his future. Man, she had no idea how right she was. She hit the head right on the nail. If it had not been for Kat and Kellie he wouldn't be where he is today and that's on top of the world. And as far as Devin Bryson he owes him big time for even attempting to do harm to his Baby. Okay, slow down man she's not yours yet.

***

Gregory got up from his desk to stretch his legs a bit. He had been at it ever since he returned from Edna. The trip was only an hour and a half drive, so he drove straight through. He couldn't get home fast enough hoping to see HER. To his disappointment she was nowhere around. He unpacked his truck and decided to do a little work. Needless to say that didn't last long before his mind began to wonder and he decided to walk over to his office window that overlooked her patio. He knew he was looking in vain, she was probably...His face lit up, he couldn't believe it. There she was breathtaking as ever reading a book. He continued invading her privacy as he admired the view...ample ice tea colored cleavage...thick thighs and long shapely legs. Gregory silently wished she would get up so...wish granted! Not only did she get up, but she had to walk over to the other side of the table to retrieve something she dropped. He loved the easy sway of her body when she walks. Smiling to himself, he now knew how David felt when he watched Bathsheba. She must have been sitting for a while because she did a cat stretch that made his whole body...He needed to stop this craziness. Man up and go over there and join her...he did have something sweet from Ms. Lois Bell...

94

Kellie couldn't believe it. There he was standing on his patio looking her way, handsome as ever. He seemed to be hesitant as whether or not he was coming over. A satisfied smile slipped passed her lips. She was glad he was just as uneasy as she was. With one hand in his pocket of his well-fitting jeans and a shopping bag in the other he started walking toward her. Well that didn't last long she thought, as he walked right to her side of the yard revealing his fetching seductive smile. Okay she gives up. And she may as well get used to him being next door. But she will talk to someone about putting up a fence soon.

"Hey Kellie," greeted Gregory as he gave her the shopping bag, this time kissing her on the cheek. "Compliments from Ms. Lois Bell, she sent some of your favorites."

Oooooh…Kellie didn't understand why she hadn't said anything to him about kissing her. This was the perfect opportunity to get him straight and put an end to his foolishness. They were alone and on her patio. Her mind and heart screamed you know why. As if that wasn't enough, for a split second she struggled mentally with herself whether or not she should get up or remain seated. Again her darn dress was too everything exposing cleavage, thighs, and legs. She told that Nisey when she tried the dress on it was too short. It's too late now! There's nothing else for her to do.

"Hi Gregory," accepting the bag. "I didn't mean for you to actually tell her what I said. But I sure thank you." Who was she fooling she was a happy camper. Kellie Kincaid was addicted to sugar. This means an extra walk around the track.

"Oh no, I do as I'm told," he said teasingly. So far so good he thought. Maybe he should count his blessings and leave well enough alone especially since she was being pleasant. It was getting late and dusk was beginning to set in.

"Would you like to sit for a minute? How about some tea?" Where in the world did that come from she thought? But it was too late she couldn't take the invitation back. It was clear on her face she was only being polite. He thought he'd take her off the hook this time and decline, but the next time Ms Kincaid…He told her to have a good evening and left.

***

Kellie stood in front of her closet. She couldn't believe her vacation was over. She grunted as she moved several pieces of clothing to the side, it wasn't a vacation at all. Everything had gone wrong starting with Uncle Kel's news, Sandy now married, and Gracie getting married in two weeks. As if that wasn't enough she found out she's been dreaming and fantasizing about the devil himself who's living right next door. And she's allowed him to kiss her each time they're together, and in front of Nisey. What really vexed her was the fact she's enjoyed each and every kiss. Mmmmmm...She loved being close to him and the feel of his lips on hers and ...Oooooh will you stop! Lord, where did all of that come from. Kellie pleaded with her inner self to put a halt to her frame of mind. It's like she has no control of her own thoughts and actions when it came to him, but she had to keep it together because today was THE DAY.

Kellie and Nisey did some serious damage to her mad money savings, but she was worth every dime. Nisey insisted she needed to update her wardrobe and add some new pieces. And she did exactly that trying to decide. Today she felt soft and womanly and picked the ideal outfit for her first day back at work. She selected a royal blue suit with smooth, sleek, feminine lines instead of her regular business attire. Her straight skirt with gathered side panels stopped midway her calves. The princess line five button tweed jacket was a cinch to show off her hourglass figure. A glossy black trimming adorned the edge of her collar and the hem of the three quarter length sleeves and jacket. She even found a pair of two-tone spectator pumps. Instead of her simple gold jewelry she normally wears, she completed the outfit with a bold sterling silver Hammered set which added the special touch she was seeking. After applying her makeup and ruffling her short curly hair style, she took one last look in her mirror and smiled. She was pleased with what she saw and was ready for whatever.

CHAPTER 12

Kellie pulled into her reserved parking space that said vice-president, right next to Uncle Kel's. She smiled as she recalled the day she had been given that promotion. Boy was Cynthia green with envy. Humph, she had been raised to one day run KTS. For the sake of peace, he pacified Cynthia with a promotion to office manager. It all worked out for the best. She was able to relieve him of some of his duties while Cynthia acquired some of hers which made her feel that much more important. Everyone was happy. But she didn't know how long that was going to last, with all the new changes.

Well it seems everyone was here, she thought. Kellie looked around the parking lot and found just what she was looking for, the metallic black Escalade truck parked in the front row. She imagined he'll take her uncle's space soon. No need of working yourself up into a hissy girlfriend, stay calm and work that attitude. Kellie pulled on the door and to her surprise it was locked. Using her keys she unlocked it and stepped inside. Looking around she noticed no one was minding the store. She could hear noises coming from the multi-purpose room which was located down the hall. It had been named the Blue Room because of the wall coloring and the in-door/ out-door carpet and served as their large conference room and dining. Surely they hadn't started the meeting, especially without her. Kellie followed the noise and went straight to the area with purse and briefcase hanging from her shoulder. The smell of food filled her nostrils. Mmmm bacon and eggs for sure. Kellie stood in front of the door. There was much chatter and laughter and everyone was eating.

"May I serve you something Ms. Kincaid," asked the voice from behind her. She didn't have to look around or guess who the voice belonged to. She felt his presence and recognized that low husky voice without a question. It has plagued her spirit and soul for the last few months. Kellie turned to face the inevitable. There he stood behind a table that had a spread fit for VIPs. He was wearing a chef's hat and jacket that was opened two buttons down revealing dark silky looking hair that she imagined made a sexy trail down to his navel. *Oooooh...will you stop she scold!* It seems everyone was getting the VIP treatment. Before she could answer him...

"Welcome back cuz," greeted Cynthia. "Boy don't you look great! I guess your vacation truly agreed with you. Looks like you've lost a few pounds." Cynthia always made it her business to make weight an issue with her. She was 5'8 and a perfect ten. As far as Cynthia was concerned she was every man's dream. She always had some poor soul running behind her. And that was an understatement. Cynthia Stanford was gorgeous, smart and definitely a high maintenance sistah. She saw men as a dollar sign and dropped them almost as often as she changed her hairstyle. If he doesn't suit her fancy she moves on to the next. Kellie heard through the beauty salon gossip that she had kicked her last beau to the curb. She didn't need to wonder why, her cousin was already working her show.

"Thank you Cynthia, I did lose a few pounds, nothing to write home about."

"Well I hope you're not watching your weight today. Can you believe this man? Not only is he tall dark and handsome, he's an excellent cook. You should taste his ham and cheese omelets. They melt in your mouth."

"Stop Cynthia, you're embarrassing me," said Gregory as he picked up a plate for her. He was actually blushing. She found that hard to believe. "What would you like?" *Lord give me strength she prayed.*

"While she was making up her mind," interrupted Cynthia, "I'll take another serving of those mouthwatering omelets." Thank you Cynthia! This was one time she welcomed her cousin being her usual self. He served her just what she requested but never took his eyes off of her while she pretending to be looking at the different choices.

"Now what would you like?" he asked for the second time.

"I guess I'll have what seems to be the popular pick of the house, the

98

ham and cheese omelet." He immediately scooped up a serving and put it on her plate. With a warm let's be friends smile he told her to enjoy herself with the rest of the goodies. Kellie thanked him gracefully and continued down the table, all the selections looked scrumptiously delicious. The counter was beautifully decorated and set up buffet style with fresh cut flowers and decorative paper goods. Kellie had her choice of flaky biscuits, sliced sausage, sizzling bacon, fresh fruit, jams, preserves, and sweet rolls. Various drinks were on the each covered table where the staff sat to eat. She helped herself with a couple of biscuits, both meats, and strawberry jam. She looked at the fresh fruit and sweet rolls and decided she could get that later, important eats first. Kellie moved around the room greeting and accepting welcome back wishes from the staff. Uncle Kel who was sitting at the head of the table with Aunt Juanita by his side waved her over.

"You look fantastic boss lady," said one of their drivers.

"Girlfriend you oughta quit!" said Ann. "You're working that suit!" Kellie gave her the sister girl slap. "Tell me girlfriend how long have you known about this new CEO?" she whispered. "You trying to keep this fine hunk to yourself?" Both ladies laughed.

Kellie explained how her uncle had dropped the news right before she started her vacation. And as far as being interested in him she assured her she was not. Besides, Ann knew Kellie better than that. A man was nowhere in her present agenda nor did it go with her outfit. They had talked about men too many times, often revealing their wants and desires. They knew their soul mate was out there somewhere and would find them when the time was right. Kellie recalls their first meeting. Ann was the first female driver to be hired at KTS and it was Kellie who brought her on board. She could never forget the gratitude and enthusiasm Ann had and still does. She was desperate and real pitiful back then. Andrea Henry was hiding out from her abusive crack addicted husband, penniless with three small children under ten and living in a shelter. It seems like that was ages ago. Since then Ann has managed to rise above all of that drama with a divorce behind her, a new home, and a man in her life that loves her and her three children. She credits Kellie and KTS for giving her a chance to start over and make a decent salary to support herself and family.

That's what KTS was all about, helping people help themselves by giving them the opportunity to work and earn a decent respectable living. They were a close knit family that worked together and always there for each other. Kellie couldn't help wondering how Gregory Larson was going to fit into their little family. One thing for sure he was certainly on the right track as KTS's CEO. Although his cool persona was smooth, suave, and sensuous you can tell he was about business. Everyone seemed to be happy and pleased with her uncle's decision. And his friendly VIP breakfast clinched the deal.

Kellie took her seat beside her aunt and uncle who seemed to be enjoying their meals like the rest of the KTS family. Their plates were practically empty. Aunt Juanita stopped with her last bite to say hello and tell her how good and well rested she looked. For some unknown reason she continued staring at her as if something was different about her. "I mean it Kellie, you look stunning, doesn't she Kel?" He gave her a quick inspection and agreed with his wife. Aunt Juanita shook her head and continued her previous conversation about their upcoming cruise.

Mmm…this is good thought Kellie, she had to agree with Cynthia he has skills. Everything was delicious including HIM. *Where did that come from? Lord please do something!*

"What do you think of Gregory, Kellie," asked her Aunt. "He did this whole breakfast by himself." Humph, all he had to do was order from the deli and use a microwave. What's so hard about that thought Kellie? She sure hope her aunt was not getting ready to start singing Gregory Larson praises, she's heard enough of that for a life time. "And Kellie he's so smart and handsome. Kel has shared with me some of his ideas he has for KTS. You're lucky that you two will be running KTS together…two great minds." Aunt Juanita continued nonstop without giving her a chance to say a single word. But Kellie's puzzling look said it all and her uncle was well aware of what she was thinking. He knew she wanted to ask what she meant by them running the business together. According to the plans they had made she was to spearhead the new hotel project. Nevertheless that has changed now and for the best, whether she accepts it or not. But of course the expression on her face told him she knew something was going on. Her aunt stopped

100

eating and turned to look at her niece. "Well Kellie what do you think?"

"Hello folks, enjoying yourself." The devil himself appeared and took a seat right beside her. Turning himself so he could face her he asked how was her omelet?

All eyes were on her as they waited for her comment. Dang she hated when she was put into situations like this. "Mr. Larson everything was delicious. Who's your caterer?"

"Kellie I told you he did all of this himself and must you be so formal," said her aunt. "Gregory, everything was just lovely."

"You out did yourself Son," added Uncle Kel.

"Thanks, but I can't take all the credit. See there I knew it, she smirked to herself. "The fruit and sweet rolls were from the deli and the biscuits are from a can. But the omelets were done by yours truly. Cynthia also helped me set everything up." Good old Cynthia, thought Kellie.

"Well everything was real nice," said her uncle. "How's your new place?"

"It's beautiful thanks to your sister and lovely niece." Once again she had everyone's attention including his.

"Well now, our Kellie is very talented and quite resourceful," said Aunt Juanita.

"That she is," agreed Gregory with a big smile. He patted her hand lightly that was right next to his and felt the slight tremble. He couldn't help not to make some kind of physical contact with her. He knew he had pressed his luck with his simple kisses and dare not at this time. Just the touch of her hand was enough to satisfy his need to feel her softness. He was thrilled that she was experiencing the same sentiment that's been slowly absorbing his being…mind…body…and soul.

Kellie eyes were glued to his sensuous full lips when she thanked him for the compliment. He was very much aware of his affect he had on her whenever they were close, and the twinkle in his eyes confirmed her suspicion he was enjoying every minute of it. It was evident he was toying with her. She was going to have to show him she was not to be played with, not in this day and time. Humph, she would also get him straight about kissing her whenever he pleases too! But how could she make her body and mind understand not to take pleasure in his display of affections. Like right now she was shame the way she watched his sexy lips form each and every syllable as he spoke. What is it about this man? He was the same Gregory Larson that lived in Edna when they were children. Why is it she can't control her own eyes less known the way her body reacts each time they are near? *Lord, this was going to have to stop.* She could feel the magnetic force that was drawing her to him. He had invaded her space when he chose the seat next to her. When his muscular leg brushed against her, a warm gentle flame flickered inside. It was like he was some kind of human torch that provided heat for her body. Just watching him made her feel soft and mushy inside. She hasn't felt like this since she had that terrible crush when, okay so it was not a crush. It was still ages ago! Kellie screamed inside, how was this going to work?

To move the conversation on and off of her Kellie asked why he wasn't eating. Leave it to him, with a big smile on his face he told her he was one of those cooks that tastes the entire time he cooks. He didn't have room for anything right now. But he was happy to know she cared about him getting his daily nourishments. Gregory continued his teasing by asking her if that was going to be her daily concern. That snapped her back to her senses. Of course she took his last remark as a joke and didn't reply. After several minutes of small talk he excused himself and moved to the front of the room to make an announcement.

"The kitchen was now closed, but everyone is welcome to take any of the remaining refreshments back to their workstation. In other words breakfast was over." KTS employees broke out in laughter including him. Kellie liked the way he laughed. She wondered whether or not he was aware that when he laughs he rocks back and forth on his legs while his sexy eyebrows arches even higher in a V. *Stop it Kellie!* Gregory strolled out of the door, but not without leaving memoirs of his presence and every woman following his every step including her. Kellie took a deep breath and exhaled.

"I know that's right cuz. Godfather where did you find him? That man is something else," said Cynthia. "He makes my blood boil." She flopped down

102

in the seat that he had taken and started fanning herself like she had encountered a heat wave. "Kellie I must admit I am looking forward to working with him."

"Well help yourself." They all looked at her with question marks stamped on their foreheads. Of course she didn't mean for it to come out like that but it did. Plus, she couldn't let Cynthia know the effect he had on her and prayed silently that it wasn't obvious. Kellie finished her breakfast and excused herself. She needed to get away and get it together because she knew this was going to be a long mind draining day. Her senses had already dwindled down due to his overpowering scent. Kellie felt like she was already defeated. It was evident Mr. Larson had everyone in the palm of his hand. She watched him work the room with his magical charms as he chatted with the staff in a warm and cordial manner. Well she's not that easily manipulated. No sir, Mr. Larson not by a long shot! Her defenses just needed to be refueled.

CHAPTER 13

Mrs. Williams buzzed Kellie to let her know everyone was in the Ivory Room instead of her uncle's office. Not only had he invaded their family business, he was calling the shots. Kellie shut down her computer and pulled out her compact to apply a little coloring to her lips. She couldn't imagine where the time had gone. For once she left KTS business right on the premises and had been taking care of some KTS email that needed her attention.

Because KTS was a small business ran by family members they usually had their meetings in her office or Uncle Kel's. But he has now taken over her uncle's office so they're gathering in her favorite room that she personally decorated. It was cozily set up for clients or staff's family members, comfortable seating for six and beautiful ivies which made the area serene and cheery. Of course she was sure he was not aware of the Ivory Room being her favorite. Picking up her daily planner Kellie opened the door to leave. Once again she walked down the corridor. She was not ready for this, but knew it was time and soon everything would be out in the open.

Kellie paused and took a deep breath before she opened the door. Just as she stepped inside the doorway she collided into a hard massive chest that knocked that same breath right out and caused her to drop everything in her arms. She was embraced immediately by two powerful arms that belong to none other than Gregory Larson himself. As he held her close they both agreed silently at that very moment there was definitely a strong chemistry between them that was absolutely real. Kellie knew she should at least say something or attempt to move out of his grasp, but she didn't. Her hushed silence and motionless body reveled in his magical fiery touch…This time she was experiencing more than a flickering warmth or gentle flame inside. Her body was intense and blazing.

Gregory knew he should release her, but he couldn't... at least not until he was sure she was all right. Liar, he knew holding her this way was far more than he had ever anticipated, especially not today and this soon. With her in his grasp, it was everything he had imagined. Her soft warm body was pleasantly inviting, which caused his to become heated, hot, and needy. Instead of letting go he wanted to continue holding and snuggling her even closer. She was in his arms and it wasn't a dream. He wanted to tell her how beautiful she was...And how his breath was sucked right out of him when he laid eyes on her the first time in Atlanta...He wanted her to know about the countless sleepless nights he's had since that day. She needed to know how messed up he really was when it came to her. But he knew it was not the time. He had to have a little more patience for now. And Lord knows that's been his constant prayer since he's been back.

"I'm sorry," they both said in unison. Smiling down at her he grudgingly set her free. She returned the smile and cautiously stepped aside but not without brushing gently against his taunt body. Kellie was pleased, he was just as uptight as she was. She wished that made her feel better but it didn't. She resents the sultry state her body was experiencing because of his closeness. But what could she do? Kellie watched him bend down to retrieve her daily planner. Lord the buns and thighs on this man! If it weren't a sin she would just grab him like a whoochie and not turn him loose until she was a well-satisfied woman in every aspect! Get it all over with. Humph, that'll serve him right toying with me!

Gregory picked up her planner and gave it to her with the biggest grin ever. He knew she was checking him out and it thrilled him more so. Once again she admired the way his connecting V shaped eyebrows raised higher when he smiles. Dang that smile was potent. She wondered whether or not he was aware how deadly his smile really was. Of course silly, she scold... this is Gregory Larson remember. That's how he works his magical charm. Kellie cleared her head as she accepted her planner and politely thanked him.

"Is there something wrong?" Gregory sensed she was preoccupied and a bit agitated. That was not a good sign. He was hoping the breakfast feast would have eased some of the tension and uneasiness she had when it came to him. He was well aware of how she felt about him becoming a part of the family business. Mr. Kincaid had warned him of her feelings about him being the CEO of KTS. He wanted so much for her to leave the past behind and start a fresh new beginning, at least for the sake of the company. He needed her to understand everything that's being done is strictly for upgrading KTS. He had invested a generous amount of his life savings in rescuing this company and couldn't allow anyone or anything to jeopardize his agenda. As much as he would like to please and make her happy, he couldn't afford to allow even her to cause any kind of conflict or opposition.

"No, everything is fine." *Just like you.* I guess I ate a bit too much. The food was so delicious, especially the omelets." *Dang he doesn't miss a thing. Fool no telling how long you were standing there staring.* Kellie felt if she brought up the breakfast that would throw him off. In the meantime she cleared her head so she could focus and be the businesswoman she was known for. But for some strange reason she had the feeling her entire career was about to take some serious changes and in a big way.

"Is it safe to say you enjoyed yourself then," he said with that contagious grin of his.

Kellie found herself with an appreciative grin also. "What are you doing, fishing for more compliments," she asked sarcastically. The minute it came out she wanted to take it back. That wasn't called for, he was genuinely sincere, plus she was raised better than that. Why give a compliment and then turn it into something ugly. But she felt compelled to put a sour note on this conversation. She found herself grinning with him and he was doing a good job in reeling her in.

"No Kellie, I'm just pleased you found everything satisfactory to your taste." Good he was able to pull a smile from her too. "Why don't you join the others, I need to help Mrs. Williams with some present business. I'll only be a few minutes." Who was he fooling, he knew no one needs to help Mrs. Williams with anything she was efficient and thorough in everything she does. The problem was he wasn't ready and needed to get himself together before the meeting. A cold shower is what he really needed, but deep breaths would have to do.

Kellie opened the door, and to her surprised Aunt Juanita was still there and was sitting in on the meeting. RJ McHarding, their lawyer was also present. This was a strong indication her suspicions were right and she was definitely going to have a career change for sure. After speaking to RJ, Kellie took a seat next to the loveseat where her aunt and uncle were sitting. She was glad Cynthia had their attention. She didn't feel like talking and just wanted whatever was going to happen to take place so it could be over. Then she could start putting the pieces back together. Nerves caused her to get up and straighten the magazines that were on the small table. Although the room had a cheery atmosphere, she was edgy and tensed.

The door opened and all heads turned. She didn't have to, she was now familiar with his male scent of musk blended with other fragrances. Kellie quietly took a deep breath, it was time. He took the seat that was on the side of her and for some unknown reason she wasn't the least bit agitated or offended. As a matter of fact his closeness eased the aggravation and tension right out of her. Why was that? Their eyes locked, but she blinked to break his spell. She had to stay focused. She must!

Kelley Kincaid stood and tapped the small table like he's done so many times before to get their attention. "Now that all persons are accounted for and I have your attention, I'd like to start the meeting off by first thanking each one of you for your support, dedication, and sacrifices you've made over the years. I know we are all family here in some way or another and we've been through so much for the sake of KTS. I just want you to know you all hold a very special place in my heart.

First, I would like to thank my beautiful wife who has been by my side since day one and continued to stand by me during the struggling years. Sometimes we didn't know if we were going to have a roof over our heads or where our next meal was coming from because of my foolish pride. When she put her foot down and insisted on getting a job teaching school to bring in the income that was needed, she still allowed me to be the man and followed my lead. For that I love you so much Nita." Aunt Juanita wiped her eyes and smiled up at him as she gently tapped his hand to show he still had her support.

"Secondly, I would like to thank Gloria Williams who's served as my secretary and right hand for many years. We had some lean ones but we made it." Aunt Juanita gave her a gift wrapped package with a card, while her assistant Cherri Dickerson, who had been trained to take her place, patted her on the hand as she wiped her face. It was so true she and her uncle had gone through some trying times.

Third, I want to thank my goddaughter for her dedication and support. She's kept her father and my best friend's memory alive along with doing an excellent job, and he would be so proud. He was always there encouraging me while others were constantly saying how foolish my ideas and dreams were. Every time I look at her I see his watchful eyes. Cynthia I know KTS was not what you had in mind when you finished college and you only took this job for us. But Sweetheart you made two old men happy."

"Oh Godfather if I had to do it all over again I wouldn't go anywhere else," sniffed Cynthia. She stood and gave him a big hug. Kellie couldn't help becoming a bit emotional herself. She knew how close he was to her mother's brother Uncle Issac. She had heard over and over how he introduced him to Aunt Juanita. Uncle Issac died after a lengthy illness before Cynthia finished high school. Kelly Kincaid promised him he would take care of her and his wife and has kept that promise along with spoiling her rotten.

Gregory Larson was taking everything in. The love, dedication, and support were invincible among this family and especially his wife. Mr. Kincaid had told him about his wife getting a job to support them while he was getting his business off the ground. She was definitely his helpmate. He was proud to be a witness at such an occasion. The respect and admiration was phenomenal. He only hoped she would one day feel the same about him.

Uncle Kel then looked at Kellie his namesake, "Now to my namesake, Kellie Renee Kincaid."

Kellie interrupted him immediately, "Uncle Kel you don't have to say anything. I know how you feel about me. After all, just like you said I'm your namesake. And besides I'm the niece you made work without pay ever since

I was big enough to hold a water hose. Remember?" He burst into laughter. Thank God! This was getting to be too emotional even for her. Everyone joined in, including Gregory Larson who had been quiet so far. Now he can see how much KTS means to all of us. Their business was built on love, devotion, and sacrifice. How was he going to fit in? Money wasn't everything at least not in this family.

After all the laughter subsided, Uncle Kel continued. "Niece, you're absolutely right about working here since you were big enough to hold a water hose."

"And don't forget for free!" Kellie said with a big smile.

"Yes, and for free, but your dedication goes much deeper than that. You've made more sacrifices that others weren't willing to make and at a young age." Kellie left her seat, she knew exactly where this was going. She didn't want her Uncle to bring up the past. She did what she wanted to with her life and had not missed out on a thing as far as she was concerned. It wasn't like she had men trying to break her door down that suited her fancy. Uncle Kel held up his hands. He assured her he was not going into details because he knew she was not one for public praises. Her feelings and emotions were private. "But Kellie you…"

Kellie was now by his side. She knew when it came to her and KTS he could be very emotional. There were times when she actually worked without a salary. And no one knew, not even her parents or Aunt Juanita, she had cashed in her bonds that were given to her by her great-grand mother. They had reached maturity and were collecting interest. KTS needed her help. She didn't hesitate to help with the financial troubles. All of that was in the past and as far as she was concerned it was for a good cause. Not only did her uncle pay her back with interest, he also gave her five percent of the company. "Uncle Kel please don't," she whispered giving him a reassuring hug. She loved him and KTS. She never would have sat by and watched him become financially ruined. She knew how hard he worked to make this company what it is. That's why Kellie couldn't understand why he needed HIM.

Again Gregory watched quietly as niece and uncle embraced. He knew there was a strong bond and lots of love in the Kincaid family. He had to admit the respect and dedication they have shown through the years was touching, even to him. He could only hope and pray that she give him half as much of that same kind of loyalty and devotion. He needed her in so many ways, but right now he knew he should accept the fact that she was only going to tolerate him mainly because they would be working partners and nothing more. Gregory shifted in his seat as he made his mind up to accept her cordiality and professional respect for now.

"Okay niece you win this time, but I do want you to understand and always remember that everything that's going to take place now or in the future is for the benefit of KTS to maintain success and prosperity." He slightly lifted her chin just a bit so they could have eye contact. "Will you promise me that no matter what happens I will still have your understanding and support?" Kellie was a bit skeptical of his request, she couldn't help but wonder what was the purpose. He knew she would support him no matter what. She acknowledged with a nod, but still had reservations as to what he was not saying. Her instincts assure her that HE was responsible for whatever Uncle Kel was not saying.

"Now let's get down to KTS business. *Here it comes thought Gregory Larson who had been sitting quietly, but very attentive. It was show time!* Kelley Kincaid took a deep breath as if that was going to make him stronger and give him the courage needed for what he was about to say next. He knew only one way to be with his niece and that was straight forward and to the point. All he wanted was   for her to be patient and work with him. She had no choice if she truly loved KTS. Kellie sensed her uncle was struggling with something, but she was clueless as to what. One thing for sure she had a strong suspicion Gregory Larson was the reason. Kellie was about to say something when her uncle spoke.   "Now as you all know Mr. Larson is now our CEO. There are changes that will be made that we both agreed would be an advantage for the company. "   Before he continued Kelley Kincaid looked directly at his niece silently pleading with her to handle what he was about to say next. He continued, "Kellie I know how important," pausing for what seemed like eternity, "no we all know how important this company is to you and how hard you've worked in moving us forward." She felt it throughout her entire body something was dreadfully wrong. What was he trying to say?

"Your new position as President will involve working diligently with the CEO along with additional responsibilities." RJ was right on time as she pulled out a folder with her name on the front and handed it to her. Inside were her new job descriptions, salary, contract, and an envelope with her name handwritten on the front. Uncle Kel continued," Cynthia you will have the position as director of our hotel business." Again like clockwork RJ gave Cynthia her folder with the same information that related to her new position. Both ladies showed their approval with smiles. Kellie was uneasy and trembled inside with what she just heard. What did he mean by director of the hotel business? That's not how it was supposed to go, something was terribly wrong. "Now ladies, if you will take your folders and return to your offices, read them carefully, and I will visit each of you before I leave the building today. But before you go I want you to open your envelope which holds your inheritance."

Gregory Larson escorted Mrs. Williams and the others out. He knew this was going to be a touching moment and it should be between family. He had to give it to Mr. Kincaid. He had everything under control. Once Kellie sees her inheritance and her new salary she should be pleased. Who was he fooling, her contract states she has to work closely with the CEO and that would be him! Maybe the catered lunch will soften her up a little more. He had ordered her favorites plus two desserts. He's pulled all the punches he could for now. He was luring her in, any way he could.

For once Kellie didn't notice he had left the room. She had been too caught up with the fact that Uncle Kel was actually going through with carrying out his will. He was honestly giving them their inheritance right now. Kellie looked to her uncle then her aunt who was standing beside her husband. Sadly she shook her head and did what was asked. She took out her envelope and opened it, thinking what was she going to do without her uncle's daily presence. Cynthia had already open her enveloped and was kissing and hugging her godparents. She couldn't believe her eyes as she examined her gifts closely. All she saw were dollar signs, CD's and IRA's that valued at least a quarter of a million dollars.

Kellie couldn't believe her eyes. She now owns forty-five percent of KTS. "Uncle Kel, I can't...I don't know what to say...I just wasn't expecting this," exclaimed Kellie. She looked at her aunt who was smiling at her.

"You both deserve it," said Aunt Juanita as they all stood together holding hands.

"She's right. I wanted you to have your inheritance now while I'm alive and well." Kellie embraced them both as she whispered her thanks. "Okay so much for that," said Kelley Kincaid as he coughed back his emotions. Looking at his watch, "our catered lunch will be ready soon, so why don't you two get started with taking care of your business while it's being set up."

***

Cynthia Elaine Stanford couldn't believe it. They wanted her to be director of the company's hotel business plus she's going to receive a healthy raise. She had secretly desired to have that job but knew it was hopeless. After all it was Kellie's project. She did the proposal and secured the contracts. She couldn't hold back the smile that was spreading across her face. Cynthia was absolutely ecstatic over her new position, and no question about it today has turned out to be incredible! She couldn't wait to share her news with her mother. Picking up the phone she thought about that fine new CEO. She knew he had to be responsible for her good fortune and she must thank him properly. "Mommy, you're not going to believe what happened today."

***

Kellie Renee Kincaid glanced at her watch, it was finally the end of her first day back at work. Mondays were usually their slow days, but not today. This Monday had been the busiest ever with all the extra meetings plus the daily services they normally provide. Although today had been surprising and overwhelming, she made it. She had to admit there were two disappointments, her not spearheading the hotel transportation and having to work closely with Him. It was true she had been looking forward to putting the hotel project into action and managing it, but that was no longer a reality. What shocked her most was the fact that instead of her feeling anger,

112

distress and betrayal, she was calm, relieved, and satisfied. A smile slipped past her lips as she thought about the biggest surprise ever...a hefty new salary and partnership in the company, that's what her contract stated. She was now a partner.

Kellie recalls the conversation she had with her uncle earlier. She was on the verge of tears throughout their talk. He was so sincere but frank. He made it clear the success of KTS would fall upon her shoulders, as well as the new CEO. He let her know under no circumstances would their company continue to be successful unless she remains a team player. He reminded her of the promise she made and needed her to trust him and allow Larson to take up where he left off. He wanted her to be supportive like she's always been. Her uncle assured her that this had been difficult for him too, but he couldn't move on to the next phase of his life unless he knew she would continue to show that Kincaid resilience and fortitude that they were known for. Although her mind was flooded with all kinds of questions she kept them to herself even the one that puzzled her most...why was Gregory Larson calling all the shots, after all they owned the company. But what was the use she thought. What was done was for the sake of KTS. Besides Kellie was not going to let her uncle down even if it did require her to work closely with Gregory Larson. She did have to look after her forty-five percent, plus she was a partner! That was the main reason RJ was present today. Kellie signed all the necessary documents needed to make her an official partner of Kincaid Transportation Services. Humph, it was now on paper and the thought of her good fortune placed a smile deep inside.

Kellie had to commend Gregory Larson for a successful day whether she wanted to or not. After he was introduced to the KTS family as the new CEO and she the President, the company meeting began on a positive and productive note. He was shrewd but compassionate as he gave them a new improved lifeline. His confidence and inspiration inspired the total staff with enthusiasm and excitement with moving forward. He had accomplished what she had not been able to do because of her uncle's uneasiness and always dead set on playing it safe. It was evident that Mr. Larson had done his homework and knowledgeable when it came to transportation. His vision was to have hotshot trucks, cruise vans, and black sedans for additional limousine services throughout the city and surrounding areas. Not only was he reconstructing KTS, he had designed a logo that was perfect for the company, which will make them visible throughout the region.

One of her immediate duties was to make the decision on company uniforms. She was also asked to devise a temporary employment service for additional staff, for the new services which would gradually come into operation, over the next few months. Kellie had a sneaking suspicion, but hated to admit this new CEO maybe her blessing in disguise. They had some of the same visions to bring KTS to its fullest potential in the transportation arena. Nothing was in her way now, except maybe *HIM* himself.

Kellie Renee Kincaid clutched her daily planner to her bosom as she stood at her desk. She was ready to call it a day, but before she leaves HE asked her to stop by his office. She shook her head because she was not ready to be alone with him... She straightened up her work space and pushed her chair under the desk. Kellie put her purse on one arm and briefcase on the other. She was also going to have to regroup with all this baggage she carried back and forth daily. Gracie was right, it was too much to carry at one time every day. Her shoulders were beginning to ache behind the heavy load. Kellie left her office and went next door. Yep he was that close to her. He had taken the office next door instead of Uncle Kel's. She was somewhat puzzled about his decision to take a smaller office instead of the largest one, but Kellie had to admit he was full of nothing but surprises.

As she approached his door voices were heard. So the meeting was not only with her. She knocked before opening humph, she was expected. Both men stood and RJ was gathering her things to leave. Gregory offered her a chair. Torrance Burgess, who was their personal banker, was now present. He gave her his usual greetings, a big smile and his banker's handshake. This was interesting she thought, these three seemed to be very familiar with each other, one might say good friends. RJ and Kellie exchanged a few words as she continued gathering her folders. She had to remain professional and not let their friendship get in the way with her and Mr. Larson's business. She knew her girl understood. Kellie figured Gregory and RJ must have had some personal business to attend to. If it was KTS business she would have been present since she's a partner and president.

114

Gregory excused himself to walk RJ out.

"RJ, thank you for handling this matter. As soon as I get the other information I'll get back with you. I don't have any real family and I want her to have it all, especially since she owns the remaining shares. I feel that's the only right thing to do." Gregory had RJ to draw up his will and made Kellie his sole beneficiary.

"She's a lucky young woman. When are you going to tell her you're in love with her?"

Gregory was taken by surprise. "Is it that obvious?"

"Yes, and you need to do something about it. You two would make a great team in every way. Don't miss your chance for true happiness. Kellie is a wonderful, loving, and caring person. Any man should be proud to be a part of her life."

"It's not that easy."

"Yes it is, just man up and do what you have to do. Take it from me, you'll regret it if you don't." RJ hurriedly got in her car while he held her door. Thanking him she quickly turned away and drove off while fighting back her hidden tears. She was not going to dwell on her past. Today had been very rewarding and productive.

Gregory watched her leave the parking lot and went back into the building. He couldn't help thinking about what she said. Man he had no idea it was that obvious and couldn't help wondering who else was in tune to how he felt about her. Taking deep breaths he went into his office. "Kellie, I appreciate you stopping by, I have a couple of things I would like to go over with you before the day ends. But first we need your signature on KTS bank accounts and then we need to choose new checks." Her confused expression caused him to explain why. He explained at the request of her uncle, since he's awarded her forty-five percent of the company her signature would replace his. Together they would make all the financial decisions concerning KTS. What he didn't say was the fact that she had been given her uncle's share of KTS and the remaining shares belonged to him and if necessary he would have the last say. And most of all if something unexpected happens to him she would be able to handle all of the business since she would also be his beneficiary. Kellie signed all the papers needed for adding her name to the accounts. They also picked economical duplicate checks with their new logo. She was still smiling inside. Her name along with his would appear on the front of their checks. When all business transactions were completed, Torrance Burgess thanked them and left. Although they were really through with business he needed her to stay for a few minutes. "Kellie let me walk Torrance to the door and I'll be right back." She agreed with a nod and remained seated.

While he was out she surveyed her surroundings. Everything was in its proper place. She didn't think she would handle HIM taking over her uncle's office well, but she knew the only other office left out front was hers, the reception area, and where Mrs. Williams works with her team. Although Uncle Kel's office was smaller it was easily accessible to the front office staff. She continued her assessment and recognized Cynthia's handy work right off the top. Kellie took it upon herself to place his plant stand in the corner next to the window so it would receive natural sunlight. She loved his desk which had dual roles. It was perfect for a working area and for holding small conferences. His chairs were also comfortable. Gregory stood in his doorway with his arms folded across his broad chest. In that short time she had moved his plant stand and was now removing things off his small compact wall unit. It was a good thing he didn't believe in a lot of clutter. She was just about to move it when she felt his presence. Instead of turning around to face him she requested his help. He shook his head and smiled. Man did he love this woman. *Love, where in the world did that come from, but then too he knew where. RJ saw through him, the man up above knew and he could only imagine who else.* Together they moved the wall unit and returned the items to the shelves in a shared silence. Enough of this thought Gregory, he walked over to his closet and pulled out a large gift wrapped box. He had purchased the ideal gift for now. It was something that she needed and according to Grace she would love it. He gave it to her flashing his potent smile. Kellie couldn't believe he had actually bought her something. She was like most women, she loved receiving presents.

"For me," she asked with excitement? "Why?"

116

Gregory nodded a yes and told her, "It's a piece offering and my way of apologizing for any hard feelings, now open it." He wondered if she was aware how her eyes twinkled and eyelids fluttered when she's excited.

"Gregory, you didn't have to do this. And all is forgiven."

"Do you really mean that Kellie?" She whispered yes as she gazed into his eyes. His look of sincerity touched her heart. He patted her hand and told her to open her gift. She returned to her seat with her present while he sat on the edge of his desk. He watched her every move and expression as she examined the package. Although it was beautifully wrapped she ripped the paper like an eager child on Christmas. She opened the box and removed the tissue paper. She was speechless as she picked up the designer bag to examine it closer. It was perfect in size and weight. The black soft glove leather briefcase also had small compartments which could hold all of her technology toys and cell. On the front were her initials in gold with their logo located on the inside. Kellie looked up at him in amazement. "There's more," he said. And he was right, a smaller box was in the corner also wrapped. She removed it, but not without smiling up at him. Again she didn't spare any paper as she removed it in seconds. She opened the box and couldn't believe her eyes. He had also bought her a signature soft leather coach wristlet that would fit perfectly in her new brief case. Her problem had been solved. Lord he was in tuned to her needs as well. What was she going to do with him? She dare not admit she had already put the past behind her before he even asked and was moving on with the future. She really appreciated the gifts and wanted very much to thank him properly.

"Gregory I don't know what to say. This was really nice of you. You can't imagine how much I appreciate this. Thank you so much." This time she made the first move as they both stood. She placed herself right in front of him. Their bodies touching, both filled with each other's scent. Hers exotic and feminine…His woodsy and masculine…Her feeling his hardness and him feeling her softness……Cheek to cheek…Breast to chest…Thighs to thighs. She boldly planted a kiss on his lips and hugged him tightly. Reluctantly she released him although her mind screamed one kiss was not enough. Of course she wasn't surprised when he didn't allow her to move. As usual their eyes played the locking game while being in each other's arms, both slipping into dual trances. Although they both took pleasure in each other's closeness, this was not the place. They must maintain a business relationship. It was evident the same thoughts had entered their minds as they both hesitantly let go, but not without him kissing them both breathless. Taking deep breaths they gathered her gifts and other belongings in silence.

No words were exchanged between them as he escorted her to her car. What could they say? They had already over stepped the line. What line? He was the head man, but he knew that wasn't smart unless they were...Man was he stretching it, as he refused to even think the M word. Besides he was thinking the impossible. Gregory was convinced something needed to be said, but not now. He certainly didn't want to ruin things by saying something stupid. So far the day had been good. He had to admit he was surprised when she accepted his gift and then thanked him for it. Man did she ever thank him! She had also been supportive and encouraging, a team player just like Mr. Kincaid said she would be once she got over the initial shock of the major changes. He was aware of her desires to head the hotel business, but he needed her as his right hand. Gregory knew if he wanted things to continue to run smooth, he better stay cool for now. And just look forward to seeing her every day. With that thought he waved goodbye and waited until she was safely out of the parking lot.

***

Okay, Kellie, what in the world were you thinking! What did you call yourself doing? You were practically all over that man! Just because he gave you a present! You're being taken in by him once again. His charm sophistication and sex appeal was not enough, now he's giving you gifts. Is that all it takes? At least get a diamond! Diamond! What was that all about!

Kellie Kincaid's conscience was giving her one good lashing regardless of the fact the day actually being a good one ending with a bang. She was having a difficult time controlling her wandering mind. Just thinking about their closeness, his touch and breathtaking kiss, caused her to become a bit winded with feelings of intense warmth. She knew she started it and Lord did he finish it. Kellie knew they couldn't continue in this manner unless they were...Oh Lord was she now actually entertaining marriage to Gregory Larson. What in the world was wrong with her! Kellie knew deep within her heart and soul she had to put an end to this madness regardless to the fact that every bone in her body was singing a different tune. She had the hots for HIM and needed to cool it down. That was plain and simple!

CHAPTER 14

Moderately warm October days were slowly winding down while Thanksgiving was hurriedly coming around the corner. The last few weeks had been constantly busy at a continuous fast pace. Gracie and Carl had a beautiful wedding and was now a married couple. Kellie and Kat flew together to attend the nuptials and did they have an interesting conversation. Kat told her the entire story about Gregory and that horrible incident. She knew he was innocent about trying to attack her, but what shocked her more so was Devin Bryson's involvement. He was the culprit and responsible for the nasty remarks. It was his way of framing Gregory who had never uttered one ugly word. According to Kat he really was looking out for her welfare. Devin had staged the whole incident and dared Kat to say a word or he would tell it was all her idea so she could be with Jeremy. It was true Kellie had a crush on him when they were barely teenagers, but that was just it, a teenage crush. Poor Kat, she and everyone else knew how she felt about Jeremy. Lord, she had a thought does everyone know...

Clearing her mind she returned to her laptop, but not for work. She pulled up her buddies wedding pictures for the hundredth time. Smiling, she thought how happy her married friends were and the wedding was simply beautiful. Gracie was now wearing the title of First Lady at Westend Church. Carl's church member did an excellent job with all the arrangements and decorations which was flawless.

Kellie got up to gaze out of the window into the night instead of concentrating on the financial report that she had now reviewed for the third time. She preferred enjoying the picture perfect view of the downtown skyscrapers and their unique constructional designs as darkness enveloped the city. The child play of the flickering lights bouncing from the cars to the

120

buildings lit up the night as her mind began to wander once again…This time about him. She knew she shouldn't but it was difficult with the constant reminders. The agreement made between them to maintain a professional relationship often comes to mind with her wondering what if. That was also a waste of energy. According to her cousin Cynthia, he's involved with someone else. What her cousin didn't know, she overheard the entire conversation herself. He really had no choice but to tell her he had someone. Cynthia was always making a spectacle of herself when he was around trying to get his attention. One thing about her, once she realized she didn't have a chance she moved on.

Kellie never heard the knock or the door open. It was Ann. She was concerned about her friend and boss. There was a certain loneliness about her that she had never witnessed before. Ann couldn't help but worry, she recognized the signs. She knew all about loneliness and wanting someone to love and be loved…a black prince. Thank God she was blessed with hers and if her friend would just open her eyes she could see…

"Ann, how long have you been standing here?"

"Just a few seconds," she walked over to the window. "It's a magnificent view isn't it? I love this office just for that view. You can watch the city transform into its many different faces. How about we grab some dinner and take in a movie? The kids are at their grandparents for the weekend. We can make it a girl's weekend and have a sleepover. We can see if Nisey and RJ want to hangout too!"

Kellie knew what she was trying to do. "Is it that obvious?"

"Yes, and why don't you do something about it."

"Oh Ann, I can't, I just can't." She could not go down memory lane and take a chance of being rejected again. Kellie knew what Kat told her. It wasn't him who said, she wasn't fit for nothing but a sorry piece of…but it was said alone with other degrading remarks about her shapeless body in front of her friends. Although she had put that awful day behind her, the memory was still there along with the hurt and embarrassment.

"Okay then, I'm back to my all girls' sleepover?"

She looked at her friend, "Ann not tonight. I wouldn't be any company and besides you've been looking forward to being with your man this weekend. Don't worry about me. Besides, I have a book I've being trying to complete for the last week. Hopefully I'll finish tonight. Go ahead and enjoy your weekend with Mr. Jesse."

Ann blushed when she spoke his name. It was true, she had been looking forward to a quiet weekend with her true love. But she would have given it up for her. Kellie had been so supportive during their short friendship and she wanted to be there for her as well. "Are you sure?"

Kellie hugged her friend and assured her she was positive and she would be just fine and for her to have a wonderful weekend. Ann said goodnight and left her alone. She looked over at her desk and knew she should complete her task, it was getting late. He wanted her to check his figures. Why he wanted her to check behind him was a joke within itself. She had gone over the report very carefully and everything added up to the number. Who was he fooling, he knew it was in perfect order when he gave it to her. Humph…why not, he was perfect himself she thought closing the files. It was no sense in her being vexed with him. He has truly lived up to everyone's expectations including hers. He's done everything he set out to do and more including toying with her feelings. She began clearing her desk for the evening, all she needed to do now was email everything to Lana, their CPA and call it a day.

Surprisingly enough they have maintained a civil and production relationship while developing a casual friendship, keeping in mind their agreement made during the first week. Occasionally they found themselves having business lunches and dinners. For the sake of the company they kept matters strictly on a professional level not allowing their mutual attraction to get in the way. So far he's done just that while they worked closely implementing their new services, but not her. She's allowed herself to look at him in a totally different way, especially when their meals lead to a movie or an evening stroll followed by a friendly caress and kiss. One time they found themselves at an outdoor concert because they were in the area. Her mind constantly ponders over that nagging what if…Nonetheless it was never considered they were dating, KTS was their focus and conversation, most of the time. If they found themselves crossing the line, Gregory felt compelled to get them back on track which has paid off, KTS was doing great.

Within two weeks of them being a team, KTS added a delivery and hotshot service for the Houston and surrounding areas delivering across the country. They also have employed twenty new workers full and part time. Anyone who was honest, drug and alcohol free and dependable with the desire to work were welcome to be a part of their family. Of course an extensive background check was done for security reasons and Gregory made the final decision on hiring ex-offenders. He was very passionate about giving people a second chance.

KTS's parking lot was now completely full with all types of vehicles. Gregory was already checking into a gas station that's no longer in business located across the street. His vision was more space for the vehicles plus contract and supply their own fuel and mechanics to service their vehicles.

They were doing better than she could have imagined even without her uncle's presence. They had one hundred percent cooperation from all the employees. Even the uniforms were a success. She and some of the office staff wore the polo shirts, especially on Fridays. Gregory was the main one who wore the uniform every day, a polo shirt and a pair of black jeans and he was good to go. He kept a black blazer in his office for emergencies.

Kellie could see it was no end to what he was capable of doing. Gregory Larson has been the sharp businessman everyone had expected along with being thoughtful and considerate not only to her but all the employees. Right now he was making his third delivery for the week for one of the employees whose wife went into labor early this morning. He made it possible for their employee to be present for the birth along with getting paid for all three trips that he himself made. That's the kind of man he was. Uncle Kel had done right in hiring Him as their new leader.

Kellie reached for her bag and stopped to gaze out of her picture perfect window one last time. Before she pulled down the shades she watched the sparkling bouncy lights and the busy traffic zooming down the freeway. It was the weekend and it seems everyone had somewhere to go but her. Snap out of it Kellie, she scold as she put her wristlet purse in her briefcase and picked up her keys, it was time to go.

***

Gregory Larson was coming upon his 288 exit which would take him straight to the office in about twenty minutes. He looked at the clock, he had made good time. His trip was what they call a backhaul, taking and bringing back a load. The hotshot service was really paying off. KTS was working for two major dispatches in the city thanks to Mr. K's old army buddies, one affiliated with the Hobby Airport and the other a home base operation. Next year he planned for KTS to have their own dispatch base. Running into his old Sarge has put them on another track. His daughter Jazper and her husband, along with another couple are owners of a senior citizen's facility. They have contracted them to handle their transportation business. With KTS logo visible they've acquired other contracts from similar operations to provide the same services.

He and Kellie had even managed to maintain a business relationship and control their urges, at least she has. But, she had no idea how much pressure he was under when it came to being around her. His feelings for her were constantly growing and he was thankful she was by his side even if it was all about KTS. He couldn't have gotten this far so fast without her. Their visions were the same and she was his backbone in every way. He loved the way she's encouraged and supported him. His business life was all good. It was now time to work on his personal life and Gregory Larson has made the decision to put his plan into action. He was tired of pulling back and keeping a level head. The friendly touches and kisses was no longer enough. He wanted more and intended to just that, patting his top vest pocket where he put her gift. He was going to do whatever was necessary to make her a part of his life. Starting tonight!

***

Kellie Kincaid sighed aloud as she pulled up in front of her townhouse. She stopped and picked up her mail and went inside. She didn't even stop for carry outs for the weekend. She'll just have to find something in her own kitchen for tonight and maybe go out tomorrow. Humph, she was really in a bad mood and couldn't explain why. After all it was the weekend and she certainly couldn't say she's tired and rest broken. Her nights had been all good as well as her job. With the way he's taken control she does not have to work pass six o'clock nor has she substituted for any of the drivers. She's had lots of time for herself now to do nothing she thought.

In spite of her life now being simple and him as a part of their team, she still didn't have a social life. Who was she fooling, she didn't have anyone to date or hang out with that she cared to. Her best friends were in different states with their own lives which now involved husbands. Her sisters were busy with their own families. Ann was with her sweetie. RJ was out of the city on some big court case. She did think about calling Carl's friend Walter, who was living here in Houston now. But, she was too embarrassed for that. Maybe she'll just have to let Auntie E set her up with another date. Lord she was really acting desperate. For the first time in her life Kellie had to admit she was lonely and wanted someone for herself.

She went upstairs and straight to her room and pulled off her Friday uniform and put on one of her after work hack-a-rounds. Something she let Nisey talk her into buying and wouldn't be caught wearing it in public. She did like the oversized ruffled blouse and the spandex leggings were comfortable, but they were strictly for around the house. She didn't care if the blouse did come down above her knees.

Kellie went downstairs to see what in the world was she going to eat. She closed the door to the cupboard then went to the refrigerator, there was nothing there that suited her taste buds. Shoots she didn't know what she had a taste for, she was just hungry.

Gregory Larson pulled up in his driveway and the biggest grin spread across his face, she was home. She must have decided to go to Edna tomorrow. Wow another great idea. They could go together! He was at her door in record time ringing her door bell.

Who in the world could this be thought Kellie as she walked to her front door? She looked through the side glass and couldn't believe her eyes. The air that she was supposed to use for breathing was caught in her throat. She looked down at herself and knew she was not dressed for him. Forget it silly, he knows you're standing here, he can see you too. Kellie opened her door and without being invited he walked straight in. She gave him a breathless hi. His was an excited hello. They both stood at the now closed door which seems like minutes without saying another word. But it was only seconds. Man, did she look good to him. Forget about dinner, all he wanted was her in his arms. Not yet, breaking the silence he asked if she had her dinner yet. Before she could answer her phone rang. She turned to leave, but he caught her hand. He was not letting her go. Not this time!

"Gregory, I need to get that," was all she spoke.

"Not before I do this." He snuggled her in his strong arms and kissed her like there was no tomorrow. With a mind of their own her arms reached up and were around his neck before she knew it. Their tongues danced around while sensuous moans escaped the both of them. They silently agreed how good it felt to be in each other's arms. He released her lips but not her voluptuous body. All she could do was hold on to him while his powerful hands continued caressing up and down her body and showering her with cinnamon flavored kisses. His touch was potent and caused her nipples to harden. She moaned his name as she placed her check against his and planted kisses down the side of his face. She loved the texture of his shadowy beard...and he loved the feel of her petal soft skin. Kellie heard bells. She gasped. He stopped immediately. They gazed into each other's eyes that were filled with lust and desire. Kellie tried to clear her head, but it was hard being in his arms this way.

"I guess you better get that." He released her but not without kissing her lips once more. He held her hand and walked over to the phone with her.

"Well, it's about time. What in the world were you doing?" It was Lynette, her oldest sister.

"I was trying to get to the phone," she explained through short gasping breaths. Gregory had wrapped his arms tightly around her while pinning himself against the wall with her body. She could feel every hard muscle. Lord, everything was hard. He planted sizzling hot kisses in the bend of her neck...the side of her mouth...All Kellie could do was take it as she tried to talk to her sister sensibly. He was not being fair and he knew it. She whispered please. He stopped, but then began caressing her breasts gently while still holding her captive. His lips were pressed against her cheek. She felt his hot cinnamon breath. A sweltering blaze was steadily growing inside her. She looked up at him with pleading eyes. She needed to catch her breath so she could at least have a decent conversation. She heard her sister scream her name. This time it was that messy Nisey. That's it thought Kellie. She pulled away from him and pointed to the swivel asymmetrical back chair next to a small pedestal accent table. "Sisters, I'm here. What's wrong?"

"Are you sure you're alright? You seem to be preoccupied."

"I told you, something is going on with her. Listen to her, she can hardly talk."

Taking a deep breath, she told them she was good. He was about to get up and she shook her hand at him like he was two years old. He sat there grinning at her like he was innocent. Humph, two can play this game, she thought as she walked right over to him and straddled his lap. While Lynette and Nisey were going on with their third degree, she unbuttoned his vest and fingered his soft hairs on his rippled chest. She then caressed his taunt nipples. He sucked in whatever air he could. That'll teach him to come over here with only a vest and no shirt.

"Kellie, do you hear me?" He reached up to caress her and she knocked his hand down. She was so glad she was multi-task.

"Yes, sisters I hear you. And yes I did forget this was homecoming Sunday and yes I'll be there. If Nisey had reminded me I would have come down with her." She heard Nisey give some flimsy excuse. "Sisters, my cell is now ringing can I please get back to you," she hit him again with the same hand that was massaging his nipple. It wasn't her cell it was his. Now let's see how you like this she said silently giving him a wicked grin.

"You be sure you do," they both said in unison. She didn't know if they said goodbye or not. Kellie placed the phone on the base. Before he could reach his cell she replaced her hand with her tongue and suckled his tight nipple. Gregory dropped his cell and pulled them both to the floor. He pinned her body down with his and held her hands over her head, as he tried to steady his heavy breathing. He knew he started this and had to put a stop to it before something happened that neither was ready for. They smiled at each other with their eyes signaling truce. He kissed her one last time then pulled her up with him.

"Let's go get something to eat." Looking down at herself she was about to say she couldn't leave in what she had on but she knew she couldn't chance going upstairs, especially not in their present state. "You look fine, and no you don't need to go upstairs."

"Let me get my purse and you might need to check your cell that could have been your woman." *Why did she say that?* If she felt like he had someone else why in the world was she kissing him. His hurt expression tore at her heart, but she needed him to ease her mind. After all she heard him with her own ears tell Cynthia he was involved with someone else.

"Are you serious? Do you actually think there's someone else in my life? After what's just happened here?" He couldn't believe she uttered those words or did he, after all she didn't acknowledge he was even there. He waited for her response.

"Gregory, I'm"…was all that left her lips.

"Cynthia! Now Kellie you know better." She put her finger to his lips and reached up to kiss him hoping the hurt he felt would vanish. He was right, she did know better and if anyone knew her cousin she was the one. She's seen her in action so many times.

"Give me a few minutes." She looked in the mirror ruffled her hair, added color to her lips and put on gold hoop earrings that she kept in her purse for emergencies. "I'm ready."

Yes you are, thought Gregory taking in the whole picture. She had been thoroughly kissed and caressed and it shows. Of course he wasn't any better. She had ignited a fuse inside of him that's been growing stronger each day. He was sure it wouldn't be long before he explodes, but not yet, he had to continue being strong and maintain self-control. Anyway he didn't intend for it to go this far tonight. All he wanted was a kiss and hold her for just a minute, but he sees now that was impossible when he comes to Kellie Renee Kincaid.

He asked her what did she have a taste for. She just looked at him with dreamy eyes. He understood exactly, but it was his responsibility to have self-control for the both of them. He knew he had not been fair with her and had to back all the way down. It was getting kind of late and they didn't need anything heavy. Besides when they go to the homecoming celebration there will be a variety of the best home cooked dishes and they get to share another meal. That drew a smile that was stamped in his heart as well. Gregory Larson made up his mind right then and there. He has always been a man of action and didn't believe in dragging things out. Now, if he could just get her to see it his way, their life would be perfect. He suggested grilled fish and salad at Janet's, an intimate family owned diner that's become one of his favorites when he didn't feel like cooking. She agreed and they were on their way.

CHAPTER 15

Kellie and Gregory were enjoying a quiet dinner with barely any conversation, both savoring the taste while making eyes at each other. He made it a point not bring up what happened back at her place, but they would definitely address it later before the night was over. Furthermore it was time they admitted what they had was more than a friendship and stop the pretending. They were both over twenty-one, mature, intelligent, sensible, and caring adults. He knew what he wanted and she has thrown some serious hints herself. Nevertheless he'll deal with that later, right now he was taking great pleasure in watching her eat. He loves seeing a woman enjoy a good meal, and Kellie was doing just that as she took each bite. She had a habit of pausing every few minutes to slowly lick her lips. The fact she had no clue the effect she had in doing such made him smile.

Kellie was aware he was no longer eating himself and was watching her. There had been very little talking during their meal, and now he was staring at her. What is wrong with HIM? She had made it a point not to hold much conversation for fear of him bringing up what had taken place earlier. Besides, she loved taking quick glances at him while he ate. Lord he was so sexy the way he opened his mouth wide to stuff it with food. Anyone else would have looked disgusting, but not him. His lips moved with a smooth sensuous rhythm that caused any healthy woman to have wicked thoughts. Once again they gazed into each other's eyes and were mesmerized. Just as she was about to tell him he was letting his food get cold, her cell rang. She pulled it out to answer, but she was not quick enough, the party hung up. Kellie looked at her phone and couldn't believe the missed calls she had, several and all from Gracie and her sisters. That was not good. Knowing Gracie she had phoned her sisters trying to locate her. That's why they were so upset which caused her to now feel agitated. She dialed Gracie's number and had to hold the phone away from her ears. Her girl was in rare form. She chewed her out royally without giving her a chance to say anything and loud enough for Gregory to hear her.

"Gracie please stop." Her voice trembled as she tried desperately not to become upset. She could hear the hurt in her buddy's voice. But she'll understand once they get a chance to talk and she explain. But right now she was emotional which was not helping the situation. Gregory could tell she was being giving a hard time and was fighting to hold her composure. He got up from his seat and kneeled down beside her. He caressed her gently to give her support, but when the tears started flowing, that was it. He took the phone, there was silence. Gregory figured Grace was probably running tears like Kellie and told her to give the phone to Carl. Carl explained that they had been trying to get in touch with her before they left Atlanta to let her know they were coming to Houston tonight. They wanted her to pick them up at Hobby Airport and of course they thought they would spend the night. Grace panicked when neither she nor her sisters could get in touch with her. Unfortunately they were already in the city and decided to stay in the hotel across the way. Gregory assured them that would not be necessary and they would be there shortly, they were just down the street. Before leaving Janet's, he placed a family order of the same meal plus dessert and had the waitress to put the rest of their dinner in carryouts and he would be back to pick it up.

As Gregory and Kellie walked to his truck he asked her if she was alright, she shook her head indicating yes. Before letting her get in, he gave her a comforting hug anyway. During their ride they held hands while being surrounded by a peaceful silence. Arriving at the airport in minutes, Kellie spotted Gracie first then Carl who was coming out with their luggage. Gregory couldn't get the truck in park fast enough before the door was flung open. Gracie saw her and they both ran to each other. Both friends apologized while embracing. The guys put the luggage in the truck, settled the best friends in the back seat and left the terminal. They had a private conversation during the ride texting. When Kellie confessed to Gracie what she was actually doing that kept her from answering her cell, she wrote the word shame three times in all caps. She ended with a visual that showed a screaming woman with her hair standing on top of her head. They both giggled like teenagers with Gracie ending the texting because she preferred hearing the details...

The two couples finished their delicious dinner and mouth-watering dessert. Janet had surprised them with her scrumptious homemade strawberry shortcakes. Everyone was stuffed and well satisfied. Patting his stomach Carl thanked his host and hostess for a fine meal. Gregory insisted that Grace and Carl make themselves comfortable and relax while he helped Kellie clean the kitchen. They needed to talk about their relationship and where it was headed, that's what he wanted to say, but he knew that would not have been fair to Kellie for the time being. She had been on edge ever since they arrived back at her townhouse. Gracie wanted to protest but his look said not now.

The married couple did as they were asked and settled in Kellie's modest den. Although the area was small, it was cozy and provided comfortable seating for at least four people. Gracie and Carl snuggled on her small sofa. It was a perfect fit in the living space with her dual role upholstered chair in a plush cobalt-blue with its own matching ottoman. It was too early to call it a night, especially after their meal, therefore Gracie decided to find something on television. They had no idea how long it was going to take those two to clean up so they settled for the comedy *Barbershop*. Meanwhile in the kitchen Kellie and Gregory hurriedly put up the left overs. They put her brown, blue, and cream paisley print napkins with bamboo napkin rings back on top of the dark natural bamboo place mats which were on the table.

"You definitely have a love for plants," he said putting her crystal vase which held fresh blooms and ivies back in the center of her small round table.

"Yes I do," she said. "I love to see them grow, but only this kind because they are easy to take care of. The flowers I get from the florist section in the grocery store weekly."

"It's evident," he said smiling at her. She had plants all over his place, plus they were throughout KTS. He looked around her kitchen area and asked if they were finished getting everything in order. She nodded yes. He

132

needed to talk to her in private. He had made up his mind no more tip toeing around her anymore. Tonight he was prepared to tell her how much she meant to him. For once he was putting his heart on the line. He just prayed she wouldn't reject him. He took her hand and walked into the area where they heard the TV to ask Carl and Gracie to excuse them for a few minutes. To their surprise the couple was actually asleep. They quietly backed away.

Gregory led her to the patio to make sure they would have an uninterrupted conversation. He asked her to have a seat and he took the other seat. Thank God there was a small wooden table between them. He needed his space to maintain control and stay focused. Kellie sensed he was troubled and what he had to say was hard for him. She looked into his handsome weary face and her heart ached. He had driven for three days, took her out to eat and then picked up her friends. He had to be tired and worn out and should be resting. She knew she was grasping for any excuse to not have this conversation. She really was not ready for this, but she knew with all that has happened between them it was *Destined to Be!*

He took a deep breath and began. "Kellie, we need to talk about this chemistry between us. Furthermore I need to make you full aware of my true feelings I have for you. I know what we agreed on, but things are just not working out like we planned. I don't know how you're going to take what I have to say but I need to get this off my heart."

Lord, what was he trying to say. Had she put him in a situation because she's allowed him to kiss her whenever they were alone? Yes there's a sexual attraction and perhaps that's the so call chemistry that's consuming the both of them. Is he trying to tell her…tell her…she couldn't even say the words to herself. What has she done? Had she made him feel he was…Lord, all she's done is made a fool of herself with this man. She's put him in a difficult position that he didn't intend to be in. Okay, she'll put a stop to all of this and take him out of his misery while she still had a little bit of dignity left.

"Gregory, you don't' have to say another word. I am so sorry I've caused you to," her voice cracked. Before she could gather her composure and stop the flow of tears he was now kneeling in front of her.

"Sorry for what, Kellie? That I love you and need you by my side? I don't want to spend another day without you. I want to spend the rest of my life growing old with you. I want you to be the mother of my children. I love you Kellie Renee Kincaid, more than life itself." He didn't mean to be so blunt, and knew he should give her a chance to consume all that's been said, but he couldn't for fear she would say something he couldn't stand to hear. He's never utter the words I love you to any woman. She was his first and he silently prayed she would be the one and only. He might as well do it all and take another step, what did he have to lose but his heart. He said it again, "I love you Kellie Renee Kincaid with all my heart and soul. Will you marry me?"

Kellie could not believe this man. Tears were streaming down her face. He loved her. He wanted to spend the rest of their lives together. He wanted her to have his children. He stood and pulled her into his arms. She laid her head on his chest. He kissed her softly on her cheek then the corner of her mouth. He could feel her heart pounding with his. He whispered her name softly and said, "Kellie, please say something Baby."

Before she could speak, "There you two are," said Gracie with Carl right behind her. They had found themselves alone and asleep on her sofa. "We were looking for you two." Gracie was about to step out onto the patio, but Carl stopped her. He could sense something special was going down and they did not need to be disturbed yet. She was about to protest but he shushed her and closed the patio door. The embraced couple never acknowledged their presence.

He called her name for the third time, "Kellie." She looked up into his sensuous piercing dark eyes that showed his love for her and realized that she's been here before. Lord her dreams! But that's it they were only dreams that's now come true! Lord she couldn't believe it, she loved Gregory Adams Larson. She smiled up at him and confessed just that. "Gregory, I love you too. And yes I'll marry you." They kissed passionately with their tongues tasting each other's essence. When it ended he told her he had something for her. She looked at him with a puzzled expression. He smiled and walked her inside to get her gift, which he had hid in one of her decorative jars on the table by the front door.

134

"Auh...Auh..." was all Gracie could get out. By the look of her best friend something wonderful had just happened. The evidence was all over their faces. Kellie and Gracie reached for each other and embraced like best friends do. She whispered to her buddy that he asked her to marry him and she said yes. Gracie screamed with excitement and happiness. "You said yes?" Kellie shook her head. She couldn't believe she actually said yes. After all they've only been back in each other's life for a few weeks. Gracie recognized that look. "Don't even try it." She knew her buddy to well.

"Kellie." She looked at HIM. He was holding a small box. Was he that sure she was going to say yes? "It's not what you think." She took the gift and sat down on one of the twin loveseats in her living room. He sat beside her and Gracie and Carl sat on the other. She opened the box and gasped, inside was an expensive gold bracelet that was simply gorgeous. It had an outrageous large heart shaped diamond in the center of a flat gold heart which was surrounded with smaller diamonds that connected three gold link chains. She knew diamonds and the heart alone had to be at least three carats or more. She leaned against him and with a shaky hand she gavd him the bracelet to put it around her right wrist. It was even more beautiful on her arm.

"Oh Kellie it's simply magnificent," exclaimed Gracie. "It's one of a kind."

She was right about that. Gregory had a vision and had his jeweler in Atlanta make it a reality. He was just waiting for the right time to give it to her. He told her to look on the back. It was engraved with the inscription G luvs K always & forever. After she read it, she gazed into his eyes and rewarded him with a kiss.

Carl and Gracie congratulated them both with hugs and kisses. Carl, being a minister requested a word of prayer for their forthcoming union. He thanked God for bringing them together and to continue blessing them with his mercy and grace, and fill their lives with much love, happiness, and joy. Carl also reminded them to always put God first in whatever they do.

"When's the big day," asked Gracie with eager anticipation.

Kellie and Gregory looked at each other and then at Gracie. "We haven't set a date yet," said Gregory. He looked at Kellie to make sure she was in agreement. She gave him a smile of approval. "I think it's also safe to say soon. I can't wait too long." They did a group hug and burst into laughter. Gregory looked at his watch and knew it was getting late. They were all riding together to Edna around noon. Carl was going to be the guest minister for homecoming service. Bro. Kellogg was supposed to be there but his wife, Felicia was threatening a miscarriage and he couldn't bear not being by her side.

"I think I should call it a night. I haven't had much sleep these last few days," admitted Gregory.

"You look tired, I'll walk you out." He took her hand and kissed it. He told Carl and Gracie goodnight and they walked to the front door. He stopped and declared his love for her once again before opening the door. Kellie smiled as she made up in her mind she would never get tired of hearing him say those words. She never dreamed in a million years she would be in his arms conveying her love for him and only him. She was past happy. He held her tightly as they kissed and said good night.

Carl decided to turn in too. He knew his wife was on pins and needles and couldn't wait to interrogate her friend. Although she was ecstatic about her getting married, he sensed she was anxious for Gregory to leave. He kissed her goodnight and headed up the stairs. Gracie loved her some Carl. He was so in tune to her in every way. He knew she wanted to be alone with her buddy. She found Kellie standing on her front door step watching him go in the house. Before she could say a word the darn telephone rang.

"Kellie, the phone's ringing," announced Gracie. Kellie knew it was her sisters and for once she welcomed their call. Kellie and Gracie were behaving like two teenage girls as they sat together on the love seat. Kellie put her sisters on speaker. With her buddy by her side and through all the questions and tears she told them the entire story starting with the exciting news of course. She made them promise not to tell their parents. She wanted to tell them tomorrow when she gets home. After everyone was satisfied that she had given detailed step by step account of how she and Gregory arrived at the decision of matrimony they called it a night...

As tired as he was, he couldn't go to sleep. He knew what he needed, but that was out of the question. It's been so long since he's been with someone, he's lost count. He didn't know if it was four or five years. He knew he was looked upon as a stud and a womanizer, but that was just a myth. Gregory can't count the women that have tried to break him, but none were successful. He had made up his mind to put a halt to being promiscuous and wait until he finds his true soul mate. Lord, he had no idea it would be Kellie Renee Kincaid, soon to be Mrs. Gregory Adams Larson. He smiled as he took it all in, it was just *Destined to Be!*...

Kellie needed to go to sleep, she had to get up early because she needed to pack and be ready to go by noon. She, her sisters, and Gracie talked past midnight. You would think she would be sleepy by now, but she was too excited to sleep. She had been gazing at her beautiful bracelet for at least thirty minutes. Enough of this she thought, she was behaving like a teenager instead of a mature adult. Humph, who was she fooling as she traced the engraving on the back for the last time. She felt like a teenager in love for the first time. Lord, she was now able to admit her true feelings for HIM. With a smile Kellie reached over to her lamp and turned off the light...

He looked at his clock, it was two in the morning and he was still awake. That's it he said out aloud, as he reached for his cell. He put on his slides and punched in her number all at the same time. Before she answered on the second ring he was downstairs disarming his alarm system and out the back door. "Meet me on the patio now!" was all he said.

Before leaving from upstairs she peeped out her window. There he was on her patio with only dark blue pajama bottoms and slides. She rushed down the stairs, grabbed her keys to turn the alarm off and went straight to her patio door. Before she could ask any questions, she was snatched up in his arms and pressed tightly against his chest. He kissed her fiercely. When he finally allowed them to catch their breath, he looked down at her and chuckled, her full melon size breasts were wearing pink piglets with purple ribbons tied around their necks. She had on her favorite three little pigs pajama set and fluffy piggy slippers that were gag gifts from her sisters. They bought them on one of their many shopping sprees and thought they were just perfect for her.

"I know I look very…"

"You look beautiful," he said as he interrupted her with a soft and tender kiss this time. "Now," he started," we need to set a date."

"Right now," she asked?

"Yes, I don't think I can rest unless you're by my side. I've been tossing and turning for hours and I"… She put a finger across his lips.

"I've always wanted a spring wedding."

"Kellie, that's so far away," he exclaimed. He walked off with his hands up in the air. Gregory turned his back to her. He didn't want her to see his disappointment.

She immediately stepped around him and looked into his weary face. She reached up and caressed away the frown in his forehead. Taking his hand she calmly asked, "When would you like for us to get married?"

"Before I answer that question, let me ask, are you one of these women that must have all the fluffs and frills?"

She wanted to be honest. She had secretly planned her wedding some time ago with all the fluffs, frills, and trimmings, but never gave it much thought until now. She had shared her wants with Gracie when they were planning her wedding, but again it wasn't a big deal not until this very moment. Looking at him anticipating her answer, she told him no she didn't have to have all the fluff, but would like to have a comfortable amount of frills with a little bit of trimmings.

"Thank you Kellie, you've made what I want to say next easy." He gathered her back into his arms. "Marry me tomorrow in Edna at the Bed and Breakfast Inn!"

Her mouth flew wide open as she repeated in high pitch, "Tomorrow? Gregory how in the world can we put together a wedding by tomorrow?"

"You have your mother, sisters, and friends who are all in Edna and I

138

have a few connections to get the marriage licenses and you know food will not be a problem. The only thing we won't be able to do is have a honeymoon right now. But I promise you a honeymoon of your dreams later. What do you say? Please Kellie, say yes." He flashed his intoxicating potent smile that was very effective. Is this the way things were going to be, she give in to his every whim.

"What in the world is going on out here," asked Gracie?

"Oh Gracie, I'm sorry we woke you. Is Carl up too?"

"Girl please, he can sleep through a Texas hurricane! Now, again what's going on?"

"He wants to get married tomorrow at the Bed and Breakfast Inn," exclaimed Kellie!

"Get out of here! I think that's a wonderful idea. All your family is already there for homecoming. With your sisters and Kat's help we can have a beautiful small ceremony with all the frills and trimmings."

"Do you actually think we can do it?"

"Of course we can."

Kellie looked at him and then to her buddy. "Okay, but I want you to know one thing Gregory Adams Larson don't you plan on having your way every time!"

"Yes dear!" They all laughed. He held her in his arms for the last time and told her how happy she's made him. Right then he promised he would spend the rest of his days making her as happy as she has made him agreeing to become his wife tomorrow. He winked at Gracie and then kissed the woman that had his heart and soul…his future… the love of his life.

CHAPTER 16

Kellie was awakened by the smell of coffee and bacon. Knowing Gracie she probably had a full breakfast fixed for her husband. Remembering last night put a big smile on her face, after today she would have a husband too. Today was her wedding day. She looked at her clock to see the time, it was almost ten. Oh my goodness she had slept the entire morning. She didn't have time for that, she needed to call her family. The phone rang, Lord, this family had ESP. It was her mother. Dang that Lynette and Nisey, she told them she wanted to tell her parents.

"Mommy, I wanted to tell you. I told them not to say anything."

"Kellie, Baby they didn't," said her daddy. "It was the man you're marrying. Baby are you sure about this?"

"Don't you think you're rushing things a bit?" asked her mother who she knew was just concerned.

"Yes Mommy and Daddy, I really love him. He's my soul mate and true love." She knew that would convince them, because they had often referred to each other as soul mates. Her parents married very young after only knowing each other for four weeks.

"Okay Baby, your sisters, and Eula are making the preparations. Cynthia is also here helping. Lois Bell and Daddy are taking care of the food. Kat has gotten one of her co-workers Ms Virginia, to do the cakes. Gregory and Bro. Carl got here around nine and they are assisting with setting up the church and the fellowship hall instead of Lois Bell's because of the light rain. We all have our dresses, including the girls. Nisey and little Robert were the only ones who had to go out and get something. She went to Ms Arva's

140

boutique early this morning and found the perfect dress in a beautiful fall floral that blends in perfectly with Lynette's. Robert took little Robert to get a black suit. Everything is taken care of, so you have a good morning Baby and we'll see you sometime later today." Both parents told her they loved her and hung up.

Kellie couldn't believe it, he and Carl were already in Edna. He had allowed her to sleep late while he took care of everything. Who in the world was Gracie fixing breakfast for? There's that ESP again, Gracie walked in with a tray fit for a queen and a red rose.

"Gracie, you shouldn't have."

"I had no choice, orders from your future husband." There was also a card on the tray from him. She decided to save the card for later, and ask Gracie to put it on top of her jewelry box for safe keepings.

"Oh, I forgot your living room looks like a garden too."

"You're kidding!"

"Nope, you'll see when you go downstairs. Now move over so we can eat," they laughed. That was her buddy. After having breakfast burritos, juice, banana and strawberry yogurt, they were ready to put Gracie's plans into action. Gracie took the tray back to the kitchen, but not before giving orders for her to take a nice hot shower. They didn't have time for a bubble bath because she had slept the morning away. They had a full schedule before leaving for the big city Edna. She and her sisters had actually put together an agenda / checklist for the day.

Delana was on her way over with a couple of dresses and headpieces for them to choose from. Bronwyn would be there around noon to give her a complete beauty treatment. Once that's done they can pack and hit the road. Gracie even had the number of outfits needed and suggestions for accessories. They had planned for her to wear white practically the entire weekend. Delana was also bringing a tiara to wear until the wedding. Gracie said if anyone wears white it should be her. Kellie had a nervous thought. She had not told HIM she was a twenty-nine year old virgin! How could she, everything had happened so fast. Oh well it's too late now!

***

Gregory had one more task to do. All had been pretty much a breeze. The church and fellowship hall were ready thanks to Kellie's family and hired help from the inn. The license and rings were being delivered to her parents' home, they would be responsible for getting them to the church. Gregory didn't have a bit of trouble securing them. Sheriff Griffin came to his rescue once again, with the help of his son Jeffery who's the Mayor. He personally saw to it that their marriage permit was issued without any delays. All he needed was the appropriate identification which had not been a problem.

Gregory had contacted his personal jeweler who recommended a reliable substitute in Houston. He told him what he wanted. Gracie had been a big help in letting him know her desires, which made the rush job that much easier. Kellie always thought his and hers matching gold bands were so romantic. It was his idea to add diamonds and of course her diamonds were larger. Tony was given instructions to get the rings before picking up Kellie and Gracie. When they arrive in Edna, he was to give them to her father.

Now he was getting ready to deal with the most difficult mission ever, he thought, as he pulled up in front of his Aunt Marie's house. Gregory was ready to bury the past and wanted to extend an invitation to his family that was still living in Edna and Ganado to his wedding. He had already talked on the phone to his father's only sister to invite her. He explained the reason for a call the day of the nuptials. He couldn't believe she accepted and offered to call his grandparents and the rest of his family who still lived in Ganado. Now it was time to deal with his mother's side. With both sides being a small family you would think... It was no need going there. He took a deep breath and got out of his car. He hadn't walked the steps that led to her front door since he was a kid with his great Aunt, thought Gregory as he knocked on the door. According to Ms. Lois Bell his grandparents were living with his Aunt Marie, his grandmother's baby sister. Thanks to him, they were able to build an apartment on the side of their home which was handicap accessible and connected with a shared screen in porch. What luck, his mother's sister was also there, she opened the door...

Well everything was taken care of, he could finally relax until it was time. He was still a little stunned by the warm reception he received from his mother's family. They had nothing but apologies and hugs. He accepted and expressed he wanted nothing more than for them to be a family. What was really a surprise they had already made plans to attend. They had received the email and text like everyone else. He knew Bro. David Coleman and wife was responsible for that. He called him before leaving Houston to ask about performing the ceremony, he was honored. Bro. David also volunteered to use the church directory to extend the invitation to family and church members. Gregory requested him to hold off until he was able to tell Kellie's parents face to face. He knew his great auntie would be so proud of him right now. He has finally let go of the past and was starting a new life with the one woman who has always held his heart and soul.

***

Delana bought two of the most exquisite wedding dresses ever that she thought would be perfect for Kellie. She was so right, they both fit like they had been made just for her. Although she brought her sewing machine, the alterations needed were hand stitched. She was stunning and looked absolutely beautiful in both dresses. Delana specializes in dresses for plus size women and she knew her business well. Under no circumstances could Kellie make a decision. She was so glad she was able to include the women in her family and best friends in making the right choice, thanks to cell phones. Together they chose the perfect dress and headpiece.

Her floor length strapless A-line gown was absolutely gorgeous. A lovely detailed fitted bodice flowed into a soft flowing chiffon skirt. The empire waist was accented with exquisite hand beaded lace and ruching details that gathered up on the side to give it an asymmetric look. The 3D flowers that held the side drape were embellished with pearls, sequins, and rhinestones. A charming laced up back created an hourglass shape with a sweep train adorned in the same ornaments. Her headpiece and veil consisted of a white satin headband featuring different sizes of feathered flowers with detailed embellishments like her dress and train. Yards of soft bridal tulle cascaded to the floor creating a romantic and elegant look was attached. There was not a need for accessories, she was going to wear her grandmothers' pearls and crystals along with some of her own for a chic but classic look. Delana also brought two sets of white sexy lingerie and three sets of lace undies. She even brought a dress for Gracie in a beautiful rich coral. According to Nisey the color blends perfectly with Lynette's chestnut spaghetti strap dress and her fall floral strapless print. You would think everything had been planned and purchased months ago.

Bronwyn had arrived earlier which allowed her to complete her job in less time than Gracie had allocated on her so call schedule. Everything was done and they had time to spare according to her buddy. Bronwyn had even applied her make-up and told her where to add the finishing touches for a more dramatic look for the wedding. During her beauty treatments, Gracie had actually packed her clothes which was really easy…everything was white. Kellie still checked behind her and added jeans, and a coordinating top. After making sure she was satisfied with her selections, she put on the outfit that had been laid out for her. She was glad Gracie chose something simple and comfortable to travel in, a pair of white skinny jeans and a long soft knit pullover top with an asymmetrical shark tooth hemline, rolled V-neckline, and ribbed sleeves. She even picked out her jewelry, gold and silver chain with dangling discs, matching earrings and bangle bracelets was chosen so it wouldn't clash with her gift. Kellie didn't care if it did or not, she was wearing her gift everyday regardless of what she had on. She slipped her feet into silver shoes and picked up the matching bag to make sure his card was in the side pocket. A pleasant smile spread across her lips as she thought about him.

Gracie was right, her living room did look like a beautiful fall garden. When he called she wouldn't let her talk to him. "*Time wouldn't permit*", *she said*. All she wanted to ask was his ring size but that had been taken care of too. Of course it was Gracie's chance to pay her back for not allowing her to talk to Carl on their day.

"Kellie are you ready? It's time to go. The limo is here and the driver is ready to get your bags," announced Gracie as she entered her bedroom. She looked at her buddy and fought back her tears. She was a vision of pure loveliness if she says so herself in the outfit she chose, and the tiara made it special and official. "Don't, you'll start me and I don't want to mess up my make-up."

144

"You're right, let's go!" They pulled her small luggage in the hallway. Her clothes bag and wedding ensemble were already downstairs. Tony, their driver met them in the hallway. The two friends followed him downstairs, secured the townhouse, and went to the limo. Being driven to Edna in a limo was a bit much thought Kellie, but Uncle Kel insisted.

The first thing Kellie did was tell him she needed to stop at a jewelry store in the Sugarland Mall. She and Gracie thought of the perfect gift for him. Tony couldn't believe his ears. He had just left the jewelry store in the underground mall downtown, but did what he was told.

After settling back in the limo, Gracie announced she was going to take a short nap, and to wake her when they hit the big city. She was the one who had been up at the crack of dawn to see Carl and Gregory off and made plans with Nisey and Lynette. She needed to get at least a few winks before they arrived. Once they get there it will be non-stop once again. The Kincaid women had put together a little brunch in her honor. Gracie smiled, she had kept her schedule to the minute. They would have been forty-five minutes ahead of time, but the jewelry store delayed them a bit. It was a good thing Kellie was able to call in a favor from one of her patrons and all they had to do was pick it up. Humph…they were still on schedule. Dang she was good, bragged Grace silently.

After holding a little small talk with Tony, Kellie took out her card to finally read it. It was so beautiful and touching, she messed up her makeup anyway.

Kellie I will never be able to express in words how much love I have for you, nor how much you've always meant to me. I know you may not remember the first time we met, but as you continue reading you will see I never forgot. It was my first day in Ms. Mason's kindergarten class. You were the only one who reached out to me and made me welcome. You took me by the hand and showed me where to put my raincoat and backpack. You also invited me to sit next to you during lunch along with Kat, Jeremy, and Bryson. Although Bryson and I became homeys afterwards, it was that little skinny girl that stole my heart at six years old. I was the one who secretly put little trinkets in your backpack the entire time we were in the same grades. I was crushed when they separated us in the fourth. It seems my whole life changed after that. I entered into a dark lonely place and remained there which seemed like forever, acting out whenever I could. When we finally crossed paths again, well you know the story. We had been victims of betrayal and deception. Thank God we both survived and went on with our lives. I can truthfully say my heart never belonged to anyone but you. Of course I must confess that I did foolishly fall in love with a perfect stranger. You see we met on an airplane on the way to Houston. In that short time when our paths crossed, I felt a powerful connection that I couldn't explain. I can't count the times I dreamt about that very day. The man up above was the only one who knew how my feelings continued to grow for her even though we were strangers. I prayed that our paths would cross again. It was fate itself Kellie, that woman was you. I thanked God then and now for bringing my six year old love back into my life. Ever since that wonderful day in Atlanta and we met again, my mission was to love you and only you Kellie Renee Kincaid. I thought the love I have was enough for the both of us. Baby when I saw your eyes filled with love for me, my heart and soul melted. You loving me was far beyond my expectations and dreams. Giving me your love is the greatest gift ever and has added an abundance of joy and happiness to my life. So my love, I want you to relax and look forward to starting our life together. I'm asking you to meet me at the altar at 6:45 where I will make my undying promise to love and cherish you forever.

Love always and forevermore

Gregory

Gracie heard her sniffling and sat up to look at her buddy. She asked what was the problem? Kellie handed her the letter, while dabbing at her face to keep from ruining her makeup. "Ahhh," sang Gracie, "How beautiful and touching. "Oh Kellie he has loved you for so long. Give me some tissue," she sniffed. "You know what's so ironic about this whole situation?"

"No, what?"

"I've always had strong feelings for him too. Maybe not when we were

146

six years old, but I did have a terrible crush on him all through middle school until I was told he didn't like me anymore. I was even going to ask him to attend one of the church socials and I let Kat talk me out of it. And then that incident ... well you know that story. Poor Kat thought it was all her fault because she wanted to make sure I ask anyone but Jeremy. She actually encouraged me to invite him in the beginning. Then right in the midst she changed her mind and wanted me to invite Devin instead. Gregory was supposed to be this terrible person who said some awful things about me. She really didn't know that I knew the real reason was Jeremy. We know now Devin Bryson was the culprit and responsible for that entire mess."

"Well, that's all in the past and you two will finally have that happily ever after that you so much deserve, because of the true love you have for each other." Gracie was right, thought Kellie. She didn't have a clue as to why she brought all of this up now, especially on her wedding day. After all this was her past and she was very much above that foolishness. Kellie knew she couldn't deny the fact that she had been hurt behind the *"he say, she say"* mess, but it was that incident that has definitely made her the strong powerful woman she is today. Besides, this was her wedding day and nothing was going to spoil this glorious and happy occasion. She was truly happy to be able to spend the rest of her life with this man that was so giving, understanding, passionate, and loving. And she certainly couldn't leave out the fact that he was handsome and fine!

Gracie made a call to let everyone know they were taking the Edna exit and would be their shortly. They made good time to enjoy the family plans.

CHAPTER 17

The off and on light drizzle had stopped and left a clean fresh smell of fall foliage with a mixture of late blooming flowers. The fragrance helped set the ambiance for a wonderful romantic affair. Peabody Church of Christ had a full house. Chairs had been set up wherever there was room without blocking the aisle. The church was elegantly decorated in simplicity. In the foyer was a small decorative table which held the guest book and a basket filled with white scrolls and bird seed pouches tied with apricot, chestnut, and yellow ribbons. Hung on the end of each pew were white organza ribbons, tied into pretty eye-catching bows with dyed berry branches and colored strings of accent pearls. Potted trees with clear lights threaded around their trunks and branches, were placed on layers of white shimmery netting in front of the church and pulpit, leaving space for the minister and wedding party. The unmovable pulpit stand was completely covered with two white tablecloths and decorated in the same fashion with the netting and lights. A planter with a bouquet of fall flowers, berries, and greenery sat on top. To the right was a charming antique accent table which held unity candles in gold candleholders on a bed of berries and leaves.

The table was special, it belonged to Gregory's great aunt. Ms. Lois Bell said she loved that table because it was made by a lost love. She thought its sentiments would be perfect, and knew he would recognize it immediately. It represented a gift of love and a part of her would be present with the two lost loves that have found themselves again. Ms. Lois Bell always knew how Gregory felt about Kellie. It was so obvious since he always asked about her whenever he called or visited.

The air was filled with excitement, love, and happiness as their guest waited patiently for the wedding to begin. Surprisingly, Gregory had a

148

wonderful representative of family members who seemed to be elated they were in attendance. Both sets of his grandparents were present and sitting in the back along with Kellie's. They were the ones who would start the procession. He had asked his Aunt Cheryl and Ms. Lois Bell to represent his mother and great aunt to light their family unity candle, of course they both agreed through tears…

Kat and Cynthia checked one more time to make sure everyone was in place and ready. Boutonnières and corsages had been pinned. The runner was at the front of the sanctuary ready to be rolled down. Acappella singers were serenading the audience with love songs. While the guest were enjoying the entertainment, the groom was nervous and impatient, which was expected. They had gotten the word that the bride would be ready in about twenty minutes or less. So far everything was going according to schedule.

"Oh baby sister, you look absolutely gorgeous," said Nisey. Both of her sisters stood in front of her with Gracie and her mother, who were dabbing at her face. Lynette had just finished adorning her in their grandmothers' jewelry. Her dress and veil was stunning and make-up just like Bronwyn wanted, sensuous and dramatic. The satin headband encircled her short curly hair with the feathered flowers crowning her face. Once again they all agreed she was a vision of pure loveliness.

"Mommy please don't cry," pleaded Kellie. She had fought tears ever since she and her daddy had their father and daughter talk. She couldn't believe the admiration her father had for Gregory and how he always felt that he would do well. He said it took a strong individual to live with the hearsays and scandals that surrounded his life while growing up as a young man, and the humiliation he encountered was just plain disgraceful. He was a prime example of what does not kill us, makes us stronger. His determination and stamina personified his character and integrity as a man. He was going to be proud to call him son and add him to their family.

"I think we're ready ladies," announced Lynette. They needed to get started before their mother had them all in tears. Lynette gave her one last look as she gave her the beautiful bouquet that she had made especially for her. A cluster of white roses accented with bear grass, dyed pearl accents and bouquet jewelry hand wrapped in white satin ribbon. After she was satisfied that everything was exactly like she wanted, she gave Nisey instructions to call their father and Cynthia to tell them they were ready. The ladies blew her kisses as they left the room...

There was a hush silence as everyone watched the procession began with the photographer on hand. The minister, groom, and groomsmen walked in, then the grandparents, followed by Ms. Lois Bell and Gregory's Aunt Cheryl who was escorted by the best man, Carl. He walked them over to light Gregory's family candle, escorted them to their seats and took his place beside the groom. Mrs. Kincaid stood in the doorway dressed in a light taupe two piece with a matching hat. Gregory came down the aisle to escort his future mother–in–law. The guest marveled at how handsome he was in his black tux and tuxedo shirt with a diamond clustered pin at the neck and diamond earrings to match which was a gift from Kellie. He walked Mrs. Kincaid over to light Kellie's family candle and then escorted her to her seat.

The guests anxiously waited for the bridesmaids and matron of honor. Lynette then Nisey walked in with their small bouquets of fall flowers that were a replica of the bouquet centered on the pulpit stand. Gracie was next with her matching bouquet. Lynette's son and daughter stepped out from opposite sides to pull the white runner down, and did a fantastic job. Little Robert and his twin sisters Reesa and Reisha were next. Little Robert held the flower basket while the girls dropped orange, yellow, and beige rose petals. He set the basket down in front of his mother, ran down the aisle and back with the ring bearer's pillow, then stood beside his father. The room was full of laughter.

Cynthia and Kat closed the doors. Once again Taryn and Trey appeared in front of the church and rang wedding bells. The singers began singing the traditional wedding song as the audience stood. The doors opened slowly. Gregory was not ready for what his eyes beheld. She was more beautiful than he could ever imagine. He was simply overwhelmed and captivated by her very essence. He considered himself a strong tough black man that had to overcome obstacles in every shape form and fashion. But today she has turned him soft. Kellie and her father stood in the doorway for a quick second and then walked slowly down the aisle. The *ahhhhs* and *oohhhhs* filled the room as father and daughter walked gracefully down the

150

aisle. Gregory was grinning from ear to ear as old school would say. He was glad they had a short walk as he stood to claim his bride. After her father officially gave her away, the striking and loving couple took turns declaring their love for one another. He couldn't handle the promises she made in front of the world as far as he was concerned. Tears slowly flowed down his face. The last time he shed a tear was at his great aunt's funeral. She wiped his tears with her blue lace handkerchief. In a broken voice filled with tender emotions he declared his love for her which caused her to step even closer in his arms. They held on to each other for joint strength and loving support during the remaining of the vows and Bro. Coleman's words of encouragement. He had a time getting them to let go long enough to exchange rings, which brought smiles and chuckles from the audience. They exchanged their customized two-tone matching diamond wedding bands. The minister then announced it was time to light the unity candle. Instead of moving, they stood locked together both physically and emotionally. Bro. Coleman shook his head and repeated his request this time raising his voice. They still stood smiling at each other as if their feet were glued to the floor. Lynette gave her bouquet to Nisey and stepped over to the couple and freed one of Kellie's hands and led her to the unity candle. She knew he would follow and he did. Giving them their tapered family candles, she pointed to the unity candle. Together they lit the candle and Lynette lead them back to Bro. Coleman. He thanked her loudly. The audience was now laughing and saying amen. Bro. Coleman did not waste another minute as he said "You may now kiss your bride!" They looked into each other's eyes. As if they were given a clue the singers croon out Issac Hayes classic *"The Look of Love."* Gregory held his gorgeous wife snugly as he kissed her with genuine love and passion. She now belonged to him...his true love and soul mate. They were then introduced as Mr. and Mrs. Gregory Adams Larson with the audience giving them a round of applause. After both took deep breaths she removed the lipstick from his lips and together they turned to face their audience.

Next the bride and groom did the traditional Kincaid's stroll to the popular old school song... *"As We Stroll Together"* As they walked down the aisle they were congratulated and given well wishes.

***

"Harold, I'm so glad you answered the phone. I'm up the creek man without a paddle." He wanted to say he was SOL, but knew he couldn't use that kind of language with Harold Grimes. He was a member of the old school no nonsense gent. He was helleva and the top of the line in of his profession. He had some bad dogs working for him and G-Man was his best. Right now that's who he needed his top man. He had heard through the channels that G-Man had left the company and relocated in Texas, but still contracted his self out for special jobs. "I've been trying to get in touch with your top dog G-Man for the last six hours. Has he changed his digits?" Thomas Jarell Wiltz shared partnership with his two brothers of Hit Factory Enterprise in Detroit. They were a fresh company that was steadily climbing to the top. They had just signed a contract with a well sought out singer. She was making her comeback in the music industry after a stretch in television and needed a body guard for a few days. They had put together a little PR for promoting her new single and wanted G-Man to provide security while they wait for Big Shasta to return to the country.

"Thomas J, G-Man is getting married as we speak. And no he has not changed his contact number. He has slowed down on his jobs though. So why don't you give him a call sometime next week to see if he's interested. How's Griff and MC?" Those were Thomas J older brothers who Harold generally did business with. Thomas J was too flip for him. After the small talk they hung up.

Harold thought about Gregory. He couldn't believe he was actually getting married to that young lady he had carried a torch for ever since they were kids. He was happy for his young friend. And expressed just that in the telegram he sent from GAL.

***

Finally, thought Gregory as he looked at the time on his watch, while sitting at the table with the other men. Everything had been done according to etiquettes (a receiving line, drinking sparkling cider out of stemware, the cutting of the cake, and throwing the bouquet and garter) which satisfied the Kincaid women and Gracie. They wanted Kellie to have it all and she did. As a matter of fact his wife (he loved the sound of that) and the other Kincaid

152

women were still taking group pictures in a corner that had been set up in the foyer of the reception hall. They had to bring the remaining of the picture taking inside because of the sudden outburst of rain. The weather had been perfect long enough for them to take a few group pictures outside on the lush lawn.

He and the guys had taken their last set and were relaxing. Gregory observed his surroundings and was pleased with the results. Soft music was playing while the guests enjoyed themselves. Kellie's family had done a superb job along with Ms. Lois Bell. The reception hall was smartly decorated with the same color pattern used for the wedding. The trees had been moved into the hall to keep the ambiance. The tables were dressed in white tablecloths with fall floral arrangements in lovely decorative vases, and lighted candles of various sizes inside fancy candleholders. It was evident they belonged to family. There were two buffet tables with a variety of finger filling foods and desserts placed in the corners to keep the guest from having to stand in long lines. Gregory was so happy he built a fellowship hall for the church that his great aunt loved dearly. She would have been pleased and proud he thought popping a chocolate mint in his mouth…

The Kincaid women entered the hall. Gregory and the other gentlemen stood. Kellie had exchanged her wedding gown and veil for a sexy white strapless tea length dress and a decorative jeweled comb. The flattering draped bodice and flirty box pleated skirt was stunning with a rhinestone brooch at her waist which added a touch of sparkle. She walked across the floor straight in the waiting arms of her husband in white satin sandals with rhinestone anklets and ribbon ties. He wanted so much to bury his head in her ample bosom and kiss her twin peaks, but knew this was not the time and place. Oh but later, thought Gregory. She knew exactly where his mind had wandered to as she caressed his sexy eyebrows that now belonged to her. He kissed his lovely wife and they walked back to their table. Kat and his Aunt Cheryl brought them refreshments. Ms. Lois Bell had made her special cream cheese sandwiches that resembled a layered cake. It was a delicious decorative dish she made just for him. Although he didn't have much of an appetite he couldn't wait to taste Ms. Lois Bell's sandwiches…

The beautiful wedding cake was now being served. Ms. Virginia Hart had really out done herself in such a short time frame. She had three different sizes of square layers stacked on top of each other with butter cream icing, chocolate trimmed border, and decorative candy crystal flowers of apricot and yellow. A small bride and groom were nestled on the top layer which had been taken off for the couple for later. The cake was enjoyed by all, especially the children.

Uncle Kel tapped his glass, to get everyone's attention. Gracie and Carl stood to start the toasting celebrations and wished the joyous couple much love and happiness. The guests were then asked to toast the bride and groom.

Uncle Kel took his turn next. "You all know how special Kellie is to me," he started. "She's my namesake and I have always been so proud of her. She's the daughter Nita and I never had. So it goes without saying we want to wish her and her husband who I've become very fond of these last few months a blessed and wonderful new life. Always remember this day and how David Coleman had a hard time marrying you two and" … Aunt Juanita pulled his coat. "Wait Nita, I'm almost finished. See how you're smiling at each other at this very moment with the look of love in your eyes…Humph, I sound like Issac Hayes." Now Aunt Juanita was now standing by his side. She held her glass up with everyone else following her lead.

"To Kellie and Gregory." Uncle Kel announced he was still not through. Aunt Juanita teacher's skills surfaced. "Put it in writing darling." The family and friends laughed.

Gregory's Aunt Marie stood next. With tears in her eyes she spoke for his grandparents and herself. She told her nephew that his family was so thankful for his forgiveness and was proud that they were able to share this day with him. He will always remain in their heart of understanding under the word love. His Aunt Cheryl then stood next with tears streaming down her face. She had a card in her hand pressed against her chest. Gregory was on his feet as he reached for his wife's hand, he needed her strength. Together, hand in hand, they walked over to his aunts and grandparents and embraced them all. Aunt Cheryl whispered she put it in writing and gave him her card. There was not a dry eye in the room.

His grandfather stood to represent his father's side and expressed the same sentiments. They were thankful that he grew up to be a loving and productive young man in spite of his obstacles. They were especially proud because he wore the Larson's name.

"Okay people, it's her Daddy's time."

The guests laughed as her mother said, "Oh Lord."

"I want to say I'm happy for my babygirl. I must admit her mother and I were surprised. I'd be lying if I said we weren't. But I have to be honest. We're going to be proud to call this young man son and add him to our family. And I know my baby is in good hands." Mr. Kincaid held his glass up with everyone following his lead, "To the bride and groom, may your life be filled with love, understanding, and support for one another. Look around this room, you have some wonderful role models to pattern your marriage after. Always remember," Kellie's mother touched her husband's hand. "I know put it in writing." Again laughter filled the hall.

Gregory and his bride were standing in the middle of their guest. He cleared his throat, looked around the room and then at his beautiful bride by his side. He was touched by the love and support that was shown. Squeezing Kellie who was now in his arms he took a deep breath and began. "First, I want to thank Mr. and Mrs. Kincaid for producing such a beautiful and loving daughter. I promise to spend the rest of my life making sure her life is filled with nothing but love and happiness. I also want to thank this great family that I've always admired for welcoming me as a new member. I want to especially thank both sides of my family for sharing this day. It meant so much to have you here. Special thanks to our friends from Atlanta, and again the Kincaid family for making this day perfect." Taking a deep breath, Ms. Lois Bell, I don't know where to begin. You have always been there for me. You've listened to my woe is me humdrum countless times, put me on the right track numerous times, fed me, gave me the love and support I needed when there was no one else." His voice cracked but he continued, as he wiped the tear that fell. "You always knew when I needed someone to hold me and say I care. I love you son. You have always been in my corner cheering me on and I want you to know you will always have a special place in my heart. I love you Ms. Lois Bell." Again not a dry eye in the room as he and Kellie walked over and embraced her with a kiss on each cheek.

Kellie wiped her husband's face with a napkin and kissed him gently on the lips and then each cheek. She whispered, "I love you Gregory Adams Larson," and hugged him ever so tight. The look in his eyes said it all, it was time to go. Together they said good night and hugged their family and friends for the last time.

***

The newlyweds had the surprise of their lives as Uncle Kel pulled up in front of the house he grew up in. Gregory had already asked Jeremy to pull his truck in front of the hall and he was going to drive them to their destination which they thought was the inn. Instead, when they got ready to leave the hall a path of rose petals lead them to Uncle Kel's black vintage Rolls Royce. He had been given strict instructions to chauffeur them to their new country home. Aunt Marie and the rest of his family had gotten together and made it possible for them to spend their first night as husband and wife in their own master suite. In spite of the weather they had managed to give them the ideal gift. Gregory really wanted to do just that but knew time wouldn't permit such, especially with her family doing the wedding preparations in record time.

They got out and walked up the wraparound porch. Jeremy and Kat greeted them at the door with big smiles. This is where they disappeared to, assumed the surprised couple.

"Welcome to your new home," they said together. "Everything is ready for you to"…Kat paused. She knew there was going to be very little sleeping tonight. "Aunt Marie and Aunt Lois Bell have a scrumptious food basket prepared and the refrigerator has been stocked and"… Jeremy told his wife that was enough as he pulled her out of the doorway.

"Goodnight you two," said Jeremy with Kat echoing.

Gregory looked at his bride with a devilish grin. Before she could say a word he scooped her up. She gave him a sistah girl look and shook her head. Setting her down after crossing the threshold they glanced around the room.

156

Although there was no furniture, large candleholders were on the floor with luminous scented candles glowing and providing just enough light while soft romantic music played in the background. Kellie recognized Kat's handiwork, but where was the music coming from. Her husband drew her close to his heart. His dark sensuous eyes said it all as he kissed her tenderly on the lips. With the room set for romance and love, they did their first dance as husband and wife to one of Kat's special CDs that Kellie recognized. She had named it *For Lovers Only* which featured old school love songs. They held each other intimately as they moved to the sultry melody of *Gladys Knight's You're the Best Thing*…

They were engrossed in each other's essence exchanging sweet kisses and tender caresses. Their senses were pampered with the fragrant scents they both had found exciting, seductive, and pleasurable. Her memorable soft perfume of exotic treasures of dreamy florals and softly spiced amber has clouded his senses since their first encounter in the sky. Since then he has longed to do more than just hold and feel her opulent full size body, he wanted no needed to now taste her sweet nectar. Tonight there was nothing to hold him back. She belonged to him and only him. He had her in his arms now…Her soft fleshy body was pressed against his…He could feel her heartbeat while his did a fast rhythmic dance. She moved her arms from his shoulders and encircled his waist which pressed her even closer to his strapping hard chest. Lord she smelled and felt so good he thought. He leaned down and assaulted the top of her twin melons that were peeping up at him with sweet kisses, something he's been wanting to do since she walked down the aisle. She gasped with her breathing becoming intense as he continued planting butterfly kisses on her cheek then neck. Gregory rested his cheek on top of her head as they continued moving slowly to the tempo of the music.

Kellie reveled in his masculine scent as she placed her face on his wide shoulder. Nudging the side of his broad neck she inhaled his male cologne. The rich and smooth masculine fragrance of tempting citrus, rich spices and smothering woods created the ultimate seduction. She loved the feel of his rock-solid body as they danced to the second slow jam, *The O Jays…Let Me Make Love*…Her mind wandered to the countless times she dreamed about being in this man's arms this very way. Her man now…He belongs to her and only her…He was now holding and caressing her like there was no tomorrow. Kissing her with such tenderness and passion caused her to become feverish as her temp began to slowly rise. Lord he felt so good she thought as she lightly stroked his cheek. She loved the baby soft texture of his facial hairs that was silky smooth. She held his face to position it so she could place tender kisses on his forehead, right where his sexy eyebrows met. She then pressed her soft lips at the corner of his mouth. How long had she dreamed of doing just that? Kellie gently nipped his neck that caused bolts of lightning to shoot through his body dispersing excitement and pleasure to both of them…their breathing now becoming hard and winded.

"Kellie sweetheart, it seems like I've waited for you all my life," he whispered as he nibbled her earlobe and caressed her bare shoulder with more kisses. "You don't know how many times I've dreamed of us being together like this…in this house."

She gazed into his bedroom eyes and couldn't believe what she was hearing. She had been here before. It was dejvu. "Gregory you won't believe how many times I've dreamed of hearing you say those very words to me and now it's finally happening," she confessed.

Gregory abruptly stopped dancing and stood still, raising her chin and gaze into her bedroom eyes filled with love and desire. He kissed her eyelids which caused them to flutter shut. What were they waiting for it was their wedding night? He took her hand and kissed the inside and held it to his chest. The warmth from his touch caused her to shiver. As he led her to the master suite he blew out the candles. Entering the hallway was another surprise. Trails of rose petals lead to the master suite. You could hear the music coming from the bedroom. Flickering dancing lights glistened on the walls which provide the mood for lovemaking.

Gregory couldn't believe his eyes when he saw his own bedroom furniture from the inn with other special pieces along with an exquisite quilt and matching shams that he recognized immediately. It was his great aunt's that she had quilted herself for her own king-size bed. He also recognized present accent pieces that had disappeared after her death. They had done this for him. He picked up one of the shams and held it to his heart. He was now filled with mixed emotions as he sat them both on the pillow-top bench in front of the bed. He then pulled back the quilt like he had seen her do so many nights.

Kellie saw his sadness and gently caressed his cheek as she told him how beautiful the quilt was. He refused to step back into that dark place and reached for her. Taking the hand that touched his skin, he kissed each fingertip. The impact was startling, it caused her to gasp. He covered her mouth with his, kissing her in a way she had never experience before. Kellie had read dozens of romance novels about these things, but Lord none of them had prepared her for this man. She was now lying on their bed and didn't know when or how. He was on top fondling her breasts through her dress. Their bodies were entwined with her rubbing and stroking his. There was just too much clothing between them.

"Kellie I need you now," he whispered as he continued his caresses gazing into her adorable face. He needed her to see the longing in his eyes for her.

"I want you to," she said softly. "Let me do something about all of these clothes.'"

"You read my mind," he said smiling. He pulled her up and held her in his arms. He whispered in her ear, "Can I help?"

She didn't know if she could handle being totally nude in front of him…after all this was her first time, but he is her husband. This is what she wanted. Lord he doesn't know she's still a virgin, she thought. Kellie looked up into her handsome husband's face and confessed that she was a virgin. She made it clear she was not shame because it was her decision to wait until she married, but thought he needed to know. What she didn't say she was like any other woman being intimate for the first   time…anxious…self-conscious…awkward…and…unsure of herself, especially on her wedding night.

Gregory's heart grew two sizes larger during her revelation. He was going to be her first. She had saved herself for her wedding night…her own man…her husband…HIM! He was touched and honored. He turned her around so he could begin the undressing of his virgin baby. First he relieved her of her jewelry except her diamond studs nibbling each earlobe and leaving tantalizing kisses around both wrists. He slowly unzipped her dress and let it fall to the floor while dragging steaming enticing kisses wherever his hand touched. Kellie leaned back against her husband for support as her temp began to rise again. Tingling little tremors danced inside. Her breathing was quickening with each touch and squeeze. She was now left exposed in her strapless lace bra and body shaper that was an absolute essential for big girls. *Thank God Gracie talked her into buying a lace body shaper instead of the plain ones. She will be forever thankful.*

Gregory pressed her close to him so she could feel how much he wanted her as he caressed and stroked her softness. She shuddered at the hardness she felt while her heart skipped several beats. Again her thoughts went back to her extensive reading which had not prepared her for what was happening to her at this very moment.

He felt her trembling and knew he had to take his time and make sure she was good and ready to receive all of him. He wanted her first time to be a mind blowing experience. Gregory wanted…no he needed her mind as well as her heart, since she definitely had his as long as there was breath in his body. He turned her around so they would be face to face. Her eyes were closed tight. He kissed each eyelid as he whispered how much he loved her. Slowly he unsnapped her bra and melon sized breasts leaped out with dark erect nipples that begged for attention. He consented as he took turns suckling and massaging each breast. She called out to him softly, she didn't know how much longer she could remain standing. Gradually he pulled down her lace body shaper that was concealing her virtue and sweet nectar. He planted wet kisses on her velvety skin as he exposed it bit by bit. He helped her step out of the lace garment and untied and removed her shoes. Gregory knelt in front of his wife to continue fondling and caressing her now completely nude body. Wrapping one arm around her waist he dragged more kisses from her navel down to her feminine core while using his free hand to gently stroke the essence of her passion. He touched her where she had never been touched before. She was losing it as her mind and inner self slowly soared out of her body. She had no control of the smothering moans that were now escaping from her trembling lips while desperately struggling

160

to stay on her feet. He recognized the signs as he moved her to their bed, but not without kissing the shield that was guarding her nectar. While she screamed his name every nerve in her body screeched right along with her as he plucked and toyed with her nipples.

Gregory stripped in record time and covered her nakedness with his. She welcomed him and took great pleasure in his touch. He started his seductive assault to her body again. His hand and tongue were all over her suckling and caressing her with a fever of need and wild desire. Dragging intoxicating kisses between her full bosoms down to her feminine core drew thunderous moans and cries of passion from deep within. Kellie grabbed hold to his shoulders as she exploded into pure ecstasy. He whispered words of love as her body slowly calmed down. Her eyes fluttered open...she gazed into his handsome face. She wanted to speak but was speechless. He suspected as much as he covered her mouth with more kisses. She felt his heart pounding and his hardness throbbing as a shudder of delight continued to course through her entire being. He now knew every inch of her and what pleasures and excites her more. He made his way to her feminine core that held her sweet nectar and began his teasing and coaxing to start their lovemaking all over again. She was ready for him and it was time for them to take a lover's journey to a rapturous blissful paradise.

"I love you Kellie Kincaid Larson," he whispered as he trailed moist kisses at the curve of her neck down to her full bosom straight to her feminine core. Once again her breathing became uneven with passionate cries and moans as she anticipated the inevitable. He slowly eased his taut hardness into her soft tenderness joining them together making them one. With the union of their inflamed bodies...soul...and mind, their breathing became erratic and ragged, with their blood boiling into a sweltering intense fervor. They both were absorbed in sizzling sultry passion while reaching their sexual pinnacle that sealed their bond forever that was *Destined to Be*.

***

Kellie stirred and opened her eyes. She discovered she was alone and heard noises in the bathroom. It was her husband and that thought put a smile on her face. She couldn't help recalling their night of passion and how her body had been pleasured and satisfied to no end even if she was tender to the touch. Her husband accused her of being greedy and she was. When he insisted that they take a bubble bath after midnight she had no idea the fulfillment and pleasures she would experience from getting a bath. She had been blessed with the most magnificent and passionate man who knew how to use his God given talents. Mr. Larson was something else she thought as she stretched and purred in her white silky nightshirt. Kellie never dreamed it would be so wonderful and mind blowing. Everybody was right she needed a man and Lord a man he is.

There standing in the doorway was her husband with his arms folded across his chest. He was wearing a big grin and towel around his waist. Gregory had been watching his beautiful wife stir around for several minutes. "Good morning, Mrs. Larson, you're finally awake." He walked over to their bed and kissed her on the forehead then lips.

"Good morning yourself Mr. Larson. How long have you been up?" Kellie reached up to give her husband a hug and a smack on the cheek. Her nostrils were filled with his scented bath soap and cologne.

"About thirty or forty minutes or so. I'm an early riser. I see you're not," he said smiling down at her. She gave him that look that said it all.

"You are kidding I know. I do believe you were here last night and insisted we take a bubble bath at one in the morning." His devilish grin acknowledged just that. He let her know it was getting late and they needed to get ready for church. Kellie smiled as she got up. He was so right everyone would be looking for them…

The Larsons were ready to leave in their coordinated black and white outfits. Gregory had on black linen slacks and matching short sleeve shirt with black and white spectators. Kellie wore a black and white soft print dress. Her V-neckline and short sleeves had dramatic layers of ruffles. The bodice featured a midriff band for a flattering stylish fit. Fashionable black and white jewelry, black sandals, with a matching bag accessorized her outfit.

"Kellie, there's something I need to tell you about last night." She looked at her husband, what in the world did he have to say. He glanced over at her and saw her worried look. "Calm down Baby, it's not that serious

162

unless you're not ready to start a family yet." Her sudden smile eased his mind. There was nothing to worry about at all. "Did I tell you how beautiful you look this fine morning Mrs. Larson?"

"Yes, you did, but I don't mind hearing it again." She reached over and kissed him on the check as they pulled into the church parking lot. He winked at her as he parked the car.

CHAPTER 18

On the way home the two couples talked about the events of the wedding and the homecoming celebrations. It was wonderful seeing all their old friends and family members. This year Gregory was able to visit with people he hadn't seen since he left Edna during his dark somber days. He even signed them up to participate in the annual class reunion this summer. The nicest visit of all was his visit with Devin Bryson's parents who expressed how proud they were of him. They were glad he had made something of himself and not end up like their son. Mr. and Mrs. Bryson informed him that Devin was doing time and would be out sometime before the year was out. Carl had an amazing surprise when Bro. Frank Melton and Bro. Roy Beaty attended the two o'clock homecoming service. They were responsible for him getting a scholarship at Harding Christian College and becoming the minister he is today.   It was agreed it had been a fantastic weekend.

The also discussed the living accommodations for the newlyweds, neither had given it much thought. Before they could come up with a solution Kellie's brother-in-law called to inquire about her townhouse. It seems his sister was relocating to Houston from New York and needed something ASP. The plan was for her to move into his place with the help of professional movers and whatever furniture they were not using would be taken to their country home in Edna. With her having the smaller unit and him with empty rooms everything should work out. But for tonight they would stay in her townhouse since her bedrooms were furnished...

"Well we're back where we started," announced Gracie as they entered Kellie's townhouse. The men carried the luggage and took them upstairs while the ladies put up the food that was brought back. Gracie and Carl had an early morning flight tomorrow. Besides, they were all exhausted and

164

decided to call it a night. The townhouse was secured and everyone went upstairs. Kellie and Gregory couldn't decide to unpack or leave the luggage as it was since they were only spending one night. He left her pondering over what to do and decided to run water for their shower. The sound of the water caused her body to tingle with a bit of excitement. She decided to push their suitcases in the corner wondering what her husband could possibly have in store for her...in a shower. Whatever, was far beyond her imagination? Smiling to herself, she knew what she wanted to do but had to be realistic. Anyway not tonight!

"Baby are you ready for your shower?" Kellie stepped away from her closet and couldn't believe her eyes. Her black prince was standing in the doorway smiling striped down to his natural self. Flashbacks plagued her mind. "Girl, you may as well stop looking at me that way. You'll be out of commission for at least another day or two. Remember, you had a good workout last night. Besides we have company and you are quite noisy."

She threw a pillow at his ducking head. "You said what happens in our bedroom stays in the bedroom," she pouted.

"Kellie, we are in the bedroom. Come on let's take a shower." He took her by the hand and led her in the bathroom.

"No bath this time," mocked Kellie.

"Come on Mrs. Larson be nice, besides I think you'll enjoy your shower just as much as you did your bubble bath."

"Promises, promises, promises," she said with a smirk slipping her shoes off. Kellie pulled down her white hareem crop pants and vowed not to wear white until summer...maybe. She was just about to pull her lace corsage sweater off when he took hold of her and carefully walked backwards to the shower. Pulling her top off himself he pinned her arms above her head. Just as she was about to speak, he covered her mouth with a kiss while pressing her against the shower wall with his nude body. He then began kissing her passionately on his favorite spots that excited them both to no end, not giving her a chance to think or talk. Massaging water jets were hitting them from all sides. He placed suckling kisses around her neck...up and down her throat...each earlobe... and then over to her out stretched arms. Pressing harder into her fleshy body he could feel her rapid heartbeat or was it his as a smothered gasp tore from her throat. Using one hand he released her breasts but not without capturing a hardened nipple in his mouth. Her body squirmed and shuddered as she began to slowly break down. He had no mercy as he continued his potent assault. Finally, she let out a strangled scream of surrender as her passion exploded. Kellie held on to her husband for support. She didn't have the strength to say a word.

Giving her a few minutes to calm down and catch her breath, her husband held her lovingly in his arms kissing her gently on her nose. Through short breaths she inquired about his... He didn't allow her to finish as he assured her his time will come. These two nights were for her. He removed her bottoms and together they gave each other a shower. Kellie never dreamed a shower could be so erotic. Her husband was even able to have a little pleasure, but of course he stopped her before they went too far. She was given his word that his time will come, they needed to be patient. As they got ready for bed, she looked at her husband and confessed her shower was absolutely fantastic.

***

It had been a hectic three days blending the two households. Gregory was anxious to get their lives in order because he had a special assignment and was leaving in a couple of days. Although he would return before Thanksgiving he still wanted to make sure their home was what she wanted it to be. The packing and moving had taken a toll on the newlyweds. What they had planned to do in a week or two they accomplished the job in three days. Thank God for Uncle Kel and Ann taking charge at KTS. Nisey and Auntie E helped make decisions about combining the two households and assisted in supervising the packing.

Their bedroom was the main room to undergo major changes. It had been transformed into a woodland retreat nestled beneath beddings of vibrant rich colors of chocolate and green. Shades of rose were added to soften the décor for a mellow romantic mood or for just plain relaxation. Their accent pieces of natural inspired elements such as driftwoods, rattan, river rocks, faux grasses, dried and fresh flowers nurtured the spirit of a lazy

166

afternoon on the beach or a walk in the woods. She and her aunt accomplished their mission in providing a serene hide-a-way right in the midst of the city.

Kellie checked the time, her husband would be coming home in a few minutes. He was going to have just enough time for a quick shower and get dress for KTS annual Halloween Bash. They were going as Beauty and the Beast. Their readymade costumes were simple. She was wearing a light shimmering gold sleeveless bridesmaid's dress with a V-neck bodice and full skirt, she's had for a couple of years. Her gold sandals crystal gold jewelry and tiara was everything she needed to look like a queen. Gregory agreed to wear his black tuxedo pants, but refused to wear a coat or vest. They compromised and settled for a gold sleeveless t-shirt, gold jewelry and a crown… gluing hair to make him hairy was also out of the question.

***

"Thomas J who are you getting to stand in for Big Shasta," asked Griff? He knew they needed someone who could handle their starlet and not have any foolishness while their number one man was unavailable.

"G-Man Griff, I got in touch with him and he'll be here next week." Thomas J was sick of his brothers doubting his ability to handle business just because he was the youngest, like he needed G-Man watching over him. He could handle *Ms Kay K* without any help. After all she had the hots for him and was under his spell. All G-Man was going to do was complicate matters with his no nonsense attitude. He was worse than Big Shasta.

"That sounds like a winner Thomas J. Remember, this is what you do best and we're depending on you to do it correct."

"Have I ever let you down?" Griff wanted to ignore his youngest brother's question, because he did not want to bring up the past. But Thomas J had cost them a pretty penny because of his hot nature and temper behind a skirt before. He wished he would find the right one and settle down so he can really handle business instead of trying to be with every fine sister he thinks have talent.

"You know you're the man little brother, just handle ya business and don't forget our meeting with BJ at Club Silver Fox."

***

"Kellie, where are you baby?" Gregory had gone in to the office to handle a little business and hurried home to change and get her. He left some of the staff getting ready for the trick or treaters that were expected tonight. It had been a tradition for KTS family and friends along with neighboring parents to bring their children to the business park for Halloween treats. The Kincaid clan along with the employees and suitemates wear costumes. There was also a delicious spread and plenty of drinks for the participating adults.

"I'm upstairs in the bedroom, sweetie." A big smile stretched across his face as he raced up the stairs. Gregory Larson never imagined life could be so wonderful. With all of his accomplishments, nothing came close to being married to the woman of his dreams. He couldn't ask for anything more, except children. That's something they need to discuss. How many do they want to have? There she was stretched out on the chocolate chaise in her gold lace undergarments. Kellie held her arms out for him. He straddled her body and laid his head on his favorite spot, right between her luscious bosoms, but not before kissing each peak. She caressed and massaged her husband as he rested for a few minutes. Lately this had been their favorite place in their room besides their bed and the bathroom which was an oasis of comfort and serenity.

Kellie kissed her husband's cheek and told him to take his shower and get in his costume. "The sooner we get there the sooner we can get back home and"…he silenced her with a kiss and did just what she suggested. He looked back at her with a big smile and she certainly knew what it meant. They were due for a good workout.

***

The Larson's finally arrived at the business park. The parking lot was well lit and practically full with children and their parents. The rule was simple, children must be accompanied with an adult and go through security. They

168

couldn't take any chances with the way things were these days. Chairs and large jack-o-lanterns were placed in front of their building. Halloween decorations were in the windows and on the doors. The idea was to keep everything outside to maintain order which they have been able to accomplish successfully.

"Come on my beast," said Kellie. He growled like a true beast as he reached for a rose from the back seat. Kellie looked at him in surprise. He told her he knew the story and Beauty needs a rose. Gregory didn't mind passing out treats to the children, he just preferred wearing jeans and a t-shirt. He looked so cute she thought. Kellie even darkened his eyebrows to give him that beastly look. She kissed his lips and pulled him all the way to the sidewalk where all the excitement was going on. Everyone was so happy to see them. Although he came by earlier, this was their first appearance as husband and wife. It had been hard for her not to come in, but Gregory insisted she stay with the movers so things would be just like she wanted. She was thankful he was thinking which kept her from having to come home and move things around. Everything was put in its proper place the first time.

"Congratulations you two," sang the office staff and friends. It seems the entire KTS staff and associates were there and dressed in costumes. There sidewalk area was well represented. They never had this much participation before. She knew Uncle Kel had to be pleased this year. Kellie knew some were just plain curious to see it for themselves that the boss man and boss lady were really Mr. and Mrs. She couldn't blame them, she was always considered a level headed woman that took her time and thought matters through before taking action. To get married like she did was out of character for her. But Kellie Kincaid Larson considered herself fortunate and was extremely happy. She was glad she didn't dwell on matters this time and followed her heart instead.

"Ummm...you're glowing boss lady, it looks good on you and I like it," exclaimed Ann as she took her hand to see her ring and diamond bracelet. "I should be upset with you, but I do understand." Ann looked over at HIM and whispered, "We must talk friend." .

"Wow Aunt Kellie...Aunt Kellie who are you supposed to be," asked RJ?

The twins shouted they knew as they skipped towards her with their parents behind them. She hugged her sister and brother-in-law who were dressed like someone from the sixties.

"Beauty and Uncle Gregory is the Beast. Huh Aunt Kellie?"

"That's right."

"But Uncle Gregory don't have on a beast mask like in the movie," exclaimed RJ. He ran to his new uncle to ask about his mask. Gregory scooped him up and asked if anyone needed something to drink as he headed toward the door.

"Guess who Mama and Daddy are Aunt Kellie," sang the twins.

"I don't' have a clue." She looked at her sister then her brother-in-law and smiled. Kellie couldn't imagine who in the world they were supposed to be. They were dressed in coordinating green and black outfits. Nisey had on a green pleated chiffon party dress with matching shoes and Robert wore a green blazer with black trousers. They knew they had her and everyone else who had given up guessing who they were pretending to be. Nisey pulled out a play microphone and the couple started singing,

"Ain't nothing like the real thing baby"

"Marvin Gaye and Tammy Terrell," shouted the onlookers as they gave them a round of applause. Leave it to Nisey thought Kellie, smiling at her sister. They both took seat with the other KTS women to join in with the fun. The children were full of energy as they raced from one station to the next. Gregory and RJ returned with drinks and announced they were going to hang out with the truck drivers who seem to have a nice crowd at the garage. Kellie couldn't imagine what was going on. If it was anything like last year it's probably turned into a man's cave with a big screen, card games, and their own refreshments with Uncle Kel leading the group. On the whole everyone seemed to be happy and having a good time.

"Cousin how's married life," asked Cynthia dressed as the tooth fairy? Taking a seat, "I must say you do look good. It seems marriage agrees with

170

you girlfriend."

"Thanks Cynthia and married life is just wonderful." Cynthia knew she had set her eyes on Mr. Larson, but he made it perfectly clear there was someone else. She had no idea it was Kellie, but it's obvious he loves her and could never be interested in another woman. She didn't care what Michelle's sister said.

CHAPTER 19

G-Man couldn't believe two weeks had passed and he was still on this assignment that was only supposed to last a few days. Big Shasta came back with pneumonia and had to be hospitalized. He hated to see his man down but he had not planned on being away from his wife this long. Thomas J was just going to have to find a replacement. He was not looking forward to any more radio and club appearances, especially the ones where a lot of drama was left behind.

Gregory knew that was putting it mildly. Although it had been some years, those days were totally disastrous and stressful. Hell it was a nightmare as for as he was concern and Thomas J was responsible for most of it. He left a trail of broken hearts up and down the east and west coast. It's true he couldn't put all the blame on Thomas J and of course they were both foolish and wet behind the ears back then. They had just finished their stretch in the army and were making up for lost time. Once they got out of that mess, but not without Thomas J's family shelling out some serious cash, he decided to leave Detroit and start over in Atlanta. The rest is history. But he still maintained a working relationship with Hit Factory Enterprise and BRIGGS' PI Security...

"G-Man, it's time to roll my brother. What are you doing texting that big gorgeous wife of yours?"

"Watch your mouth Thomas J," warned G-Man as he closed his laptop and picked up his iPod that had been on the charger. He was like every other business man he needed his toys. "Maybe if you settle down you wouldn't get into so much trouble."

"Don't do me, just because you decided to wear a ball of chains."

172

"Don't' knock it until you try it son, besides I don't have chains just diamond studs." He flipped his ear, "a gift from my baby. Anyway, how's Big Shasta?"

.   "He's doing much better. I talked to him this morning after we left the station and he'll be going home at the end of the week if his temp stays down. Doll said he just needs a little TLC. I tell you man, I can't believe you and Big Shasta jumping the broom like that and for the record I can buy my own diamonds."

"Trust me Thomas J, it's a wonderful thing and you will see one day. Let's roll." G-Man was looking his GQ self in his standard black, but new attire. He actually had to go shopping because of the weather. He bought a complete wool outfit, a heavy coat, and hat which would do the trick in keeping him warm. This Chicago weather wasn't nice at all. G-Man was glad this was the last appearance and they would be heading to the west coast...LA and Hollywood. They were making a cameo appearance at one of the upscale local clubs in Chi-town. It was going to be nice to see Satin Doll again, he thought as a smile spread across his face...

Thomas J had tried it. His first and only love was the most beautiful black Amazon sister God had put on this earth. He loved every inch of her fine thick body. He gave her his heart and soul. What did she do but refused it. She didn't believe in love at first sight and good steamy hot sex can make a man say and do just about anything. She only had one valid point...the sex...which was mind blowing and the best he had ever encountered. It was what his brother's called making unadulterated love and he would know when he meets the right woman. They were so right! He never would have put much stock in their theory until she sashayed in his life. Although they only had a weekend it was enough to convince him she was his soul mate. He meant what he said about her being the woman he's long for all of his life. It hurt that she didn't take him serious and pushed him aside.   Thomas J will never fall in love ever again...How could he when his heart already belong to someone...Yeah, he had the nerve to still be in love with her...

G-Man knocked on *Ms Kay K's* door to let her know they were ready to ride. He was a bit tired of this little number who found a way to rub up against him every chance she got. She and Ms Cutie Pie had gone too much at the radio station as far as he was concerned. The two of them had made a sandwich out of him in a few provocative pictures that he knew would be twittered on the social networks.

***

"Satin Doll, you look beautiful Baby." Her nickname was just perfect and fit her like a dream. She was smooth and sweet like chocolate kisses and nobody and he means nobody with her complexion could wear bright red like her. She was the show stopper. G-Man felt a little bad for *Ms Kay K* who was also wearing red for her performance tonight, because she was no match for Satin Doll even if she did have five years on her side.

"G-Man, love of my life, how's it going," she purred. "Is it true you are no longer a single man?" She gave him a seductive hug and held up his hand to see his ring.

"Yep, Satin Doll it's true," kissing her on the cheek.

"She must be one hellavue woman to get you down the aisle."

"She is and for the record I proposed to her.

"Umm... I must say she's one lucky young lady."

"Thanks Satin Doll." Now I would like to introduce you to *Ms Kay K*." He knew he had to get down to business because they could go on and on. He looked around for Thomas J, who was nowhere in sight. G-Man couldn't imagine what had gotten his attention that quick, for the record he thought he was hitting on baby girl…guess not.

"Follow me sweet thang." Satin Doll was a very nice upscale club…featuring lip-smacking delicious cuisine as she likes to say. Maybe that's where his boy was. Satin Doll opened the door to *Ms Kay K* dressing room. G-Man looked around to secure her safety and then hung her clothes bag up. He removed one of the chairs to set outside her door and told her he would let her know when it's time. "Can I send you something from the kitchen? The chef and I have a thing going on."

174

"Is that right, is this who I think it is?" She nodded a yes. Finally, she was happy and it showed. She had a special aura about herself that said it all. He knew just where she was coming from because he was walking on clouds himself. He declined for now and told her maybe after the show as he took his place.

"I do intend for you two to meet, and then you'll see why you were my favorite," she said as she sashayed off. G-Man agreed and told her to watch out for Thomas J. She raised her hand and disappeared around the corner...

Ms Kay K put on one fantastic show, thought G-Man as he escorted her to the dressing room to change. Next would be the signing of autographs. Thomas J was already selling CD's. The mixed crowd was very receptive and showed her how much they enjoyed her performance. The audience basically gave her standing ovations throughout her entire set. Thomas J may have just hit the jack pot, if he continues to remain professional and don't try adding another notch to his bedpost. If he play his cards right this could be a lucrative relationship that pays off very well for their company.

While waiting for *Ms Kay K* Gregory decided to call the love of his life. "Hi sweetheart, I miss you and love you so much. Kiss my twin peaks for me," he whispered.

"You're crazy and I will not," she whispered back.

"Ar'ight girl, what did I say,"...

"G-Man, I'm ready. G-Man, I'm ready!" He held his hand up to let her know he heard her the first time.

"Wait up for me Baby, please."

"Of course Sweetie and I miss and love you more." He growled and disconnected the call. Man did he ache for her shaking   his   head and taking deep breaths before acknowledging babygirl. Besides, he was not Thomas J...

"It was nice meeting you Glenn and Satin Doll you stay sweet." G-Man thanked them for their hospitality and takeouts. He knew exactly what Satin Doll meant, he and Glenn could pass for brothers. If he didn't know any better he would be concerned, but they came from two different parts of the country and his father knew nothing but Texas. Maybe... that's just it, he didn't know what roads his father traveled during his day. The handsome couple walked them to the front door. G-Man looked at Thomas J to see if he had everything in tack. He patted his breast pocket to let him know he was ready with brief case in hand. G-Man put his hand on his friendly persuader and escorted them both with the club security to their waiting car. He knew he couldn't take any chances closing the door behind Thomas J, this was Chi-town. They were carrying a nice sum of cash and had to be very careful. That was one of the many drawbacks doing this kind of work, you had to carry large sums of cash when you're promoting new talent.

After making it to the hotel safely, G-Man went about his job before calling it a night. He made sure *Ms Kay K* was tucked in safely and secured Thomas J's briefcase. He had a beautiful sexy woman waiting on him and he didn't plan on disappointing her. What's more, he had promised her a new experience and tonight he was doing just that.

***

Kellie was enjoying the beautiful view that she loved so much. Dusk was now dressing the city with sparkling glowing lights and soothing luxurious skies. A cold winter storm was drifting through the city as the prediction of a light freeze threatened the area. Traffic was moving slowly as Houston residents were trying to get home before the weather changes. The light freeze was expected with moderate to strong winds late tonight. The rustling leaves danced as the branches swayed and bowed to the same cadenced melody.

Kellie looked at her watch and realized once again she had stayed pass her time. She was not in a hurry to go home to an empty house. Gregory's security assignment had turned into two whole weeks instead of a few days. She missed him tremendously and was actually at a lost. She had been spoiled by him until the day he left. The calls and flowers were a help, but it wasn't the same. They have lived apart more than they have together as a married couple thanks to that *Ms Kay K* and Big Shasta. She wanted and needed his warm body besides her at night, especially now with the cold front

176

creeping into the city. She was almost tempted to ask for the twins for company this weekend. Kellie Kincaid Larson was lonesome and not in a pleasant mood, company was not what she needed. It was simple, she ached and wanted very much to be with her husband. She had to admit they had some passionate conversations and he did know how to bring about some scorching intense heat that caused some powerful explosives on the telephone. *Yes ma'am…yes ma'am.*

Well even that was not going to happen tonight she thought. She was not expecting a late telephone call. It was the weekend and he would be in and about the Los Angeles area for two appearances each night and it would be very late when he gets in. With the time variations it was just difficult for them to connect at night, especially with this being the weekend. She wasn't able to see any of the LA interviews because of the time difference. And she was not getting up early nor staying up late to see *Ms Kay K* and some lady DJ hit on her husband again. Besides she didn't have to see anymore interviews. When they were in Chicago she watched one of the syndicated radio stations. He had made his usual good morning call and told her how to go to the web site to actually see the complete show. Kellie was quite impressed, *Ms Kay K* is incredibly talented with a soulful old school sound.

It was during that interview the lady DJ flirted with her husband big time while she questioned *Ms Kay K* about her fine bodyguard. Ms Cutie Pie even had the camera man show the radio audience who she was speaking of. Regardless of the singer informing her he was a married man, Ms Cutie Pie still continued hitting on her man. She did allow him to give a special shout out to his beautiful wife before the interview was over. Nevertheless she still asked him what happened afterwards. Sistah girl had crossed the line even though Kellie didn't consider herself the jealous type. But she does plan on providing him a picture for his wallet. She was so proud of him for showing pictures of their wedding. Even Ms Cutie Pie was impressed and paid them a compliment for being a striking couple. She even said she was a gorgeous bride.

Kellie turned her light off and walked to the front office to say good night. Three of the evening workers were in deep conversation and didn't notice her.

"Girlfriend that's what my sister said. And she has proof, of course it's confidential." Michelle Anderson was good for a good gossip and the only reason she has this job was because of her sister Jessica who was Lana's secretary. But this time she's stepping on some serious toes thought Rhonda and the other two evening workers, plus she was jeopardizing her job as well as her sister's business.

"I don't believe it and if I were you I would drop this mess right now before she gets wind of it," demanded Rhonda as she turned around and looked Kellie in the face. "Hi boss lady, you're calling it a day." The other two ladies snatched around with guilt written all over their faces. It was obvious that she was the conversation.

Kellie didn't believe in acknowledging gossip even if it was about her. She knew their employees would be a little talkative because of her marrying as quickly as she did. Everyone was probably waiting for her to start showing or something. Pregnancy is always the first suspicion of a quickie. She could only wish. Her baby did want to start a family as soon possible. And OMG it's not like they were not trying in the midst of all their adult fun…Flashback…from the kitchen to the living room…to the stairs. Humph every room in their home had been christened. Life was wonderful! "Yes ladies, I'm calling it a night. Ya'll handle the job and have a good weekend." Kellie walked out to her car and waved to the security guard.

***

"That's her leaving now."

"Where's her husband? They usually leave together."

"I know, but he's on some kind of security job."

"And you think this is going to be an easy hit with him in security."

"Man, it's only one him. You, me, and Clyde…we can take this wantabe with no problem."

"Clyde…man since when. You know your brother is on the up and up ever since Cherri had old man Kincaid to give him a job. What makes you
178

think he would even consider doing this? He's been legit for eight years. Clyde and Steven Ray Stevens had jobs with KTS. Clyde was their full-time maintenance operator while Steven Ray was on a temporary assignment which has lasted for six months. His real job was casing the place for him and his buddy Red-Dog. His older brother had put in a word for him with the old man. Clyde even made him promise he wouldn't do anything crazy and mess up his good thing. His brother may enjoy keeping KTS nice and clean but he had other plans. He knew every Christmas the old man gave each employee a bonus the day of their Christmas party. Clyde has come home with a nice chunk of change and he was just the janitor. He could only imagine what the others received. This year they weren't gettin a dime, thought Steven Ray smiling. He and Red-Dog had it all planned. As soon as he was able to get him on as a temp, their plan would go into action. They just needed to be patient until it was time and if Clyde didn't want to go in with them, he'll be like the others, he won't get a bonus this year either.

***

At least the weather was good, thought G-Man as he got ready for tonight. It was a cool seventy-five degrees with clear skies. He dressed in his usual black attire and was ready. *Ms Kay K* was doing shows at two of the hottest clubs in LA. They had truly done some traveling this week. They were in Long Beach one day and two days in San Diego, once again she was well received. Thomas J's starlet was doing very well for herself. She was leaving audiences mesmerized wherever she performed. Thomas J had even sent for the band and had to order more CDS for the California shows. *Ms Kay K* was leaving her mark everywhere and her CDs were selling fast. It looks like his boy was finally maturing. He was showing signs of a true business man.

G-Man had him to hire two more bodyguards from BRIGGS' little family who came highly recommended by Big Shasta who was on the mend. That's why he had gotten ready earlier while everything was quite. Along with Thomas J they were going to meet number two man that was actually supposed to take his place. Big Shasta was very confident that Sam was the right person to carry on even when he returns. *Ms Kay K* was resting and Kendall was on guard. G-Man went down to Thomas J's suite to wait. On the way he couldn't help hoping this Sam was truly the man and could handle the group. If everything pans out alright he would be able to make it home for

Thanksgiving.

"He's not here yet," questioned G-Man as he took a seat at the bar. He made an assessment of his surroundings. If he could just get Thomas J to live modestly on these trips, he would be just fine. You live in luxury at home. A luxurious suite is not necessary on the road. That's how you make your money work for you. The phone interrupted his thoughts. It was the front desk letting them know their client was waiting in the lobby.

The duo entered the lobby looking around for their possibly new member. They walked over to the front desk, they didn't have time to waste. The desk clerk pointed in the visitor's direction. Samantria Alex Hamilton stood and walked over to the stunned duo. G-Man had a smile wide as the Brazos River while Thomas J stood in shock and disbelief. He couldn't believe she was the number two man. His Sam and how she had changed. He didn't know one could be more beautiful. He watched the sway of her ample hips in a colorful form fitting floral dress with a tulip skirt exposing thick firm thighs and shapely long legs. She stepped gracefully in fashionable three inch black sexy sandals. Her sleeveless plunging V-neckline bodice with a ruched waist revealed the top of her ample breasts which jiggled as she made her way to them. She was absolutely breathtaking. Her alluring smile still had that hungry effect on him to feast off of her sweet lips...while running his hand in her soft curly tangled mane that crowned her beautiful oval shape face.

"Sam!" Shouted G-Man as he grabbed her in a big bear hug and lifted her completely off the floor. More thighs were exposed. Thomas J's heart was beating fast and hard as he watched them greet one another. So they also had some history he thought as he stood there looking like a jealous lover. "I can't believe it! Big Shasta said his brother Anthony was sending someone who could handle the job single handed, but I had no idea he was speaking of you. Thomas J I want you to meet Samantria Alex Hamilton better known as Sam," not giving him a chance to respond one way or another. "It's been so long Sam, let me look at cha girl," putting her down. "You look fabulous!" While G-Man turned her completely around, their eyes locked, neither acknowledging the other.

"Thank you kind sir, you look pretty damn good yourself." Sam noticed his wedding band right off. Some lucky sister has tied him down real tight.

"What can I say, I do try hard," he said as they broke out into laughter. He was still standing there like a lump on a log looking very foolish. "Where are your things?" She pointed to her luggage beside the chair she had been sitting in. G-Man noticed Thomas J was still standing there with a strange look on his face and had been very quiet. He did say the decision was up to him and Big Shasta. But something tells him he's not cool with man number two who was really going to be the main person until Big Shasta can take full control again. He didn't have time for Thomas J's attitude or hang-ups. With Sam taking over he would be home by Sunday for sure. He picked up her bags and they headed to the elevator. G-Man first started with her accommodations as they rode up to the fifth floor. She could have his room and he would spend the rest of his time in Thomas J's suite. He needed to make sure his man was not going to start any trouble.

He barely gave her a hello, thought Sam as she walked in the opposite direction. So, she guesses he has the nerve to still be angry. She didn't care, she was protecting her heart. Furthermore she had closed the book on them. Sam shook her head to fight back the memories that were trying to surface. She didn't go into detail with Anthony and Big Shasta, but did admit she and Thomas J had some history. What she didn't say was the fact that he was her first and only love, but she did promise their past would not interfere with her performance. The Briggs' brothers assured her they had full confidence in her and everything would work out just fine. She was just standing in for Big Shasta for the time being. Her main job was to operate BRIGGS' PI& Security Services for the two brothers. They needed a roundabout person who could manage the entire business aspect of BRIGGS'. What she was engaged in now was what they considered an emergency and extra. Sam silently vowed to herself that she could do this and would.

Samantria Alex Hamilton was the family backbone and her mother's right hand since the death of her father. In addition to that she also had a baby that she was raising alone. She needed this extra income to stay afloat and maintain the life style they were accustomed to. Sam was not letting him spoil this for her. All she needed from him was professional courtesy and they would get along fine because it was a known fact they would be running into each other from time to time. She was not an insecure fat girl under any circumstances. She knew she was hellavue and handled her business well.

"Here we are Ms. Hamilton," said G-Man as he opened the door to his room. "It's getting kind of late and since I'm ready, I'll move my things out later, because we need to introduce you to our little family. So while I gather up the group you take care of your business and I'll be back for you in about twenty minutes."

"That sounds like a plan. Let me unpack and make a quick change and I'll be ready." Sam did just that as she unzipped her bag to pull out her comforts. She scooped her curly mane into a ponytail leaving out a curl on each side. She removed her dazzling jewelry and replaced it with simple functional pieces. Her intentions were not to be flashy, but to look good. She smoothed down her black slacks which were made out of that wonder fabric she likes to call it. It moves with you and that's just what she needed in her line of work. She never knew when she'll have to prove her worth. Sam pulled out a black and white plaid blouse with a draping neck which was perfect for retrieving her concealed hardware. She took down her black sweater with a cascade front just in case... the cool LA nights can be a bit chilly. Changing into her two-inch black pumps with stack heels for support and whatever else, she was ready. The little make up she wore was still good all she needed to do was add lipstick. Sam picked up her small designer purse when she heard a knock on the door. That G-Man, right on time.

***

The entourage was in route to their first club with G-Man going over the schedule and agenda for the remaining assignment. Thomas J was a total jerk throughout the entire meeting with the group. He spoke only when he was spoken to and answered questions when they were directed only to him. His eyes were filled with daggers whenever she looked his way. It was G-Man that took charge in introducing her and explaining her role. She must admit they had a nice group of real musicians and *Ms Kay K* was a DEVA for sure. Everyone made her feel welcome. Sam had made up in her mind that Thomas J can continue to be the jerk she knew he was and she was even a

182

bigger jerk for still loving him.

***

Kellie tossed and turned as she tried to sleep. She went to bed early because of pure boredom. She tried to exert herself by addressing and putting stamps on all of the thank-you cards that needed to be sent out for the gift certificates and money they received as wedding gifts. Afterwards she tried reading a new book of one of her favorite authors, but staying focused was out of the question. The same thing when she tired watching a little television…nothing was on as far as she was concerned. She had talked briefly to her sisters and parents. She could tell everyone was preoccupied and didn't want to hurt her feelings. Why wouldn't they be, it was Friday night. She should be used to being at home alone on Friday night…No that's not the way it's supposed to be now, she's married. If it wasn't a shame she would cry, that's how she felt…balling like a two year old. The phone started ringing, most likely another wrong number which she had been getting a lot lately. Gregory had already called before he left the hotel and she knew he was on the job this time of night. Although it was late here, LA party goers were just getting started. He was probably in route, thought Kellie as she looked at the caller ID. It was him…She could barely get out hello.

"Hi Sweetheart, you still up?"

Her face lit up like a small child at Christmas time as her eyes started tearing up. The sound of his voice warmed her heart regardless of the fact that he was hundreds of miles away. "Yes, I'm still up," she sniffed.

"Baby are you crying?" She hated he caught her at a weak moment and knew she was behaving like a baby but she couldn't help it.

"I'm trying not to but I can't help it," she whimpered.

"Baby don't," he pleaded. His soothing voice was encouraging and had a calming effect. "It's not going to be much longer. I promise." He hated to really say when until he was absolutely positive Sam could handle the job even though he was pretty sure about her ability. His biggest concern was Thomas J whose behavior had been somewhat strange. He told her how much he loved and missed her and as soon as he returns they were taking a lover's holiday. Gregory knew this was not how newlyweds were supposed to spend the beginning of their marriage away from each other. He knew circumstances put them in this position but thanks to Big Shasta he worked it out for him and it won't be long before she's in his arms again. Once he sensed she was better he asked about her evening. They spent another few minutes talking when…

"G-Man we're ready."

Kellie heard the voice of a woman who was probably the new security person that had been hired. They said their goodnights ending with the usual I love you with phone kisses, except this time he ask her to dream about him before they disconnected. Kellie had to admit she did feel better as she drifted right off to dreamland. She could actually smell his scent… feel his touch… and kisses.

***

Gregory had just finished checking with Sam to see if she had everything under control including Thomas J before he left the hotel. He had already said goodbye to the group and Thomas J who was still acting stand-offish, but he couldn't concern himself with that. It was evident he and Sam had some history and neither was talking which was fine with him. All he wanted to do was get home as soon as possible. He was flying standby and didn't know how long he had to wait at the airport and really didn't care as long as he was able to catch a flight out. He had prayed to God to make it possible and allow him to arrive safely. Everything was already booked to Houston, and to make matters worse, the weather was freezing cold but dry. They were expecting sleet sometime Sunday evening. That's why he had decided to leave now and take his chances. If he was lucky he could make it home before the weather gets worse. One thing about H-town, the city would come to a complete stand still in inclement weather, matters not he had to get home. He knew the man up above would see to it that he did just that because she needed him and he certainly needed her.

His heart was crushed when he called last night and found her crying.

184

He was so glad she was in a better mood when he called around noon LA time. Even though she spent the entire day in the house her spirits were still good. They both had a good laugh when she told him about her attempt to try her baking skills. The roast and cornbread turned out fine, but they both agreed the crumbled pound cake would be great with homemade icing and ice cream. He couldn't help smiling as he recalled more of their conversation. She called him naughty and he assured her she didn't know what naughty was.

"G-Man, go home to your beautiful wife," ordered Sam. He really had it bad she thought as she watched his expressions. His thoughts were constantly about her. Sam couldn't wait to meet her. He definitely wore the look of love well. If only she could be so lucky. "Don't worry about me and Thomas J. As long as we remain professional we'll do just fine. Besides, Big Shasta will meet us in Florida and then I go home. So I'll be okay." They gave each other a big hug and he left for the airport.

One thing for sure, thought Samantria Alex Hamilton, she was not going to be bullied by him. That's why she didn't have a problem making her decision. It was no longer all about him. Sam tried to be cordial, but he continued pretending she doesn't exist. That was fine with her and furthermore two can play that game and she was good at it. She had no problem letting men like him know where they can go. Besides he was too small of a kitten to tangle with a big cat like her. Sam pulled out her iPod tablet to study the schedule and the agenda for *Ms Kay K*. She had to give it to Thomas J she was impressed, he had done an excellent job in promoting his new star.

Ms Kay K was very nice with a humble spirit and lots of class. Sam noticed the way they looked at each other when they thought no one was paying them attention. She saw the looks and wondered just how involved they really were. Okay Sam why, it's none of your business. Get over it once and for all. He's gotten over you.

CHAPTER 20

Kellie had decided to attend the early morning service since she was already awake. Although she had a good night she still woke up earlier than usual. She had to admit she enjoyed the early service and it kept her from being late for Sunday school. Gregory tried to tell her it wasn't that bad once you got use to it and he was right. She was just about ready, all she had to do was add the finishing touch to her make-up. Her brother in-law was picking her and his sister up instead of them taking a chance driving. Sleet and icy rain was expected around noon.

She checked herself out in the floor length bedroom mirror and was satisfied. Kellie had on an oversized cowl neck long sleeve cashmere sweater, in a rich shade of green which was his favorite color. The asymmetric hem gave it a chic and stylish look. Her black and green tweed wool skirt stopped midway her calves and black leather boots. For accessories she wore a multi-strand burnished silver tone necklace and a gunmetal medallion pendant with dark resin accents and sparkling crystals. She completed the look with several matching bracelets and a pair of hoop earrings. Because of the weather she had pulled out her full length wool swing coat and matching hat trimmed in faux mink.

Kellie made her way downstairs just in time as the phone rang. Robert Sr. said he would call when he was outside. She grabbed her purse and headed toward the door. Honey did not like waiting, especially when he's going to worship. According to Nisey he's extremely time conscience when it comes to church and gets ready earlier than he has to and expects everyone else to be ready too. Regardless, he did not have to wait for her, because she was ready…

186

Gregory couldn't believe his luck. He was able to catch an early morning flight that got him to Houston just in time for the second morning service. Making it just in time for the opening prayer, he spotted her on the pew that's become their favorite, holding somebody's baby. They were going to have to work on getting a baby of their own he thought, standing by their pew. Kellie got the surprise of her life when she looked up and saw HIM. He sat down and pulled her into his arms. She had to contain herself as she leaned even closer. He didn't want to make a spectacle of himself but he needed her near him. She didn't care about making a spectacle as she turned to gaze into his handsome face and kissed him gently on the lips. They both were satisfied for now just being in each other's arms and sharing a kiss. Together they began their worship and joined in with the congregational singing…

Poor Bro. Bruce the minister was coming down with a bad cold and left right after the early morning service. Bro. Sowell the assistant minister stepped in and delivered a short meaningful sermon on the "Grace of God." He did a phenomenal job and his wife Earlisha was so proud. The young couple stood at the door to shake hands with the congregation. Everybody agreed that Little Walter showed up and showed out as they greeted one another while leaving the building. It was no lingering this Sunday as a cold windy mist filled the air. Freezing rain and sleet was threatening the area and was already reported in the downtown and northern part of the city. Kellie's twin nieces, Reisha and Reesa were upset because they were expecting her to come home with them today, everyone thought she was going to be alone. To pacify them she promised to take them to the movies when the weather cleared up, hopefully before they return to school. Gregory assisted Robert Sr. In putting his family in their vehicle and then he and Kellie walked over to his truck. He couldn't resist holding her to his heart in spite of the weather before helping her in. It had been two whole weeks and some days since he held her in his arms. He would do his best to make up for the time they've been apart…

They were barely in before they were engaged in a fury of passionate kisses and fondling. The two lovers latched on to each other as they discarded clothing making a path straight to the staircase. Both gasping for air as they climbed to the top of the stairs. Forget the master suite, the desperate and anxious lovers stopped at the first bedroom. Gregory snatched the bed clothing back as he laid her down with him on top. The room was filled with sweet words of love, passionate moans, and whimpers as they held on to each other moving to their own seductive melody. Taking great pleasure in each other's passion together they began their sensuous journey to ecstasy. He trailed wet hot kisses up and down her sensitive body while she kissed and stroked his damp skin, both working their own magic. Now rocking and twisting to a faster tempo little sparks of fire ignited causing their dance of love to become more and more intense and powerful. He touched that delicate spot which caused her to fall apart in his arms with screams of bliss escaping from the depths of her soul. As she ascended into the realm of ecstasy she was surrounded by soft sparkling dancing lights. He didn't let up as he continued his magical dance, stroking her like she was an expensive instrument belonging to the strings family. She held on tightly as her body began to build up once again for another overwhelming experience of tingling sensations. Deliberately taking turns with slow and swift movements he had her just where he wanted as he held her down nibbling and toying with her nipples. Once more she was on the brink of releasing her passion as she called his name over and over. She was losing control once again as her body trembled and shuddered with excitement. His thunderous groans and growls said she was not going alone, this time she was taking him with her. They held on to each other as they both traveled to a place of pure pleasure. Their hoarse cries filled the room as they burst into shattering pieces.

As their breathing became steady they gazed into each other's eyes silently agreeing they had been satisfied and fulfilled for now. He covered them with the bed clothing and whispered, "I love you," as he gathered her into his arms.

"I love you more." They kissed and drifted off to sleep.

***

The Larson's were finally settling into married life and working together was wonderful. Business was even better, thought Gregory as he pulled into the bank. He needed to make a deposit from his assignment and check with

Torrance about closing the deal on their newest business venture. KTS was able to purchase the property across the street at a very good price. He was just waiting on some additional information and the deal will be closed. KTS was now in the process of acquiring ownership of their own gas station and garage. After the holidays more jobs would be added plus a complete security system was going to be put in place. Finally he was going to be able to do what he really enjoyed, managing his own security system. One thing Gregory had to admit undertaking management of a company was not his true mission in life. His preference was investing and allowing the company owners or qualified persons to carry out the daily operations. So far his other business ventures had worked out amazingly well, mainly because he's done just that.

During this last assignment he'd come to the conclusion security was his true passion. He loved the business aspect as well as being in the field, regardless of the drama. He was mature and not out searching for whatever which has made working in the profession simple and less complicated. The only drawback was being away from his true love and soul mate, Kellie. Nevertheless he has come to the conclusion that he would prefer managing his own security at KTS which will provide him stability and a steady income, especially since they have ventured out in other areas of transportation. They could not afford to be too careful in this kind of business. Dishonest people were everywhere always trying to get over and it was important to maintain that trust the community had in them.

Kellie has done an excellent job in management and operation, which convinced him she should take complete control and get her an assistant. He was going to discuss this with her very soon because he wanted her to be in full command at the beginning of the year. He had already contacted the company's lawyer RJ to start the paper work immediately. He wanted everything legal before the new year. Gregory was going to assume the role of silent partner to the fullest, but he needed to let her know that they are the sole owners of KTS first. He's accomplished more than he's ever dreamed and being CEO was really not what it panned out to be. He was too confined and could care less about impressing people, he didn't need all of that. His main mission in life now was to spoil Kellie and keep her happy for the rest of his life. Although she was happy, she would be even more so when she's

CEO, since she had been raised to run the family business.

***

Thanksgiving holidays were over and Christmas was around the corner, thought Kellie as she pulled into their drive. They had spent a relaxing holiday in Edna...that is after Thanksgiving Day. That day had been the busiest holiday she had ever experienced and was glad when the day came to an end. She could only imagine how the next holiday was going to be. Kellie now had an appreciation for her family making Christmas a holiday for children only, which meant they did not exchange gifts. Trying to buy presents for her family was hard especially when they have practically everything they want. But there were several parties during the holiday season.

Kellie went into the kitchen to take dinner out of the refrigerator. They were sent home with enough food for a week, thanks to Ms. Lois Bell and Gregory's Aunt Marie. He had already said he wanted the beef stew and cornbread for dinner which was fine with her. They needed to eat light the way they ate during Thanksgiving and the festive holiday activities are approaching. Kellie smiled as she recalled their first Thanksgiving. They had to juggle their time between both families, breakfast with his father's family in Ganado and dinner with her family. Since both of her grandparents live in Edna they usually have their holidays with her parents along with Uncle Kel and Aunt Juanita. This year her parents' siblings joined them, both families were there for dinner and they had a wonderful family gathering. After their meal, they all gathered in the family room and watched the wedding video before Kellie and Gregory left to have dessert with his mother's family. Regardless of the running between families they were able to have their lover's holiday right there in their own country home.

The weather had been was great with awesome sunrises, clear skies during the day, and magnificent sunsets in the evening their entire stay. The temperature had also been favorable with cool days and chilly nights. They enjoyed sitting on their gallery, drinking tea or hot chocolate along with enjoying Ms. Lois Bell's delicious pastries. Now she was looking forward to spending their first Christmas.

190

Kellie knew the next few weeks were going to be busy with family gatherings and several holiday parties already on the calendar. The end of the year was also pouncing on them even faster...which meant taxes. Thanks to their reliable and dependable accountant and office clerks, taxes were never a nightmare. Lana, the company CPA was the best in her profession and she's kept KTS on the right path. This year had been successful in more ways than one with several surprises. Kellie may even have the biggest surprise yet.

CHAPTER 21

The last few weeks had been hectic and very demanding thought Gregory. Finally everything was coming to an end and he was even meeting his deadline that he had the nerve to give himself. Gregory had spent long hard hours supervising and assisting wherever he could with the simple renovations of the garage and service station across the street plus the security system that was being installed. He even hired extra men to help with the clean-up. Clyde's brother Steven and one of his homey's had turned out to be hard working and dependable men.

The truth of the matter, he had taken on two major projects at one time. He was very thankful for the accommodating Houston weather which made it possible for him to walk back and forth to the sites. Although it was cold and they needed to wear warm clothing, it was nothing like Chi-town. At least the wind wasn't blowing and the skies were clear with no rain insight.

He and Kellie had to drive separate cars to work for the last two weeks so he could work late which caused her to have dinner alone a few nights while he grabbed a sandwich or a box of chicken. At least their lovemaking was not suffering, he thought with a wicked grin on his face. That wife of his was something else and she was full of surprises too. Just last night she surprised him with dinner, dessert, and entertainment. She was a delicious treat and very entertaining. Speak of an angel, thought Gregory as he answered his cell.

***

"Cynthia, sounds like you have it all under control and it seems we're going to have a wonderful time, so I'll see you tonight cousin." The parties have started, thought Kellie as she prepared to leave for the day. The first

192

party was tonight. They were going to J & E annual holiday celebration that usually takes place two weeks before Christmas. Uncle James and Auntie E's party starts the festivities, Uncle Kel and Aunt Juanita's event is the following week, with KTS office party the week of Christmas. Kellie was glad they were back to back so they could get it all over with. She loved this time of year, just didn't like the adult drama that could take place during the parties.

Close to the holiday they usually work with a skeleton crew until after New Year's which includes security, limo drivers, a dispatcher and a manager. This year was going to be totally different. Additional office staff would be needed with drivers on call for the cruise line transportation service until after New Year's. To make sure everyone enjoys their holidays Kellie had proposed having a day and night manager, office clerk and an extra dispatcher on volunteer bases with holiday pay. The response had been overwhelming among the staff. Those who wanted to would get a chance to put in some holiday hours during those days.

***

Kellie had called her husband earlier to remind him of J & E holiday party. He had been getting home late ever since he's been back from his last security assignment, due to the new projects. Thank goodness the physical aspect was completed and the rest will take place after the holidays. They both were pleased and she was so proud of her husband. All she needed now was for him to hurry home so they could make their appearance and call it a night. A smile spread across her face as she heard the front door close. She turned the faucet on to run his bath before meeting him at the top of the staircase. She knew he had had a tough day and his face showed just that as he reached for her. He needed a special treat and that's exactly what she was going to give him as she led him straight to their bathroom. As they entered he pulled her into his arms. Just holding her energized his tired body. Although they really didn't have time for him to sit in the tub, he needed to soak and relax for a few minutes.

She kissed him lightly. "I have your bath ready for you. Why don't you get in the tube and unwind while I get your tea." She kissed him again before she walked out the room.

He had so much love for this woman and he was going to spend the rest of his life showing her just that. "Kellie"…She knew exactly what he wanted.

"Get in the tub Sweetheart," she ordered. She was going to give him a treat and they would just have to be late for the party. Besides, the invitation did say 7:30 until 10:30. They would get there before ten.

Gregory smiled and began to undress. He eased down in the tub, the water was perfect as it massaged his weary body. He leaned back and rested his eyes. Poor baby thought Kellie as she set the tray down and plugged up the tea kettle to keep the water warm. She then took her clothes off and joined him. She gently straddled his wet body and traced sensuous sweet kisses under his neck to his face. She seduced him with tantalizing strokes as she suckled his cute button nipples which forced deep growling moans to escape from within. The flapping massaging water added to their pleasure as she continued toying and teasing him. He called out her name as she replaced her hand with her soothing tongue. She could feel his accelerated heartbeat as she teased him more pressing her mounds in his face. He hurriedly switched places with her as he filled his hand with her petal soft fleshy skin. He took turns kissing and nibbling her breasts while robbing them both of the air they were supposed to breathe. Through grasping breaths she called his name as he started their rapturous dance. Twisting and trembling, she grabbed hold to his shoulders anticipating their destined journey to ecstasy.

***

Kellie and Gregory finally arrived at J & E's traditional holiday party which was being held at the Grandeur Inn. Even though the Grand (they like to call it) was gorgeous with its own decor, Auntie E and her cousins had done a magnificent job with the additional holiday decorations. The room was festive in bright holiday colors with soft music playing in the background. Decorative bulbs, crystal stars and swirling snowflakes were used to adorn their seasonal tress. Round tables were dressed in gold tablecloths and beautiful table settings of poinsettias, holly berries, pine cones with red and gold ribbons. Large vases with lit candles were also a part of the decor.

194

Buffet style tables were located in each corner with an assortment of cuisines and beverages. The complete layout was conveniently organized for the guest to socialize and serve themselves with ease. They even had a photographer on hand. Charlotte's son Darian was taking pictures near the decorative holiday trees.

"Baby, where do you want to sit?" They looked around for her sisters and their husbands. Nisey and Lynette's husband Darin both work for J & E. Nisey is their human resource director and Darin supervises the operations of their Wharton and Victoria branches. Kellie spotted Nisey waving them over from the far end of the room. That Nisey prides herself in picking the ideal spot...far away from the doorway...close to a buffet table...and a perfect view to see all.

"Over there Sweetie." She took her husband's hand and led him to her sisters' table. Gregory took her black wrap and laid it on the chair that was holding the other coats.

"Wow little sister, you look gorgeous. Is that the skirt I talked you into buying?" Kellie ignored her sister with a smile as she recalled that shopping trip. Nisey had a time convincing her to purchase several black pieces. She assured her she wouldn't be sorry and she wasn't. Before she left home her husband had already told her how good she looked.

"Yes, she does," agreed her husband along with the others. Kellie glanced down at herself like someone else had dressed her.

"Girl I don't know what to say about you. You're glowing all over the place. I wonder why?" said Lynette with a sneaky smile.

"Girlfriend you look absolutely stunning."

"Thank you Lana and you look fabulous yourself." As always Lana Harvey was fashionably dressed in her designer's outfit and expensive jewelry.

"Friend there's a certain glow about you," continued Lana. "And Mr. Larson we certainly can't leave you out. You two make a striking couple with your coordinated black and red." Kellie gave her a hug and thanked her again for the compliment. "I'll see you guys later," said Lana as she gave Kellie a squeeze.

Kellie was pleased with her selection and knew people were not use to her showing so much cleavage. But it's now all about pleasing her husband. She loves watching his expression when he sets eyes on her regardless to what she's wearing. He makes her feel desirable and sexy in anything she puts on. Tonight's outfit was really simple with her basic flattering style which accentuates her curvy figure. He was actually speechless when she came downstairs. She chose a soft gathered black velvet wrapped skirt, with a wide sash and gold jeweled buckle. The tulip hem stopped at the top of her knees. A bright red sweater with a sweetheart neckline and three quarter length sleeves that were ruched at the shoulders made her selection sexy and festive. Satin red flowers of different sizes sprinkled with gold sequins trimmed her sleeves and neckline. She wore shimmery sheer black stockings with short black three inch suede boots that had a decorative tie up bow that could be worn different ways. Sparkling gold jewelry and a black velvet bag were used to accessorize her outfit. With everyone staring she felt a bit uncomfortable and snuggled up to her husband. He hugged and kissed her forehead and then pulled out her chair so they can join her family.

Kellie looked around and noticed her sisters were pretty chic themselves. Nisey's red strapless party dress was complemented with dazzling crystal jewelry which changed colors as she moved in the light, red satin sling backs, and matching bag. Lynette wore a flowing long sleeve chiffon print in red gold and black, with an asymmetric hem over a black satin slip dress. Her customized jewelry, black satin pumps and matching bag completed her look. Like all the other men their husbands had on black suits with white or red shirts and coordinating ties except Mr. Larson. He opted not to wear a stiff neck shirt as he called it and wore a red silk t-shirt instead.

"Cousins, cousins, you all look fabulous, do you have room for two more." Of course they did, but Cynthia was alone. Everyone gave her a strange look. Why did she need two seats? Before they could question her he walked over. She introduced him as her *Boo*, Cedric Bernard Henson. He certainly did not appear to be like any of the other men she's dated in the past. He had a no nonsense look about him, very serious and could

196

definitely be someone who works for the IRS. He said good evening in a deep authoritative voice and pulled her chair out for her. Cynthia had a new look about her too thought Kellie. Talk about glowing, she was blushing. Kellie had to give it to her they made a very handsome couple. Like everybody else she had on a party dress that had a red bodice and black skirt and her date was alike the other men. While getting acquainted they found out her *Boo* did work for the IRS.

"I'm ready to eat," announced Robert.

"I'm with you brother-in-law," said Darin.

"I'm down too, besides Kellie didn't give me any dinner." Kellie looked at him and couldn't believe he uttered those words. Just as she was about to comment he leaned over and kissed her parting lips. "Come on Baby let's go get something to eat." Her sisters got up also to accompany their spouses.

Kellie glanced over to her cousin whose eyes were fixed on her friend. Correction, thought Kellie...they both seem to be mesmerized with each other "Cynthia…"

"Not now, maybe will get something sweet later."

"I already have something sweet," replied Cedric.

"Cedric you say the sweetest things," giggled Cynthia. Wow, thought Kellie. Hummm...it was time for her to dip deep into Cynthia's business now and soon…

"Girl that is one fine GQ looking man in his tailored suit," sang Jessica smacking her lips. "I see what Michelle means. Lord I would love to wake up to some him every morning… let me start from the beginning and say go to bed with some him and then…" Lana's glare stopped her right in the middle of her sentence. Jessica was a terrific secretary but a bit rough around the edges when it came to men.

"I told you that man is madly in love with him Kellie. My sources say he's loved her since they were kids. Besides can't you tell? Look at them girl. You would have to be blind not to be able to see that. He looks like he can eat her up."

Yeah I bet, thought Jessica to herself silently. Lana had no idea that she had actually seen his file that was marked confidential. Jessica really didn't intend to go that far and look at his information, but she had heard so much about him from her sister. She was curious and very much interested in the man himself. One afternoon while Lana was working on KTS business she had an emergency. She left in a hurry and ask her to secure her PC which she's done so many times. Up until then Jessica had always been a very trustworthy employee and still is, she just made that one mistake. Although she and her sister had discussed the man she never broke her employer's confidentiality. Michelle was the one who planted the doubt and she might have indicated there could be some qualm about why they had a rush marriage. Nevertheless, she did know all about Mr. Gregory Larson's business ventures but she would never breathe a word. Jessica does have her doubts about Mr. Larson and his nuptials to Ms. Kincaid though. She was convinced he was after…

"Jessica, where did you go," ask Lana as she snapped her out of her deep thoughts.

"Girl, what do you mean?" Jessica knew exactly what she meant, but she didn't have to know that.

"Good evening," greeted RJ McHarding. Both ladies said hello and invited her to sit with them. Michelle didn't know how she does it and admired her terribly. She was daring and vibrant in her dressing and whatever she puts on she looks incredible regardless of her dark complexion and large frame. Tonight she wore a metallic gold shirt waist dress which stopped slightly above her knees showing off her long legs. Cuffed longs sleeves turned back for a chic and stylish look and a red metallic sash belt was tied around her neat waist. Red jewelry with gold specks, matching shoes and evening bag were used to add more drama to her attire. RJ accepted the invite and took a seat as she surveyed the room. "Looks like J & E did it again, everything was just marvelous. They've even put me in the spirit."

"Yes, Mrs. Harris does beautiful work. I love the way she decorated her potted shrubbery. That gives me an idea too," commented Lana. "I haven't put up one decoration, but this has inspired me to do so." RJ and Michelle agreed.

"Well we still have time, it's just two weeks before Christmas," exclaimed Jessica. "But I'm like you this has truly motivated me too. Although the decorations are fabulous, it seems simple enough to copy." I agree with that, said the other ladies laughing. "Come on let's help ourselves at the buffet table."

"Wait a minute, is that Kellie over there," asked RJ. "Wow, what's come over her?"

The other two looked at each other and said in unison, "a fine man."

"You can say that again."

Kellie left Gregory reminiscing about old times with an old army buddy Mr. Johnson. She thought she would take advantage and socialize a bit. It was during these holiday gatherings great opportunities were provided for mixing, mingling, of course networking or just plain hanging out with old friends…not to mention a lavish buffet.

Kellie could feel the stares as she walked the room. She went over to speak to a couple of friends who were clients of J & E. And then took a seat at her aunt and uncle's table to spend a little time with them before the evening came to a close. Uncle Kel and Uncle J were busy discussing their hunting trip. Of course her aunts were like everyone else, complimenting her on her appearance and the special glow she was also wearing …and of course how married life certainly agrees with her. Kellie had to admit she agreed with them because she felt amazingly happy and loved married life. After she chatted with her aunts for a little while longer she kissed them all goodnight and made her way back to her table.

"Kellie, hello girlfriend," greeted RJ stopping her. "I must say I have never seen you sooo…"

"RJ don't you start. I thought you of all people…"

"Hold up," RJ held her hands up to stop her. "Girlfriend I mean you are representing. And I must say you've made me proud." The two shared a private moment for the big girls and together walked over to the dessert table.

Gregory had requested some of the chocolate sweets and a slice of cheesecake. Of course she got enough for her and everyone else at the table with RJ's help. This time Kellie knew she wasn't being watched alone. Ruby Jewel McHarding was nothing nice. She was an inspiration for all plus size women. She was wearing that liquid gold dress that moved right alone with her ample body exposing long healthy legs.

Gregory met his wife and RJ with a smile to assist, their hands were full. He had asked for more dessert and it looked like she brought enough for the entire table. He was glad. The food was delicious, but the dessert was even better. RJ decided to join them and took a seat...

Darin looked at his watch and announced it was time to call it a night and everybody agreed. It had been a long day and night. He was planning on leaving in the morning to go back home. They all had had a wonderful evening and got a chance to visit with old friends. Kellie really enjoyed herself even though most of her conversations were about her new husband and the usual that goes along with a new marriage. She even got use to the stares, plus this was her first holiday party as Mrs. Gregory Larson. The ladies retrieved their coats and wraps and they all walked out together. Kellie and Gregory said goodnight to her siblings and walked RJ to her car and then went to their truck. She didn't know about Gregory, but she was exhausted in a wonderful kind of way.

***

Kellie had been trying to talk Gregory into going shopping for their Christmas decorations. He was not interested and wanted to know what happened to her stuff she used last year. She had taken her decorations to Edna, since that's where her furnishings were. Those decorations where bought to go with her color scheme and furniture. He was not moving. Besides her family had already said during the Thanksgiving gathering Christmas was for the children. He didn't see a need for them to decorate. They didn't have any children and bought gift certificates for their nieces and nephews. The adults don't exchange gifts, they just enjoy a family meal, socialize, and call it a day. That was right up his alley. He had a wonderful joyous time with their families and even more so with her. That was all he

200

needed and was looking forward to it except the special gift he was giving her.

"Come on Gregory, why can't you go? You can help me pick out..." The ringing of the phone cut short her plea. He was glad and was about to escape into the kitchen, but not before she licked her tongue out at him. That was not a smart thing to do. He pounced on her pressing her against the wall and covered her mouth with his. Whoever was calling hung up. He then pulled her tightly against his chest pinning her arms behind her back. He dragged wet kisses down her neck to her cleavage. As she struggled for breath she whimpered and attempted to call his name. She knew this was not the time...she just couldn't say it as he continued his assault. His volcanic kisses were inflaming every nerve in her body. Kellie heard bells, then several hard knocks from the door which got his attention. He released her arms but still held her against his heated body. He wanted her to fill his need. They both pulled themselves together and then went to see who was at the door with him behind. Nisey and RJ were both standing at their door.

"How do I look," she asked between taking deep breaths and fluffing her hair? He told her she looked fine, but she couldn't say the same for him. If he stayed around they would know just what they were about to get into. Kellie told them just a minute to give her a chance to shoo him upstairs, she didn't need them teasing her. She opened the door and welcomed their guess.

"Good you have on clothes," announced Nisey. "We're going to the party store to buy Christmas decorations. RJ has not bought one ball and I need to purchase a few more pieces to complete my theme before my in-laws come." The entire time Nisey was talking she was studying her sister. She was up to something, It was all over her face.

RJ just smiled and said, "I told Nisey you needed to get your decorations too and that we all had been inspired by the party last night. But if you're busy we can leave."

"Oh no, I do need to buy my decorations. I was just surprised to see you two, that's all."

"Well we did call," replied Nisey. "You didn't answer the phone." She had that look that said and just what were you doing.

"Sister-in-law, RJ, what a pleasant surprise. What's up?" Gregory made his way into the living room and put his arms around Kellie's waist. The ladies spoke and told him why they were there. With the biggest grin he told them he and Kellie were just discussing where they were going to go and to purchase their decorations. Kellie didn't even try to look at him, he was full of it and was getting off too easy.

"Let me get my purse and we can go." Gregory was grinning harder because he knew he had gotten out of going shopping thanks to her sister and walked them to the door. He kissed his wife and told them to have fun. Kellie rolled her eyes at him and whispered, "I'll fix you."

"Kellie you have a beautiful home and I love your color scheme," complimented RJ as they walked to the car.

"Thanks RJ."

"You know Kellie and Auntie E was his interior decorator. Girl they had the whole house done except the two bedrooms upstairs. And now those bedrooms are gorgeous." Nisey went on to explain how they added some of Kellie's furniture to furnish the remaining of the house. RJ told her they did a magnificent job and that she was thinking of giving her place a face lift and would certainly keep them in mind...

Kellie was so excited when she returned from shopping. She couldn't wait to put up her decorations. Her plans were to spend the rest of the evening doing just that. She decided her color scheme would be blue and gold with a few pieces of red to give it that holiday look. The store had an excellent variety of some wonderful pieces. She bought a festive wreath for the door...a complete set of holiday dishes for four to put on their dining room table...a gold runner with matching place mats and napkins...and bell holders in red, green, and blue. Kellie also purchased decorative blue and green bulbs, holiday scented candles in assorted sizes and colors, red ribbon bows, natural pine cones trimmed in gold glitter, and all the supplies she needed to help get the look she wanted. She has always used a table for her gifts, so instead of a tree she bought a couple of live poinsettias and holly leaves with red berries to make table centerpieces. She wanted her decorations to be

202

simple but elegant and they were just that.

Gregory brought in all her bags, boxes and plants without any complaints. He was the perfect little helper. She had to give it to him, he was a good assistant and followed directions very well. Together they did a wonderful job and everything was just like she wanted it...simple and elegant. After their task was completed they admired their handiwork over a cup of raspberry tea and banana nut bread. Of course Mr. Larson insisted they use their new dishes and he even lit the candles on the table in his favorite spot. They both agreed they made a great team in more ways than one.

CHAPTER 22

Kellie couldn't believe the week was up and today was Saturday and open house at Uncle Kel and Aunt Juanita. The crisp cool weather and cloudless skies was an encouragement for a successful event. The guest would be able to enjoy the outside as well as the inside of her aunt and uncle's one story home that sets on two large lots. Although she would have to be in attendance the entire time she was thankful the weather was favorable and she didn't have to dress formal. Kellie smiled, she didn't know who was happier her or Gregory. When she told him he could wear his red shirt and black jeans he was a happy camper. The open house starts at twelve and is over with around four. Of course she generally stays a little longer to just sit and unwind afterwards. Her aunt and uncle's home is spacious, beautiful, and relaxing. Once you get there you hate to leave. She still had her own room that Aunt Juanita let her decorate the way she wanted when she was a teenager. They've kept the same color scheme over the years, just added a fresh coat of paint and changed the bed clothing.

Kellie looked at their bedroom clock as she finished making their bed. It was almost eleven and Gregory was not back from the bank. He had to make deposits this morning and run a couple of errands. Since he was already dress there should be no delay in them leaving as soon as he arrives. Kellie checked herself out before heading downstairs. Her hair was pulled back with a thin head band that you couldn't see because of the new growth of tumbling natural curls. She wore a pair of black slacks and a solid red round neck cardigan sweater set that had a ridge of ruffles around the collar and three quarter length sleeves which added a feminine touch. For accessories she wore one of her many customized pieces. Although she was not a fashion bug she did like to look good and loved to match her outfits with the right jewelry. Ingrid White did just that with her extraordinary unique

204

designs. A simple ball and cube necklace of gold and silver with matching hoop earrings and bracelets. She even had a pair of red low heel ankle leather boots and a red wristlet designer's purse for a festive touch.

Kellie heard the door and knew it was him. She knew they didn't have far to go and it was just a ten minute ride, but her aunt has always expected her there early to greet the guess with them. Regardless of Nisey and Robert living two houses down, she still expected her. When they talked last night she wanted to make sure she and Gregory would be there especially since he was one of the proprietors now. As Kellie recalls their conversation her aunt did sound a bit nervous after she made that statement, like it was a secret or something. She immediately added since they were now married. Her husband met her at the door and gave her a kiss. He locked the door behind them and turned on the alarm.

Kellie had her husband to park at Nisey's so the caterers and KTS guest could have access to the circling driveway. They walked down the street hand in hand and admired the beautiful houses. Kellie pointed out the few neighbors one buy one. She loved this neighborhood and always wanted to have a home here. Both of her uncles, sister and two of her cousins lived on this street. All the lots were taken when her time came. Uncle Kel does have a small piece of land on the side of his property where his home is built. She thought about purchasing it, but she always wanted a single story home the size of Uncle Kel's. That area was only large enough for a small house. She wanted more, especially since she's married and hoped to have children one day.

Kellie pointed and Gregory stopped. "Man this is some kind of house."

"Wait till you see the inside and backyard." Kellie knocked on the door and walked in calling her aunt and uncle. She was very careful not to knock down the wreath. "It's us auntie…" Her aunt answered from their bedroom and told her to show Gregory around and they would be out in a few minutes. They both looked at each other and couldn't contain the thought that flashed in their minds. Kellie stepped back to the foyer so he could see the complete front part of the house. The open floor plan allowed them to view living dining kitchen and family room which was decorated exquisitely for the occasion. Aunt Juanita's colors were red and gold. Poinsettias were placed in the foyer on an accent covered table of gold satin. Green potted trees were adorned with gold and red ornaments, ribbons, and crystal icicles. Garland, holly berries, and pine cones was used to dress the fireplace and buffet tables which were also draped in red and gold satin. From there they walked out to the furnished covered patio and marveled at the fantastic landscape. Decorative tables were also on the patio. Kellie pointed to the master suite which had its own private patio that was separated by shrubbery which was located on one side of the house. She took him back inside and showed him the other side where the remaining bedrooms and office were located.

They made their way back to the front and met the host and hostess who were also dressed casual in black slacks and red decorative sweaters. As long as Kellie could remember they had worn matching holiday sweaters. Today was no different. "Aunt Juanita everything is just lovely. You, Auntie E, and Cynthia did a fantastic job as always."

Gregory was still in awe with their home. "I just want to say you have a fine home and I love the layout and the back yard is terrific."

"Thank you both," she looked at her husband who was waiting on her to continue. "And this year Kellie your uncle helped."

"You're kidding. Not you Uncle Kel!"

"Yes I did. Come with me Gregory so I can show you my man cave."

"Darling don't be long the guest will be arriving soon." Kellie and her aunt knew better. He had a new buddy this time and didn't have to wait for Uncle J and Robert. They would definitely have to get them once the guess starts arriving.

Uncle Kel closed the door behind them and told him to take a seat. They needed to have a talk about their secret. He wanted to let him know it was time they leveled with Kellie before it gets out. He told him about Juanita's slip of the tongue and how she covered it up. It was a blessing she was able to do so, next time they may not be so lucky. He knew he was going to have to level with Nita also. She was still under the influence that he only owned a small portion of the company. She had no idea what

206

percentage.

Gregory told Mr. Kelley his plans for KTS. He had made up his mind to give Kellie the company with no strings attached. RJ had already drawn up the papers, but he wanted to make it a Christmas present. He went on to assure him the real reason why he owns a big percentage of the company would remain between them. Uncle Kel looked at him in amazement.

"You love her and this family that much Son?"

"With all my heart and soul sir. She's my life and it's nothing I won't do for her. I just need you to be there for her when I'm not available. You see sir, security is my real passion. I prefer handling the company's security and keeping the business safe if you know what I mean. Of course I'll take some special assignments on the side for a fee. As a matter of fact I have a job right here in the city next week at the Grandeur Inn. One of the executives and his siblings are giving their parents a fiftieth wedding anniversary party. They're flying in their favorite singing artist from back in the day as a surprise for a private concert and have hired me for the job of driver and security for the singer. I realize this is what I love doing sir and I need the flexibility."

"Tell me Son, how much are you worth if that's not being too personal."

"No sir, besides we're family. It depends on the job, circumstances and how dangerous the job may be. This job next weekend will pay a little over a grand. My starting fee is five hundred. I'm known on the circuit as G-Man, five hundred dollar man."

"That's alright Son, you just take care of yourself, because I know you'll take care of my niece. I'm glad we had this talk and got this out of the way. We better get back to the women folk, but before we do how much do you really like this house.

"What do you mean? I love this house."

"Well Nita and I are going to put it on the market if Kellie doesn't want it. We're planning on downsizing and build a much smaller place on the property next door. We don't need all of this space anymore. To be honest we never needed this much house."

"Are you serious Mr. Kincaid?"

"You'll get a better deal as my nephew."

"Uncle Kel I would love to buy this house for us. I know Kellie would love to have it. She was so proud when she gave me the grand tour."

"Okay it's done."

"But sir, we need to talk price."

"One hundred twenty-five thousand and not a dime more."

"Mr. Kincaid! I mean Uncle Kel this house is worth every bit of five hundred thousand at least and would probably appraise for even more."

"Son, I had this house built almost forty years ago, we already owned the land. It cost us under a hundred thousand to build this place back then plus the renovations when we did a few years ago. My nephew did an excellent job updating this old place. But what I'm asking for is plenty, especially for my favorite niece. Besides, she's our beneficiary and will inherit our worldly possessions. But since we decided to downsize and rebuild, we do need to sell so we won't drain our savings and continue living our life style. We were giving her first choice to buy it and that's her price. Now there is a catch you need to be aware of. We'll be right next door on that strip of land and our drive ways will be connected. Oh and I would like to have a covered walkway from the new house to this one if it's okay with you. That way we can look out for each other or should I say you young folks look out for us."

"Of course Uncle Kel. Anything you say and want. And let's let this be a surprise for Kellie too." Gregory couldn't believe his good fortune. He knew this too would make his wife very happy. He couldn't think of anyone else he would love to live next door to. "I'll have you a cashier's check next week before the holidays." Uncle Kel told him that would be just fine and he'll have RJ get the necessary papers needed to have the deed changed over to them.

"Now, if we're through we better join the ladies. It's a little early to be in the man cave now, but you watch for my signal so we can slip out real quiet and subtle like." Gregory gave him a big smile and told him it sounds like a real plan.

Gregory found Kellie at the front door welcoming their guest. He stood beside her and held her close. For the first time in years he was looking forward to Christmas. He was like an anxious child and thrilled to no end. He was ready to burst apart from the seams, but he had to maintain control if he wanted his news to be a surprise for her. Even though it was hard he forced himself to focus on the guest and together they greeted KTS clients and staff as Kellie and Gregory Larson. He was introduced to a great number of clients for the first time. That's why she needs to be CEO. This is her baby and she needs to continue nurturing it. After a couple of hours the crowd started slowing down. Uncle Kel and Aunt Juanita relieved them and they made their way to the buffet table and then the patio which was going to be their favorite spot. Nisey and Robert along with Cynthia were already enjoying the scrumptious food and wonderful scenery.

"Brother-in-law, where were you when we came in?"

"In the man cave," announced the Kincaid women.

"How do you like it?"

"It's all that and then some man."

"Tell me about it." Both sisters gave their husbands that look.

"What? What?" Of course they were ignored because they knew what.

"Sweetie, tell them about your security job for Thursday. Cynthia already knows." Robert snickered.

"Yes sweetie...honey," exclaimed Kellie looking at her brother-in-law. Gregory told them about the Collins children giving their parents a fiftieth anniversary celebration and they're surprising them with one of their favorite singing artist from the sixties. But he made it clear it was a surprise and he meant a surprise. "Isn't that the sweetest gift ever and such a wonderful surprise? I wish I could go just to see the look on their parents' faces."

"Baby..."

"I know it's a private party, just family and very close friends. It's okay Sweetie, I'll wait and let you tell me about it."

"Thanks Baby for being understanding." Gregory leaned over and kissed her.

"Enough of that," scold Cynthia, "besides Cedric is Mrs. Collins nephew I'll see what I can do.

"Yeah right, anyway where is the IRS man?" ask Nisey.

"He had a family emergency. And don't call him that."

"Girl please," said both sisters.

"Is this a private affair?" Cynthia snatched around with the biggest smile spreading across her lips while everyone else held in their laughter because that was just too close. Yep, she's been touched...bitten...and whatever else the love bugs does, thought Kellie. And knowing her she'll be next with wedding bells.

Uncle Kel came to the patio door and asked Gregory and Robert if he could see them for a minute. Of course Kellie and Nisey knew exactly what was getting ready to happen. They didn't kick up a fuss. Their husbands had been very sociable and deserved a treat. The sisters excused themselves too so they could give their cousin some privacy...

The caterers and cleaning crew began doing their job while Kellie and Nisey walked the last guest out. As usual they met the rest of the family on the patio. It was a little cool so Uncle Kel had Robert to turn on the outdoor fireplace. Aunt Juanita had the caterer to fix a nice tray of sandwiches, chips, little cakes, and condiments for a light snack. Hot water was also provided for hot beverages. That was all they needed while they relaxed and enjoyed their snack.

Robert and Nisey decided to leave first, their babysitter was expecting them by six. Gregory and Kellie choose to leave also so they could walk together and see the children before they go home. Aunt Juanita had carryouts already for them to take and have for tomorrow's dinner. Of course

210

the sisters were happy about that although cooking was not an issue for them. Kellie always said she didn't like cooking, but she enjoys preparing meals now for her husband. Besides he was very easy to please and often they prepared the meals together. The couples said their goodbyes and started their stroll down the street. It was just about dark and the street was lit up with holiday lights. A light wind was blowing and the temperature was dropping. According to Uncle Kel his knee indicated the weather was going to change. He was convinced a cold front or rain was coming. Nobody argued with him because the majority of the time he was right. He always said *Old Man Arthur* was very reliable.

Kellie and Gregory stayed and visited with her nieces and nephew long enough for them to show them their tree and their individual ornaments. They each had their picture in a snowflake hanging on the tree. The twins wanted them to see their room. Her sister had purchased new bed covers with little Christmas bears and red ribbons tied around their neck, sitting under a tree holding decorative packages. Of course Robert Jr. was not to be out done. His new holiday covers were blue with snowmen that had red ribbons tied around their necks holding candy canes. Only Nisey would go that far, thought Kellie. After *oooohing* and *aaaahing* they called it a night.

***

"Man what took you so long? You said six o'clock."

"Red-Dog will you please be cool."

"Where's Clyde?"

"He's not down with the job and he's served his purpose I've milked him for all the information we need."

"I told you in the beginning that's all he was good for and we couldn't count on him. Tell me this, did you let on any kind of way what's up?"

Steven Ray looked at him like he was crazy. "Man give me a break, you know I didn't say anything to that whimp. He's gone totally sappy since he and Cherri hooked up. Man that fool even goes to church now. Besides we don't need him, like I said he's served his purpose. I got somebody else in mind and he'll be here in a few. Let me hip you to this. It's gonna be easier than we thought. The word is security boy will be on a job that very day."

"Talk about luck," exclaimed Red-Dog. "Hey, is that cha boy?" A short mean looking dude stood at the bar looking their way. He and Red-Dog pretended not to know each other. He had already got in touch with Rapture as soon as he and Stephen Ray pulled the plan together.

"Yeah, that's him hold up." Steven Ray walked over to the man that was known as Rapture. He introduced them and together they laid out the plan.

Rapture was impressed with the young brother. He appeared to have a well thought out scheme his only concern was security cameras and heat, but his boy was taking care of all that. With the building right off the freeway getting a way would be a snap. He was down but he didn't know about this Stephen Ray. Hell, he was small fry as far as he was concerned. He didn't have any real experience in doing a job like this. He needed some bona fide thugs and it would be easy to double cross this wannabe with all the brains he thinks he have. They were to meet again Thursday night to handle the last details. In the meantime Rapture would get with Red-Dog and his buddy.

CHAPTER 23

Gregory looked at his watch and then turned his chair away from his desk and closed his tired eyes. He needed a break from setting up his security monitors on the computers and other technical toys. Monitoring the business park was his main priority right now especially with the skeleton crew for the holidays. KTS had been lucky over the years, but times are hard and they are located close to the freeways that would provide a fast getaway for a well-planned hit. For some reason he had an uneasy feeling and needed the security for his benefit. He glanced out at his magnificent view. Downtown Houston's tall buildings were visible through the early morning fog. He could even see a glimpse of the rollercoaster peeking over the freeway at the winter carnival that was set up in the stadium parking lot. KTS staff was full of merriment and holiday spirit. Holiday music was playing on their intercom system and the conference/dining room was set up with a buffet spread. There was no need to leave unless you were a driver. To furnish lunch for the entire week was KTS gift to their employees along with a small bonus. Everyone was in the spirit. He had never seen so many different kinds of Christmas sweaters, t-shirts, and sweatshirts in one place in his life. Smiling he recalls the conversation he and Kellie had. He made it clear he was not the one, a plain red sweater or polo was as far as he was going. Her pouting lips triggered other business before they left for work. Speaking of business he needed to return Sarge's call that he was unable to answer.

***

Today was like all their other Mondays, full of activity and demands for the week. Kellie would be busy from the time she arrived until she leaves. She had to admit she loved every bit of the hype and excitement when dealing with KTS operations. New contracts thrilled her to no end. She was now going over the calendar and various schedules with Ann. They needed to pencil in some last minute engagements, before stopping for lunch. Cynthia had contacted them about additional vehicles for their cruise line service. It seems the Grandeur Inn and its branches were the hotels for travelers cruising in and out of Galveston, of course being located five minutes from Hobby Airport and all the major expressways was certainly a great advantage. Their business was flourishing which caused them to do well also. She and Gregory were also looking into filling the two new positions that would be available after the beginning of the year with Michelle and Scott. Rhonda and Irving had done a good job in training those two and steering them in the right direction. Kellie had talked to Ann and they both felt the two were now ready to take on more responsibilities. She told Ann to speak to Rhonda as soon as she could. She knew she was very conscientious and a loyal employee. The company valued her opinion very much. Kellie loved it when they could promote their employees and hire new people. With the economy so tight they were blessed that their business was thriving.

Kellie Kincaid Larson was not pretentious nor was she full of herself. But she couldn't help acknowledging the fact that it was her brilliant idea which has enabled all connecting parties to profit. The best factor of these business dealings was the fact all associates involved were black own companies.

"There's our song, said Ann as they both began to sing. *What do the lonely do at Christmas time…"* Both ladies burst into laughter.

"Girlfriend no more sad songs for us," said Kellie.

"You can say that again," agreed Ann looking at her engagement ring. It was a beautiful solitaire with baguettes on both sides. She and her fiancé were planning a very small ceremony on New Year's Eve at their new home.

Kellie thought how good it was seeing her so happy as she smiled at her friend. Of course she and Cynthia were the wedding planners and responsible for all the preparations for the ceremony. That was their personal gift to her and a way to get back in her good graces because she was not notified about Kellie's wedding. Although she understood, her

214

feelings were still hurt and she held both of them responsible. On her day they were having a nice simple ceremony. She and Cynthia had everything planned and ordered to the last detail which was a snap since Ann left the preparations to them. All she wanted to do was just show up and say I do. Another favorite and the duo began singing, "*Merry Christmas how you've been...*

***

Gregory just finished talking to Sarge to finalize the agenda for his assignment. Wednesday evening he was to pick up Mr. and Mrs. Collins from their oldest son's home and take them to the Grandeur Inn. Mr. Butler's flight will arrive Thursday morning at eleven at Hobby Airport which meant he had to be there earlier to clear security. Once he picks him up he was not to leave his side until he was back on the plane for home Friday morning. That meant during rehearsal with the hotel band, and whatever else he wanted to do. His assignment was Mr. Butler and Sarge would handle the security for the event. Gregory was relieved when the Collins requested him to use one of their luxury sedans which he preferred driving instead of the limousine. They thought it would be easier for their parents to get in and out of. He had just the perfect car in mind, one of their full size classic Mercedes. Not only was he going to use it for transporting the Collins, he thought Mr. Butler would also appreciate an intimate luxury sedan as well since they were only traveling a short distance.

Kellie texted her husband to see if he was ready for lunch. Today's lunch was catered from Mrs. Claudia Williams' piazza parlor. They ordered pizza, pasta dishes, and sandwiches. For dessert Claudia made several pans of her peach cobbler which was to die for. Of course she made Kellie and Gregory their personal little pan. KTS employees were responsible for the drinks this week except for the holiday party on Friday. Just as Kellie was getting up her door opened, it was the love of her life. His wicked smile said more than him ready to eat, she walked right into his out stretched arms.

"Did I tell you how beautiful you look today," he whispered nibbling her ear lobe. "I do believe red is your color," now pressing his lips to her cheek. She had on a simple red cardigan with cascading ruffles around the hem and plunging V-neckline over one of her many black skirts. To cover her exposed bosom she wore a black lace tank and simple gold jewelry. After sharing a tender kiss they left to join some of the staff for lunch.

"Girl I'm telling you they had sandwiched him like he was a piece of meat," said Michelle.

"Was he grinning, ask Rhonda?

"No, as a matter of fact he looked a little upset."

"Well then, that says it all," replied Rhonda. She looked at Michelle and shook her head who has become obsessed with Kellie and Gregory. She was going to get caught sooner or later and she didn't want to be around when she does. "It seems you're trying to make something out of nothing. You need to stop with all these insinuations about things you don't really know about. Just keep it up."

"What I've said I can back it up. I can show you on the computer, I saved it. Like I said they were pressed so close to him it was absolutely indecent and if he was my man..." Kellie and Gregory stood in the door way which caused her to stop right in the middle of her statement. And Kellie finished it.

"Snatch their entire weaves out!" Rhonda strangled on her Sunkist while Michelle stood with a gaping mouth. Kellie rushed over to her, "Rhonda are you okay?" She shook her head yes, but still couldn't speak. She tried to tell that Michelle.

Tickled that she would go there Gregory told Michelle don't start no mess. He's already had to explain that situation and smooth over the whole incident. He was thankful he had good sense to show her the pictures himself. This could have gotten a bit ugly. But she was secure in their marriage and knew she was the only woman in his life. He lets her know constantly how much he loves and needs her. She is his existence.

Kellie and Gregory fixed their plates and took seats in front of Rhonda and Michelle. Kellie asked Rhonda if she's seen the pictures and said the exact same thing Michelle had said about the two women making a sandwich

216

out of her husband. Gregory threatened to leave the room if they didn't change the subject. By that time Ann came in and wanted to know what they were talking about.

"Two women making a sandwich out of my husband and tweeted it all over the circuit."

"That's it," barked Gregory. "I'm going to hang out with the drivers."

"Bye Sweetie," said Kellie and blew him a kiss. Everybody had a concerned look on their faces which caused Kellie to burst into laughter. "Don't look so worried ladies I got this let's enjoy our lunch." Michelle's hidden smirk said something different. Nobody noticed her smug expression but Rhonda. She loved Michelle like a sister and she's tried hard to make her put an end to this madness. All she needed was the right person to get a whole to these rumors and this mess would spread like a wild fire over the entire company. Rhonda knew Michelle had a sour disposition when it came to Kellie for not giving her a promotion this year, but she's going too far now. She was jeopardizing the job she did have with this foolishness. It was just a matter of time before it all blows up in her face and she'll have to suffer the consequences.

***

Gregory and Mr. Butler's manager met him at the airport without any complications. They went straight to the hotel and slipped him into his room so he could relax and have a meal, before meeting the hotel's band. Talking with Sarge, this was going to be a lavish event which had been planned for almost two years. Mrs. Collins is such a sentimental person and has celebrated their first date in May ever since they've been together. The family was brought up celebrating two anniversaries a year. For their first date they have an old fashion barbecue and do something very special for the wedding anniversary. Since this is their fiftieth the Collins' siblings and godsons were going way out. The father of the in-laws just happens to be from Mr. Butler's hometown and grew up together in the same housing complex. They were very good friends and still kept in touch, that's how they were able to get a reasonable contract. Mr. Butler was also very helpful informing them how they could cut the cost to a minimum. Accommodations, security, and band were on them since Nathaniel, Alton, and Tyler each owned a fourth of the hotel franchise. The fourth man just happens to be a sister who approached them with a business proposition they couldn't refuse. The four of them saw the perfect opportunity and possibilities with a dying business and the rest is history. After ten years they have had a successful partnership and have added two more inns to their enterprise.

"Son we're ready to go down stairs," announced the manager.

***

"Here he comes now with Red-Dog."

"Man, where did ya'll get that chump from?"

"Just be cool, that chump did hook us up to a job that's gonna be a snap." *The four men greeted each other and took a table in the corner of the club. According to Stephen Ray everything would take place when the caterers arrive. Since he and Red-Dog were given the job to assist the people it's gonna be a piece a cake for Rapture to join them. Cat-eyes will be right out front like he's part of the caterers' crew ready to fly as soon as his boys come out. Steven Ray told Rapture to wear a red polo so he could slip in without any suspicion.*

***

"Nathan I'm ready," announced Jazper as she walked into the living area of their suite. Silky Silk soon to be forty was still fine as wine thought his wife of twelve years. Mingled gray that's now around his temples gave him a cool flavor of sophistication. They have had a wonderful marriage with two beautiful sets of twins. The first set was now twelve and the second set is four. They both agreed two boys and two girls were more than enough and threw in the towel. Nathan looked at his gorgeous wife with the biggest smile ever. She was his whole life and was glad she fell into his world. He'll never forget that day and enjoys telling the story every chance he gets. Jazper walked over to her husband and kissed his cheek. She knew where his mind had wandered and she must say she too was glad she fell into his world.

218

Mr. and Mrs. Collins had insisted on spending the day with their grands at the hotel for an early celebration since children were not attending the special event. That was the plan for them to think the children would not be in attendance. The truth of the matter, their young grandchildren would be present, but would leave before the big surprise. Nathan and Jazper were the only ones with small children and decided the safest thing to do was stay in the hotel so they could be close to them and keep the surprise just that a Surprise!

She and Nathan even got a room for Aunt Polly and Uncle Jackson so they could assist with their great nieces and nephews. The four year olds could be a problem because they are very active. But she knew Aunt Polly and her father could handle them well, Uncle Jackson on the other hand was a push over. That's where the children were now, with Aunt Polly. Jazper had gone to her aunt's room earlier to get them ready. After the program and dinner the children will be escorted out. The hotel was providing a babysitter for the twins once they leave the ballroom. Besides, they should be sleepy by then. Their day had been full so she shouldn't have any problems. The older children were going to the game room. Once the ballroom becomes children free, the concert will begin.

"Come on Mr. Collins, let's get the children and Aunt Polly and Uncle Jackson." They were to meet the rest of the family down in the lobby around six.

"Not before I do this Mrs. Collins." He kissed her like he's done so many times with such warmth and desire. She could never grow tired of this man and every day she thanks God for him. He held her tighter moving seductively to their own music which always played in their hearts when they were this close. Silky Silk planted wet kisses on her honeydews and then lips.

"Mmmmmm...you smell good. Is this a new fragrance?" A classic mingling of fragrant flowers and rich woods filled his nostrils as he inhaled her scent.

"Yes."

"What is it called?"

"Possession."

"Mmmm. That sounds sexy. Where else did you put it?"

She whispered in his ear, "not now later." She knew his every move. He agreed and allowed her to reach in her purse for a tissue to wipe the lipstick off his face. Adding more color to her lips they left. Jazper knocked on the door and Junior peeped through the security hole and let them in.

"Mommy you look beautiful shouted the four year olds."

"You really do look nice," said her first and second born.

"Daddy you look handsome too." He scooped his girls up in his arms with the youngest giggling. Both were spoiled rotten like all the Collins' women.

All the Collins clan was in the lobby, waiting on the youngest member and his family. Although Natasha and Nathaniel were coming from home they knew Nathan would still be the last one, regardless of him staying in the hotel. They did have a few minutes before it was time to start the celebration. Since he was the youngest he would be the last sibling with his family to come in anyway. Mr. and Mrs. Collins will walk in on a love song and be met by their oldest granddaughter and grandson. They will then take them to their table which is located in the middle... right in from of the stage. They would have a perfect view and not be too close to the speakers. Each sibling would have their own table with their children and in-laws. Aunts and uncles were seated to the front on the other side with older nieces and nephews close behind. Their closest friends were seated around the family which gave it a real personal and intimate setting.

"Daddy, my tie is crooked."

"There they are I can hear, Nelson," announced Nathaniel. Natasha looked at her brother and told him to give it a rest. "Nathan does have the youngest children and you know the twins are a handful." She recalled the last time she took care of them for a whole weekend and it was nothing nice and she had help. Nathan and his family turned the corner with the twins skipping.

"Junior, you and Nat catch your brother and sister's hand," ordered Nathan.

"I don't want Junior to hold my hand," whined Nelson. "I want mommy to hold it." He reached for his mother's hand that his father was holding. They looked at each other and smiled. Nathan mouth *he was gonna put a whippin on this boy* as he let him have his way. As if the twins had planned to be difficult Nicole grabbed her daddy's hand. Jazper looked at him and mouth *now what*. Nathan shook his head and joined his siblings. Aunt Polly and Uncle Jackson went in to be seated at the table.

The Collins' clan was well dressed in their black and gold. Natasha was responsible for coordinating their attire and for once she did an excellent job. The girls wore short gold taffeta dresses with balloon hems. The dress chosen for the women was perfect for all their body types, a beautiful gold chiffon strapless gown featuring a square neckline. Exquisite gold lace appliqués rained down from the neck to the natural waist with a cascading full layered tea length skirt. Chiffon shawls were used to drape around their shoulders. Golden sandals and bag with diamond gold gems off set their glamorous appearance. The men and boys wore black tux and shoes, gold ties with matching cummerbunds.

Nathaniel called Alton and Tyler to let them know they were ready to start the celebration. Soft music played while the Collins' siblings entered the ballroom according to age with their families while Tyler and Alton took turns introducing them. Of course Nathan's four year old twins stole the show. They still would not allow their parents to hold hands. Nathan whispered to his wife they were going to have to put a stop to this foolishness soon. Mr. and Mrs. Collins entered the room to the melody of an old love song... *Only You*...and the guest gave them a standing ovation. They made a handsome couple. Mr. Collins was dressed like his sons. Mrs. Collins was the show stopper with her long flowing lovely gold gown of chiffon and lace jacket which was adorned with sequins pearls and crystals. She wore a large high dome gold hat with a four inch brim and pleated crinoline bow. Gold and pearl jewelry, gold pumps, and a small gold handbag accessorized her stunning outfit. Nathaniel Jr. and Naomi met their grandparents with two dozen roses and escorted them to their chairs and the program began…

The roast and toast was the highlight of the evening as the program came to a close. The sumptuous meal was also a major hit. The guest enjoyed a choice of grilled beef or chicken in their own special sauces with the trimmings. The children were given a simple meal that was a hit. The dessert consisted of a delicious four tier wedding cake and butter cream icing with a tint of gold. Red roses with gold ribbon were placed along the sides of each tier and golden wedding bells in a bed of red roses were used for a cake topper.

It was a joyous celebration and the guest truly enjoyed themselves as they waited for the special surprise which had been announced at the beginning of the program. While the children were being escorted out, the band began to gather on the stage. Of course granddaddy had to come for the twins, they were not ready to leave. Mr. and Mrs. Collins and their guest took this time to socialize. Tyler soon came to the stage and asked the anniversary couple to have a seat so they could begin the show. He knew if he got them to sit down the others would follow.

Sarge called G-Man to let him know it was time. Mr. Butler was to be escorted into the ball room through the side door singing his first song which was one of their many favorites.

The Collins' brothers took the stage to reveal the surprise with everyone anxiously waiting. After a few jokes to aggravate their Mom which they were both known for, they decided at the last minute it was easier for their parents to hear the surprise instead of them trying to introduce him.

"Mommy and Daddy your surprise," said the brothers as Jerry Butler's smooth baritone voice filled the room with one of his all-time top hits, "*For Your Precious Love.*" Screams, applauds, and sighs filled the room. Expressions of disbelief and shock covered faces all around. Mr. and Mrs. Collins stood in total amazement to applaud their surprise. As the crowd quieted down, Sarge in front with G-Man behind he made his way to the couple's table and then to the stage. G-Man and Sarge stationed themselves on opposite sides, being mindful not to block the view and observed the crowd before they relaxed to enjoy the concert as well. This was the anniversary of all times and no one would ever forget this grandeur affair…

The Collins' brothers were exhausted as they said goodnight to their last guest. Naomi took her grandparents upstairs, while Nathaniel Jr. checked in on the children. Their parents had decided to get adjoining rooms, one for the boys and one for the girls. Naomi also checked on Aunt Polly and the twins before going to the girls' room. The Collins' clan met Tyler and Ashley in one of the private lounges to relax and assess the evening. Alton had to go home because his wife was expected to go into labor at any time. They all agreed the anniversary celebration exceeded their expectations. Mr. Butler was fantastic. He even took time to give autographs which made the guest very happy. After talking and teasing one another about having to eat beans and cornbread for the next two years, they decided to call it an evening.

Tyler and Ashley settled on spending the night and would drive home in the morning. They were the only ones who had not made Houston their permanent residence. Although his grandmother who was eighty-five years old said she could handle their children they did not want to press their luck. Tyler Jr. who was now fifteen was given strict instructions to stay home and help his great-grandmother with his brother and sisters. *Yep Wolf and Ashley had four children of their own, two boys and two girls.*

When Nathan and Jazper decided to go into partnership with Carolyn and Thomas to establish a senior citizen housing facility, they relocated to Houston and joined the rest of his siblings. The house they had in Bryan was now their country home which they visit as often as they can. Every year they look forward to PVU homecoming to take part in the tailgating parties. It has become a family affair and a reunion with old friends. Life had been good for them and they could only be so lucky to have fifty plus years like his parents.

CHAPTER 24

"Baby as soon as I take Mr. Butler and his people to the airport, I'll be home. I love you babe see you soon." Mr. Butler's flight was leaving in about thirty-five minutes. He would not make it home before she leaves but he'll see her at the job site. Today was the office Christmas party and their last day until after the holidays. Of course they would be in and out to monitor the operation after they come back from Edna, plus his security surveillance system was now in place on two personal lap tops and his desk top at home. He was looking forward to a couple of days to just kick back with Kellie. Chill to some of their favorite artist, sip their favorite tea, eat their favorite snacks and nibble on each other in between. His lips turned into a big smile as he agreed that was a sure plan.

***

"Mr. Larson I'm so glad you answered your cell. This is Clyde."

"Hey, man what's going on." Gregory could tell he was agitated and a bit nervous.

"Mr. Larson, first I want you to know I didn't have anything to do with this at all. Well I probably gave too much information about the Christmas bonuses we get from KTS."

"Okay Clyde, what's the point?" He needed him to hurry with whatever he has to say… say it!

"I think my brother and some of his friends are going to try and rob the place during the luncheon. He and that Red-Dog have been acting strange. I caught them twice huddled up talking. I couldn't hear the whole conversation, but they said something about when the caterers come. I thought he had changed, but he was just using me to hit KTS. This is gonna kill my grandmother Mr. Larson. I know me and her are the only reason you gave that fool a job."

"Okay Clyde calm down. I'm turning my system on right as we speak. Now don't you try to be a hero. Let me, security, and the police take care of this. Just act natural and don't breathe a word of this to anyone. I'll alert security myself and Clyde thanks. I know this was hard for you."

"Mr. Larson, you and Mr. Kincaid have been real good to me, it's just my grandmother. He's always been her favorite. I just hate to see anything happen to that fool, it'll just kill her I know it."

"Don't worry man, I'll do my best to keep him safe."

"Thanks Mr. Larson." Gregory made a few calls to start his plan into motion. First he called Torrance Burgess and instructed him to give Mr. Kincaid decoy cards and he would pick up the real gift cards himself. Second he alerted his friend on the police department about his suspicions and his plan. When he mentioned the name Red Dog to his friend he told him he would place a couple of under covers on the premises right away. Third he called the caterers and told them to hold up and not leave until he got there. They needed to make a couple of changes before they left for KTS. Last he placed a call to his security guards and alerted them with the situation. Everyone was cautioned to remain calm and act normal. He knew nothing would happen until after Mr. Kincaid arrives and he would be there by then to take full control.

***

Kellie was in her office. Although they were still taking care of business, the day was going to be more merrymaking. Today was their office holiday party and the staff had been looking forward to the occasion and their end of the year bonus. According to their CPA they had a very prosperous year and their employees were getting a well-deserved incentive. KTS was blessed to have a loyal and hard group of workers and were worthy of their gift. Ann had called to inform her the breakfast had arrived and the staff was taking turns in the dining area. Kellie asked her to send a plate by one of the clerks.

She wanted to complete her report before noon. The luncheon would start around then and she was looking forward to the delicious meal that was being catered. She knew work would be over as far as she was concerned. The business would be left in the hands of their skeleton crew until after the holidays As a matter of fact the holiday team had already started.

"Hey Rhonda, you're just the person I wanted to see. Are you on your way to the dining room," asked Ann?

"Yes," answered Rhonda.

"Good, let's walk together. I have something I need to talk to you about. Where's Michelle, I know you two usually eat together?"

"She came in with the early crowd while I held down the office," replied Rhonda. What she didn't say was the she had made up her mind to put some space between them. She did not want to hear another word about Kellie and her husband...she was tired of Michelle's mouth and enough was enough.

"That's even better, Rhonda. I want to speak to you about Michelle." They got their breakfast and sat over in a corner. Most of the staff had come and gone so they would be able to have a private conversation without much interruption. *Lord she must have gotten a whiff of the rumors Michelle has started, thought Rhonda. All she could say was she had warned her more than one time.* "Kellie is in the process of developing a purchasing department since KTS has grown. She needs someone to be totally responsible for handling all the supplies and materials needed for the operation. Because of Michelle's educational background and since she worked very closely with Mrs. Williams before she retired, Kellie thought she would be the perfect candidate to be in charge of that department with a clerk and a stocker."

Rhonda couldn't believe what she was hearing and was thrilled it wasn't what she expected. She let Ann know she agrees with their choice and thought it was a great idea. Now she had to get to that big mouth friend of hers and warn her before she ruins her chances and finds herself out the front door instead of getting a promotion. Rhonda knew Michelle was well

226

qualified and a very dependable employee. She was just caught up. After Rhonda finished her breakfast she was just about to excuse herself and make a beeline to Michelle when Ann asked her to wait a second. She wanted to inquire about some office gossip she had heard and wanted to know where it was coming from.

"Rhonda, you know I don't believe in carrying mess but I overheard some workers discussing…" before she could finish her statement her cell beeped, it was her oldest. She told Rhonda they would talk later and took her call.

Thank goodness, thought Rhonda as she rushed out of the dining room. She went straight to her work station but not without first peeping into the front office where Michelle worked and for once she was alone and doing what she was being paid for, work!

Michelle was in shock with the news Rhonda texted her. She couldn't even express her happiness for feeling absolutely terrible and ashamed. As always she had put her big foot in her even bigger mouth. Rhonda had tried so many times to talk to her, but she wouldn't listen and continued with her hearsays. Her sister had never revealed the proof she claimed to have had. Michelle knew she had no explanation for her actions except jealousy. She dare not try to hide behind not being given a promotion. It was nothing but pure old green-eyed jealousy. All the women at KTS were infatuated with Mr. Larson and his sophistication and charisma, but no one went as far as she did. It has always been clear from the very beginning he was not interested in anyone but the woman he married. Now she was being considered for a big promotion, but her wagging tongue has probably ruined it for her. Michelle prayed a silent prayer… Lord please deliver me from this mess that I started and I promise to hold my tongue from this day forward…

Ann knocked on Kellie's door before entering. She decided to bring Kellie's breakfast herself and let her know that she had spoken with Rhonda concerning her decision. What's more, something else was on her heart that she wanted to speak to her about. Kellie was pleased everyone was in agreement with her choice and as far as she was concerned she would make this an early Christmas present for the both of them. She told Ann after she completes her last report she would like to speak to Michelle and then Scott.

"Hold on a minute Ann, let me read this... *through with assignment...at bank...see you soon luv u...* Kellie couldn't hold back her smile as she read her husband's text. Once again they had been separated for practically twenty-eight hours due to his real passion. Kellie knew he loved what he was doing and wouldn't dare stand in his way. She understood very well what it was like to have that kind of zeal for something you're totally passionate about. She just missed him terribly and couldn't wait to be in his arms. With her expression Ann knew it must be Gregory texting her. Once again Ann's cell beeped...her oldest again. She told Kellie to eat her breakfast before it gets cold and they would talk later.

Kellie finished her breakfast and decided to check out the dining room to see if the finger food trays were out. The caterers would bring their main meal around one.

"Girl the word is he married her so he could get full control of the company."

"How can he do that, don't he have to own some of it first?" Kellie stood quietly at the door listening to the conversation between the two employees.

"Like I said that's the word. So he must own some of KTS. Of course we wouldn't know about that only the Kincaids. Besides I don't care who owns it as long as I get to keep this part time job. I like working for the both of them."

What in the world did they mean by him owning... Her phone vibrated, it was her uncle. They were leaving the bank and were on their way to the business park and would be there shortly. Good, thought Kellie as she made her presence known. Two of the temp drivers were the ones in deep discussion about her, Gregory, and their marriage. Kellie was glad none of the other employees were present as she requested the two female drivers to come to her office as soon as they finished eating.

On the way to her office she stopped to speak to Ann about what she had overheard. Ann told her she had heard the same thing and wanted to talk to her about it earlier. They both wondered how in the world this foolishness got started. Kellie knew they may not get to the bottom of how it

228

began, but she assured her she would put a halt to this nonsense with quickness. But now she had to take care of the two temps...Keisha and Jackie.

Standing at her door were the two drivers with looks of despair. As soon as she approached them they both started to speak. Kellie told them to wait until they were inside. She wanted this to be a private conversation. Kellie relieved the ladies of expecting the worst. She was not going to terminate them this time but she made it plain and clear their behavior was unacceptable and would not be tolerated. Both ladies apologized and thanked her for giving them a second chance. They promised it would never happen again. When Kellie asked where did they get their information from, Keisha quickly pointed to Jackie. Jackie said she overheard it in the ladies room. Kellie knew she would never find out how the rumor got started, but she wanted to impress on these two not to carry it any further. Gossip was something you don't have control of unless you catch the culprit. She knew these two would not be caught up in spreading anymore hearsays. Delivering around the city part-time was working out very well for these two young mothers. They both made it clear they needed the flexible hours and extra income for their households. Keisha and Jackie left out with the expression of relief and gratitude, both silently vowing this would be a last for them...

Gregory had changed into one of their company's security polo. Sitting in the parking lot he phoned Allen to let him know he was on the premises. All the drivers were told to stay inside until they heard from him. Clyde had been given instructions to unlock the gas station across the street in about twenty minutes and stay put. As soon as the staff is safely across the street the caterers would arrive. It just so happen the department has been trying to get something on bad boy Rapture and his boys Cat Eyes and Red-Dog. So far Stephen Ray had not been a threat, he just hung with some bad company. Three workers had already been replaced with police officers and Janet was told to go to the bathroom as soon as she entered the building. She refused to allow any of her workers to be involved. She would be the only one present until the situation was taken care of. It was no discussing or arguing with her, due to the fact that she was a retired policewoman. If that wasn't a blessing, thought Gregory as he watched Rapture and his boy roll up and park, leaving just enough room for the van to pull up in. That was stupid Gregory mumbled to himself...

Her favorite uncle knocked and opened her door. He knew she was along because he saw the young ladies leave the room with faces of disciplined children. "Hey niece, what was that all about," asked Uncle Kel as he put his satchel down and took a seat in front of her desk.

Kellie smiled when she saw him with his father's day gift. She thought he could use a bag that could be thrown across his shoulders since he didn't like carrying a briefcase. It looked real chic and masculine draped across his shoulders. "Uncle Kel you wouldn't believe it if I told you. Where's Aunt Juanita?

"Help!" Kellie and her uncle both went to the door to. Her aunt and one of their workers were standing with their hands full. Kellie helped relieved them of their full trays of refreshments and thanked Cherri.

"Now niece tell me about those two young ladies that just left your office," requested her uncle between bites.

"I'm telling you, you're not going to believe this. It seems someone is going around spreading rumors about Gregory owning part of KTS and the only reason he married me was to seize full control. Can you"... Before she could complete her sentence Uncle Kel strangled on his drink. His eyes watered as he tried to control his coughs. With a weak voice he said something went down the wrong pipe. Kellie studied her uncle and aunt's faces. Something strange was going on. This was not the first time Gregory's name was mentioned concerning part ownership of their company. Last time it was her aunt who became somewhat nervous...like she made a slip of the tongue just the other night.

"Uncle Kel is there any truth in Gregory owning parts of KTS?" Kellie looked him sternly in the face then to her aunt. Their silence said it all.

Aunt Juanita spoke first, "Kellie it has nothing to do with you and your marriage. Kelley darling you need to level with her now." His wife stood and put her arms around his shoulders. She knew the turmoil he had been going through. A million times his mind was plagued with what he had done. He looked into his niece and wife's faces for understanding and forgiveness because he still had not told Nita everything.

"Nita and Kellie I want you to listen to me real good. I made a terrible mistake and yes Gregory is my silent partner and he use to own fifty-five percent of KTS. I had to put the company in his name and yours Kellie for security reasons, it was just that serious. I'm shame of what I've done and I know I've disappointed you both terribly."

"Oh my God Uncle Kel, use to," shock and disbelief covered her face. He held his trembling hand up pleading with her to allow him to go on. She didn't want him too, her mind was stuck on "*use to*." Kellie felt helpless and frightened. Had he placed their company in the hands of others? She shook her head, under no circumstances could she believe such...just like she didn't believe HE married her to gain full control of KTS. Aunt Juanita massaged her uncle's tensed shoulders. She always felt there was more, but she never pressured him after Gregory came aboard. That young man makes her feel safe and gave her back the love of her life.

Kelley Kincaid continued with an unbelievable story. He had invested a large sum of money to a friend for a legitimate business deal he thought. He had been scammed by a good friend in a bad way. When he revealed that he had actually embezzled money from KTS both ladies gasped in horror. Not only did he have a delinquent bank loan facing him, the IRS was also breathing down his neck. Single-handedly he had put KTS in jeopardy. It was Gregory Larson who saved them from financial ruins and public embarrassment. No one knew the company was on the edge of bankruptcy and they were close to losing it altogether. Gregory had been a God sent. Uncle Kel asked them both for their forgiveness as he became emotional.

Tears streamed down Kellie and her aunt's faces as they watched him break down and sob... Both were deeply hurt that he went through this ordeal alone. He's always had them. Kellie would have sold everything she owned and borrowed the rest to help him. He meant that much to her.

Aunt Juanita held her husband of fifty years and caressed his throbbing temples as he continued weeping. How could he think they would feel anything but love and admiration for him. He was her life and fell in love with him when she first set eyes on him. It was love at first sight for the both of them. She's had nothing but happiness with this man and could care less if they had to sell everything they owned as long as they were together. Juanita Kincaid soothed her husband with tender kisses.

Kellie kissed them both and left her office to give them some privacy. It would be time for the caterers to arrive in a little while. She needed to pull herself together and wanted something hot to calm her insides. She decided to go to the dining room and ran into Ann at the door. She could tell she was upset. Kellie shook her head to say not now, but she knew Ann better than that. She was going to have to tell her if no one else.

"It's true Ann. He does own this company, well according to my uncle use to. Uncle Kel is so upset right now I didn't have the heart to ask any more questions."

"Don't worry about it Kellie I'm sure Gregory has everything under control. He knows how important this company is to you and Mr. Kincaid." The two friends took a seat and had a hot cup of Wassail that Cherri makes every year. Kellie always looked forward to her special drink. She always makes her a container full for the holidays to take home.

"Kellie I'm glad I found you, your uncle and aunt want to go over to our new site and wanted all the office staff to go with him. He sent me to find you two. It's a field trip." Cherri was so excited as she grabbed her hand. "Come on Ann, catch Kellie's other hand." They knew Cherri was young at heart but this was going too far even for her.

"There you are! Come on, we were all waiting on you three. I had a great idea to take the office staff across the street on a field trip as Cherri puts it. Here's your cape, Ann get your coat. Everyone is outside. Son don't forget to keep your eye on my satchel."

"Will do Mr. Kincaid," said Stephen Ray grinning like he had just won the lottery. Pulling out his cell, he watched the ladies and Mr. K walk across the street.

232

"Man where the hell is everybody going," asked Rapture who was standing on the side of the building pretending to be a KTS worker with a trash bag and broom.

"Across the street to check out the new facility. Me and Red-Dog are supposed to wait for the caterers. And guess what, the old man asked me to keep an eye on his satchel. The store front is clear no one is here but us and I've already put the bag in the dining room in a chair at the first table. All you have to do is pick it up when you come in with the caterers."

"Well they just rolled up, let's get this play started." Janet's truck pulled up right in front of the door and Rapture dropped his props.

After the van parked to unload, Gregory pulled his truck around to the garage to make sure none of his drivers come out when the action starts. The undercover helper got out and started unloading the van. He gave all three men a serving pan. Stephen Ray led the way to the dining room with the others behind him. All three hoods put their pans down. Rapture spotted the satchel and draped it across his shoulder and followed his comrades out to the van. Janet did just like she was told and went to the ladies room. Rapture began walking over to where Green-Eyes was parked with Red-Dog behind him leaving Stephen Ray at the caterer's van.

When he saw what was happening he shouted to Rapture to wait. Red-Dog stopped and pointed a gun. Stephen Ray backed up without another word said. He knew then he had been double crossed.

Green-Eyes attempted to pull off. "What the"...HPD was everywhere. They had no place to go and jumping out shooting was not an option. They were told to throw out their weapons, get out with their hands up, and lay face down on the ground... which brought the play to an end. They cooperated and gave themselves up without a fight. After they were handcuffed and put in the patrol cars, Stephen Ray was brought out. He was trying to convince the officers he had nothing to do with the other three, but he was put in a car anyway.

Gregory sent out the text everything was well and under control as he walked across the street to meet the office staff and his wife. Uncle Kel had informed him everything was out in the open and she was upset. The first one out of the door was Kellie. She ran to meet him with tears streaming down her face. She jumped in his arms and held on for dear life. Her uncle tried to tell her HPD had everything under control. But she couldn't help being on edge when she saw his truck pull up at the barn. When he got out she saw that he was holstered down, that didn't help at all. Although she had on her cape she was trembling. As they made it to the storefront she became weak and nauseous. Gregory lifted her and carried her inside to the nearest area with a couch…The Ivory Room.

"Kellie Baby, talk to me." Gregory held her hand and caressed her temple. He could hear voices in the background. Someone said call for an ambulance.

"What's wrong with her Kel?"

"I don't know Nita, she just passed out in his arms. It's probably too much excitement." He just said that to make her feel better. He knew his Kellie was a strong willed young woman. Something must be wrong.

"Kellie please open your eyes Baby." Ann came in with the first aid kit. She put a cool towel on her forehead and then held a handkerchief that had a drop of peppermint oil under her nose. She moaned and her eyelids fluttered. "That's it Baby open your eyes. Ann continued to bathe her brow with the cool towel.

Kellie opened her eyes and was gathered up in his arms. "Gregory, I was so scared." He held her tightly to his heart as she released her tears and cried in his chest. He rocked her gently.

"It's okay Baby. Everything is going to be just fine." Someone reached Ann a cup of warm tea for her to drink. "Here Baby stop crying so you can take a few sips of this." Gregory kissed her forehead then her cheek. She quieted down long enough to take a couple of swallows. Someone announced the paramedics were there. Everyone cleared the room except him.

Uncle Kel had the staff to go to the dining room. The caterers were ready to serve. After they gathered in the area Mr. Kincaid said a prayer of

234

thanks for the prosperous year, his loyal employees, and the new partnership with Gregory Larson. He continued and asked for special blessing for Kellie, the meal, and the preparers...with an Amen from the KTS family and the feast began. Not one word of *I told you so* was uttered from anyone.

"Well Mrs. Larson your vital signs are fine. I think the excitement had a lot to/ do with your fainting. Is there any possibility you could be pregnant?" Kellie looked shocked because of his question and really didn't want to say anything about her suspicions, especially in front of her husband. She wanted them to fine out together alone. That was going to be his Christmas gift. She had already bought three kits. She figured two out three would confirm what she was certain of. Well so much for her plans, she had three people waiting on her answer.

"Yes, it's a very strong possibility." Gregory fell to his knees as his eyes watered. The paramedics patted him on the shoulders, congratulated them both and left the room. With tears in his eyes he told her he needed to hear her say the words. She took his face in her hands and told him of her plans for them to find out together and that it was supposed to be his Christmas present. "Yes Gregory Adams Larson, I'm having your baby." His chest swelled. He couldn't ask for a better gift than his baby giving him a baby.

"Kellie, I love you so much."

"I know you do and I love you even more."

"Even after what you found out today... that I was your uncle's silent partner."

Again she told him, "Yes." Breathing deeply to ask the inevitable, she continued. "Gregory I do have one question. Why did Uncle Kel speak in past tense and you're doing the same thing. It's like you don't own the company anymore."

"The answer to that question is your Christmas present. But since you've given me mine I guess I can give you one of yours," he said with a big smile on his face. He had a strong feeling it was *Destined to Be* anyway for him to give her the gift before time. He called Allen to meet him at his office with his backpack. He had been carrying it around since the attempted robbery. He pulled his wife to her feet and together they walked to his office. Allen was waiting by the door.

"How are you feeling Mrs. Larson?"

"Much better Allen and thank you. Please tell the rest of the staff all is well we'll be in the dining room shortly." He acknowledged with a nod and left.

"Mrs. Larson," he reached for her to sit on his lap and gave her the envelope. She opened it and found documents that awarded her complete ownership of KTS. It was dated the 3rd day of November this year. There was also his last will and testament that named her beneficiary of all of his worldly possessions dated before they were even married. He was giving her everything he owned regardless of her marrying him. She was speechless as she looked in the face of her true love…her soul mate…her baby's daddy.

"I love you and I'm so glad you're a part of my life. Thank you for wanting and loving me."

"Thank you for loving and trusting me in spite of everything that's happened between us. I promised you on our wedding day then I would love honor and cherish you for the rest of my life and I want to reaffirm I will…always and forever. Baby our love was *DESTINED TO BE*." It was like they were saying their vows again. "Come on let's go join the rest and pass out the bonuses.

"I thought they…" He smiled and patted his backpack. Like her uncle said he had everything under control. When they entered the dining room they were given a round of applause. Uncle Kel had explained to the staff how he had saved the day with the help of Clyde Stevens and their Christmas bonuses were safe. Of course Gregory had to share the news of his Christmas present which brought down the house. Kellie told him he was going to have some serious trouble because her family didn't know yet. He assured her he could handle them with no problem and she believed he could do just that, including Nisey and Lynette.

CHAPTER 25

Christmas Eve

The first part of Kellie's morning was spent on the phone bringing Gracie and Kat up to date on the Larson's excitement. She started with the office gossip…Uncle Kel revealing the identity of his secret partner…the attempted robbery…her wonderful brave husband… she was the owner of KTS thanks to her loving soul mate…and lastly she was pregnant. They had a great telephone visit that puzzled Gregory. He understood her talking to Gracie, but he couldn't understand why Kat was also on the line since their plans were to leave for Edna right after they left the business park. He just didn't know once they get together they would start all over. And that's exactly what they did.

Kellie has spent Christmas Eve at Kat's ever since she became a mother. They usually wrap children's gifts and put toys together till almost midnight. This year Jeremy helped, which made it possible for them to get through earlier. Before they left for Edna they spent the previous night over to Nisey's doing the exact same thing. Gregory said next year he was organizing a gift wrapping party, which would include everybody with children at one time…in one place. Of course every one told him that would not work. But they knew Mr. Larson would come up with a plan.

Kellie was worse than the children, she knew Gregory had one more gift for her and she wanted it at midnight. She whined and begged until midnight. She even had her sisters and Kat helping her. But he didn't budged.

"Baby it's time to go to bed. Turn the light out and go to sleep," he ordered. Of course his request fell on deaf ears. She claimed she and the baby couldn't sleep unless she got her gift right now. She knew that would get him as she set up in their bed waiting for him to give in. He reached under his pillow and gave her the envelope. *Another envelope. Hummm…* What else could be on paper she thought as she slowly opened it? Kellie let out a scream.

"You bought Uncle Kel and Aunt Juanita's house! I can't believe you actually bought their house. It's ours now! Oh thank you Sweetheart!"

"As soon as their new house is built next door," he said. She screamed again. "Okay Mrs. Thomas is going to hear you." She showered him with kisses as she continued thanking him over and over.

"Okay, my babies need their rest we have a big day in about," he looked at his watch, "eight hours. Come here." He pulled her in his arms and caressed her stomach. "Go to sleep son."

Christmas Day

The Kincaid family all gathered once again in her parents' home for their holiday feast. Of course the Larsons had to make their rounds and truly enjoyed their visits as they revealed their news to those who didn't know. Everyone was excited about the new member that was expected sometime in the month of August if not sooner according to Nisey and Lynette. Kellie couldn't wait to share the additional news. Her husband had bought her the house of her dreams. To make life even better she would be living next door to her favorite uncle. As if that wasn't good enough Aunt Juanita announced she and Uncle Kel were staying in their country home until their new house was built. That meant as soon as they moved out Kellie and Gregory could move in. The month of January was going to be one busy month.

New Year's Eve

Kellie and Cynthia stood back as they watched their friend say I do. The small ceremony was taking place in their great room with about twenty-five guest which included immediate family and very close friends. They were proud of their work. The décor was simple but elegant. They had removed all of their furniture except the sofa and chairs that were pushed against the wall. Her beautiful coffee table was put in the foyer for gifts. Chocolate cushioned stacking chairs with pink and cream satin bows tied

238

around them were place around the room encircling the bride and groom. Pink satin bulbs were also used to add color to the shrubbery. Of course Cynthia went over board and had pink and cream throw pillows for Ann's coffee cream sofa. Kellie had to give it to her, the pillows did bring the colors together which created the atmosphere she was determined to achieve.

The loving couple stood between two large green plants with pink and cream ribbons and said their vows in the midst of a quest filled room. Ann was simply gorgeous. She wore a beautiful soft satin cream dress with a lace embellished empire bodice and flowing skirt. Her braids were scooped up with pearl jeweled combs. Pearl jewelry and cream shoes were the perfect accessories. She held a small bouquet of pink roses and baby's breath tied with a cream satin ribbon. Jesse was debonair in his brown suit, cream collarless shirt, and matching shoes. They made a handsome and adorable couple.

Their dining room was set up for a buffet style reception with a menu of delicious foods and Auntie E's famous punch. A satin cream tablecloth covered the table with a medium size vase of long stem pink roses and baby's breath which was placed in the center. Two small card tables were also draped in satin cream with various sizes of pink ribbon bows positioned on top of the tables for color and additional decorations. They sat the two layered wedding cake on one of the tables which was located in the corner of the room. A beautiful floral arrangement sat on the bar with clear matching eating utensils and napkins. The two cousins did not leave out one single detail. After the ceremony they set up the other card table in the center of the room for the bride and groom with cream covered chairs and pink satin ribbons tied around them. They even had a smaller floral centerpiece for their table. They had done a fantastic job! And knew just that when they saw Ann's expression. She was brought to tears and that was just the response they wanted.

"Show time," said Cynthia who had been the perfect host. The ceremony was over and it was time for them to do their job. If this didn't put them back in Ann's good grace nothing would. Hummm...as far as Kellie was concerned they were already in her good grace.

***

"Happy New Years, Sweetie." Kellie kissed her husband as they brought in the new year together. Gregory said he did not mind spending holidays with her family, but he was starting a family tradition of his own. At eleven o'clock he intended to be home with her doing just what he was doing now as long as God allows him to. That's why he loves him some Bro. Bruce, he was one understanding minister. They had their New Year's Eve watch night early so the congregation could be safely home before midnight. This gave the church enough time to do whatever else they had planned to bring in the New Year.

The twosome cuddled on their oversized chaise with a refreshment tray and sparkling cider chilling in the ice bucket. A CD made especially for them of the smooth sexy sounds of their favorite artists was playing. Yeah, this was his new tradition, he thought as he dragged tantalizing kisses down her soft silky skin. He touched his favorite spot that caused her to show him he was right on target as she whispered his name. Yep, this was going to be his New Year's tradition, spending a romantic sensuous evening with the love of his life.

Six months later

"Kellie, your husband called and said he would be here in five minutes."

"Thanks Michelle. I'll be out in just a few."

"Please don't leave the office Kellie until I get there."

"Michelle that is not necessary. I'll be out in just a minute and you stay where you are." She was still bending over backwards behind the drama she started. Kellie was surprised when she confessed after their holiday luncheon that she was the one and how sorry she was. Of course she was reprimanded like the other workers and given a second chance. She had learned her lesson and has been a model employee even more so.

Kellie recalled that day and couldn't believe the ordeal they encountered. Gregory's security system was truly something and he's enjoying every bit of being their security engineer. He even had the word security put on the pocket of his teams' polos. Right now he's training Clyde

Stevens to be part of their unit. He feels he has that inner sense to recognize trouble, because it was Clyde who alerted him to his brother's plan. Stephen Ray was doing alright now. He had to spend one year and would be out on five year probation for his part of the foiled robbery. The fact Uncle Kel and Gregory were character witnesses and promised to give him employment, the judge was lenient and gave him a second chance. In Clyde's own words, he said that fool cried like a baby during the entire trial.

Closing down her office she moved to another chair that had been placed at the front desk just for her. Gregory insists she waits for him on the inside. She is not allowed to drive nor go anywhere alone except the bathroom. Those were Gregory Larsons rules, not the doctor's. She had Gracie cracking up about him when they talked last week. As a matter of fact she had some good news herself, they were expecting their first baby too. Two best friends were expecting in the same year. Of course she wasn't due until November. Gracie said she could tell her about childbirth since she told her about everything else. Kellie smiled as she recalled that conversation, she knew exactly what Gracie meant.

"Kellie, Baby are you ready?" He kissed her lips then her stomach.

"Yes Sweetie." Today they were doing another ultra sound to check on the twins. Kellie couldn't believe her luck. If she was having twins at least she could have one of each like her sister Lynette. Oh no, not her, she had to do everything the hard way, two boys.

"Well Kellie and Gregory the twins are doing just fine. Their weight is a little light but nothing to be alarmed about since their mother is not gaining excessive weight herself. We are just in the... wait a minute." The doctor moves the monitor over to the left of her stomach and then to the right side. The boys were very active today. They've been doing jumping jacks all day. Dr. Spurlock had a strange look on her face.

"What is it doctor?" asked Gregory getting up from his seat. He looks at the monitor too. "Is that what I think it is?" His breathing was becoming loud and laborious.

"I see it too. Three instead of two! Three babies instead of two!" A loud thump caused the doctor and Kellie to take their eyes off the monitor to look where Gregory had been standing. Dr. Spurlock called for assistance. Mr. Larson had passed smooth out. Nurse Fowler came in to help…

"Thanks Roy and Tony." They walked a still stunned Gregory straight to his room and put him to bed. He was still in shock. Dr. Spurlock said he would be alright. He just needs to calm down and rest. A nice cup of hot raspberry tea would do the trick thought Kellie as she walked their two drivers to the door.

"You're welcome Boss Lady. I hope Mr. G feels better."

"I'm sure he will and thanks again." They had to be driven home from their doctor's visit. Kellie was not about to let her overreacting husband drive her anywhere. Dr. Spurlock was able to get excellent pictures of all three babies. Although you couldn't determine the sex of the third infant she couldn't help praying for a girl and already had solicited everybody in her family and church to do the same thing.

"K…e…l…lie…" Lord is this what I'm going to have to put up with, baby number four, thought Kellie.

"Yes Sweetie, I'm coming with your tea.

August 4

Today was Kellie's last day at work. She had been working only half days…orders from Dr. Larson and Nurse Juanita for the last four weeks. She had not experienced any complications during her pregnancy. Dr. Spurlock was pleased that she had gained more weight though. That was a switch thought Kellie. The babies even allowed her to sleep at night after their father caresses her stomach while reading a story. Dr. Seuss was their favorite author according to Dr. Larson.

Kellie's parents were on their way and planned to stay until after the birth of the trio. Her mother was going to stay a little longer to assist Aunt Juanita. Their entire family was anxious and ready for the birth of the triplets who were due at the end of the month. She had to admit she was ready to drop her load now. She was tired of rocking and reeling when she walked.

All the preparations were completed with the help of her family and friends. They were just waiting for the arrival of their new family. Although they still could not determine the sex of the third child she played it safe and purchased a few girlie pieces just in case. Gregory had to give up his office that was right off from the master suite so the babies would be in the room with them. Her aunt and uncle had built the master suite with a connecting room which was to be used as a nursery during their day, of course that didn't happen. That's why Kellie and Gregory allowed them to have a major part in the preparations. They purchased everything the twin boys needed before they even discovered the third baby. Lord was that an ordeal thought Kellie as she remembers Gregory reaction. It took a couple of days before he really calmed down.

"Hey Kellie, how are you feeling," asked Ann?

"Good come in and keep me company for a while." She had just finished talking to Gracie and Kat which was not the norm. She knew they were both at work but she was bored stiff. Gregory had assigned most of her work load to Ann who had been promoted as her assistant with Rhonda taking up the slack. He then hired a personal office clerk to assist only her until she leaves. She might as well be at home for the work she was doing. "I really don't have anything to do. You and Rhonda have done a terrific job in taking over my responsibilities. I..."

"Don't even try it. We need you here, Boss Lady."

"I'll be back whenever Dr. Larson releases me."

"He is truly a mess isn't he?"

"Girl I don't have a word for all of his foolishness and his dos and don'ts. I'm so sick of Baby I'm just looking out for you and the children," sneered Kellie. "Come on walk me to the ladies room. I'm also sick of this running back and forth to the rest room. I can't hold my water long at all. Just last night I..." Oooooooo...she grabbed her stomach. "Man that was a hard kick. These   hard heads...Oooo."

"Kellie you might need to..." Her water broke. She immediately went into her breathing exercise as the contractions started. Ann being an old pro calmly took control as she walked her to the designated chair in the front and called to Gregory who just happened to be coming through the front door. He was on his baby monitoring routine…every two hours he would come to the office to check on her. "Her water broke, bring the truck." Somebody reached them a hand full of towels.

He rushed to her side and fell to his knees. "Kellie Baby are you alright? Kellie say something!"

She reached for her husband as another contraction started. "Ooooooo…"

"Kellie! Kellie!" He's not going to be any help thought Ann as she waved Clyde over.

"Rhonda call for one of the drivers."

"I already did, here's Tony now. I did that too. Dr. Spurlock is waiting.

"Ooooooooooooooo…"

"Kellie! Kellie!" Tony and Clyde helped her into the limo. Gregory fell in. Ann ran to the other side as she called Rhonda's name one more time.

"I know take care of the fort and I'm calling Mr. Kincaid and Nisey now." By then KTS staff was standing around cheering them on. The Lord was good her parents pulled up at the business park. She could hear her mom say she had a strong feeling it was time. What luck, she needed them as she squeezed her weeping husband through another contraction.

Fifteen minutes later

They made it to the hospital in record time. Gregory had stopped crying with encouragement from her mother and Ann. When they told him he was going to miss the birth of his children that seemed to work as he pulled himself together. Tony got out to get a wheel chair, Ann told him to get two just in case. Smart girl thought Kellie as they rolled them both right to the elevator. Dr. Larson was having a hard time being steady on his feet.

Three hours later

Two six pound boys and a seven and a half pound girl made their grand debut between 2:30 and 3:15 pm. Gregory was able to coach her from his wheel chair. He turned out to be a real trooper after all, regardless of him not being able to stand. Of course when he saw his little girl the faucet was turned on once again. Thank God she came last. Uncle Kel couldn't resist teasing him. He told him he didn't need to tell anybody what kind of hustle he did on the side. Gregory knew it was going to take years before he could live down his performance, but he was okay with that. Dr. Spurlock tried to make him feel better by telling him stories of the unexpected behaviors of some of her other fathers. Kellie was sure he would be added to her story collection.

After her family admired their babies they left to give them some time alone. Her husband kissed her and thanked her again for having his children. He would have been happy with just one right now, but God blessed them with three. You can't beat that he thought as he took a gold chain from around his neck. On the end was a beautiful heart shaped ring with a peridot stone in the center surrounded by large diamonds, her children's birthstone. He put it on her finger and told her how much he loves her again. Kellie could hardly keep her eyes open. Delivering three babies was hard work.

"Rest Baby," he said as he laid his head on the edge of her bed. He was exhausted and worn-out, delivering three babies was definitely hard work as he closed his eyes.

Four days later

Once again Tony picked them up, this time they needed the room for three car seats and flowers. Dr. Larson had regained his strength and once again he was on top of it. He became an old pro assisting with the diaper changing and bottle feeding during their stay in the hospital. As they pulled up in the driveway the family was outside waiting on the arrival of the triplets. Gregory had a bigger surprise…Mrs. D and her husband was present along with his Aunt Cheryl and Aunt Marie.

Their front yard was full of pink and blue balloons. A sign was stretched

245

across the lawn and door that said *it's a girl and two boys*. Tony opened her door and helped her out of the limo while Gregory unhooked the seat belts. The Kincaid women crowded around the vehicle but got the shock of their lives when they were moved aside. They thought they were going to carry a baby to the house, which was a joke.

"I'll take little Kyla Renée," that was Uncle Kel.

"I got Grayson Adams," that was her father.

"And we got Gregory Jr.," and that was Robert Sr. and Jr. Gregory stood at the car stunned. Kellie reached for his hand and together they walked in their home.

"Enjoy it while you can Sweetie."

Three months later

"Kellie it's your turn!" She reached him the phone and told him to call his man cave buddies and turned over.

Dear Readers,

First I would like to apologize for taking so long to get back into writing. I will not waste any time with the excuses I've used over the years. But I promise you will not have to wait this long again. I'm so thankful I still have the ability to write and people who want to read my stories. Thanks! Okay, so much for apologies. I hope you have enjoyed reading Kellie and Gregory's story as much as I enjoyed writing it. I trust visiting my first loves Silky Silk and Jazper from Senseless Misconceptions was a delightful surprise. I will not say (because I don't want to lie) whose story is next, but I will promise it will be soon. As always be sure to hit my face book page and let me know your thoughts. Until next time, here's wishing you lots of love and happiness.

Email address wparksbrigham@writeme.com

W Parks Brigham

 PO Box 330353

Houston,   Texas77233

ABOUT THE AUTHOR

W Parks Brigham lives in Houston, Texas. She has two grown daughters and no grandchildren yet. She holds two degrees; a BS in Social Work with a Child Development / Psychology minor and M.Ed. in Education. She has spent her adult life teaching small children and loved every minute of it. Well most of the time. She is now a retired (Halleluiah) teacher of thirty plus years and loves every minute of that for sure. Her main interest and hobbies includes active participation in her church, listening to her own radio station designed especially for her, playing spider solitaire, working bent and wiggly word search and Sudoku puzzles, and an avid reader of Black Romance.

www.ingramcontent.com/pod-product-compliance
Lightning Source LLC
Chambersburg PA
CBHW022005170626
46808CB00001B/294